TASTING RED

HOLLY ROBERDS

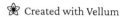 Created with Vellum

BOOKS BY HOLLY ROBERDS

* For recommended reading order, visit www.hollyroberds.com

To my mother.

What I write is not your jam, but you still tell people all about it. My favorite part is when your conflicting parts of aversion and pride mix for a delicious sales pitch of your daughter's work, no one can resist.

Not even when you slip in the words 'creepy' or 'nasty.'

Weirdest marketing representative ever.

CHAPTER I

THE FAVOR

THE BIG BAD WOLF

"Why did you call me here?" I ask, though I know perfectly well why the grizzled old son of a bitch sent for me. I spin the titanium ring around my forefinger with my thumb.

He frowns under his thick beard, across from me at the wooden table. He pushes a pint of ale over before grabbing his own. I don't pick up the mug, but the man shrugs and takes a swig.

How did I end up here? For most of my life, I've lived on my terms with no consideration for anyone else. Not even the women I sometimes let in my bed. I follow the jobs that bring the most money and that has served me perfectly well until now.

"It's been a long time, Brexley," he says.

Nineteen years, if one were counting. And for nineteen years, I've felt the ghostly shackle, tying me to someone else. Nearly two-thirds of my life, waiting for the shoe to drop.

"Not long enough," I say gruffly, finally grabbing the

mug and taking a healthy swallow of the stuff. I hate to admit the shit is good. So I don't.

I've done everything I could to be free of social ties. There is no place for me among mage, man, or fae. But today is the day my only marker is called.

I owe one being a favor in this entire world and he has summoned me here to the musty backroom of his tavern. Boxes pile high around the room, surrounding us. He named the joint *Sam's*, though his name is Jameson. I never asked who he named it after, and I still won't ask.

The drizzle kicks up a heavy mist that clings to the windows. The cold seeps its way into my bones despite my knit sweater and leather jacket. On a shitty day like this, I'd normally be at home by the fire with a book. But this old son of a bitch has me by the balls.

"You owe me, Brexley," Jameson starts, as if he expects a fight.

I wipe my mouth with the back of my hand. "I'm aware, you old bastard. Just tell me what you want so we can get this over with."

His calloused fingers drum on the manilla folder next to him before sliding it over. "I need you to take care of her."

His tone tells me he doesn't mean take her out for lunch and shopping. He must have been keeping tabs on me to know what kind of business I'm in now. Or maybe he's just a sadistic son of a bitch, and I could be a florist and he'd still give me the same mission.

I push the mug away, despite wanting more. Drinking won't make this problem disappear. But once my only debt is paid, I won't have anything hanging over me. I'll truly be free.

I flip the folder open to a picture and a single page of details: name, occupation, home addresses. But I didn't need any of that info. I instantly recognize the older woman in the photo. I've seen her many times—on billboards, commercials, packages of food, enamel pins that people stick on their jackets.

A dry snort escapes me. "You've got to be joking."

The old bastard doesn't crack a smile, doesn't move a muscle.

Fuck me.

I run a hand through my already unruly silver hair. "Grandma. You want me to go after Grandma from 'Grandma's House?' The face of the most popular household brand, and one of the most powerful witches known to the world?"

Jameson repeats himself in slow, steady words. "You owe me." Coiled tension is locked up behind his dark eyes and in the set of his broad shoulders. Blood lust shines out from his face. This is business from his past. But I don't ask questions, and I'm not about to start now.

I study him, observing how he's changed since I last saw him. Even more gray strands pepper his black hair and beard. His scowl has only deepened with the years, multiplying the lines at the corners of his eyes. He must be nearing his fifties, but under his flannel shirt vest is a body still packed with the sturdy muscles of a heavyweight boxer.

Once upon a time, I considered this man to be like a father to me. He quickly dispelled me of that notion with an unholy vengeance. He taught me the truth. Dependence is death. Don't buy into the lie. You don't need others to survive in this world. It is a gilded lie that ends with getting stabbed in the back.

Or, in my case, a set of claws raked across my face.

But finally, I'm given the opportunity to dissolve my

last tie to another being, and this is my chance. As one of the most beloved celebrity icons, this also may be my chance to get killed.

My fingers wrap around the cold handle of the mug, suddenly thirsty. "She won't be easy to get to. And afterward, I'll be hunted like an animal."

His chair creaks with a loud groan as he leans back with a smirk. I've already accepted his terms. "Good thing you're used to it."

So he does know my business.

I shoot him a cutting look over the edge of the mug as I swallow the rest of the amber liquid.

"After all," he folds his arms across his chest, "you are the Big Bad Wolf."

My grin is half-grimace. "And that is very bad news for grandmas right now."

CHAPTER 2

TRASH TROLL

RED

"Hey, I know you," someone exclaims, cutting through the music in my ears.

My combat boots drop off the table and slam into the ground as I jackknife up in the chair, my heart taking off like a shot. Sweat pools in my palms, and I swipe them down my rumpled black rock band sweatshirt.

I pull out my earbuds with clumsy fingers. A guy hovers over me in the library, excitement and recognition sparking in his eyes. His friend stands next to him, watching me with curiosity.

Witchtits, I knew I should have receded into the depths of the university stacks. Curse my dependence on mochas. They only allow students to drink cafe drinks in the study room. Here, people talk quietly and work in groups.

I traded my usual solitude for four shots of espresso to cure my trash troll state. I love working nights, but I'm getting only about two hours of sleep before my nine AM class. And right now, I feel like absolute garbage.

Which begs the question, how did this guy recognize me in trash troll mode, and why would he bother me?

Because he knows who you really are.

My heart pounds like a jackrabbit's at the nasty little thought.

The guy adjusts the strap of his backpack over his shoulder. "You're that redheaded girl who works at the Poison Apple. Aren't you a bartender?"

His shorter buddy chimes in. "Oh yeah, that's your name, Red."

Of course. My hair is a bright fucking beacon, announcing me everywhere I go. Vibrant red, most people assume it's a dye job, but it's pure genetics. And right now, it's a shaggy mess, in a haphazard bun.

I almost sag in relief. "Yeah," I force the word out, though I feel shaky to my core.

"Well, shit. I'm Alan and this is Jimi. Think you could hook us up with free drinks some time?" the first guy asks, before shooting me a flirtatious look that comes off more like a leer.

Rolling my shoulders backward, I regain my balance. I'm used to this kind of coercion, but usually it's after midnight, and I'm behind a bar. Right now, I'm too exhausted and on edge to deal with entitled little boys thinking they can charm something out of me today.

"Sorry, they don't let me do that," I coolly lie, readjusting my textbooks on the long, shared table.

People start to take notice from a few seats down and look up with interest.

"Of course they do," Alan says with a cheerful scoff.

"I've heard you can be a lot of fun." He leans in and traces his fingertip down my neck.

Goosebumps immediately rise and race down my entire body at the touch, and it's like a switch is clicked into the "on" position.

"I can be a lot of fun," I purr, despite myself.

My legs instantly press together as I think about first taking Alan and then Jimi on the ride of their lives. The images come almost violently, as they are unbidden. Heat rushes through my body as I glance up through my lashes in a way that I know is pure seductress.

Calm down, I order my hormones. You can control yourself.

My chair scoots back with a loud metal shriek. The second he's out of reach, my body dramatically wails, wanting to be touched, wanting more touch everywhere. But I've cooled it, and I regained control.

Wiping away the sultry vixen trying to muscle her way out, I shoot the two boys a stony look. "But I'm not interested in having fun with either of you."

The playful air evaporates immediately and Alan scowls. He leaves with his friend in tow, but not before muttering an audible, "bitch."

I pull the hood of my sweatshirt up over my head, covering my bright red hair, trying to disappear. I could dye it to a less noticeable shade, but I'm too vain. Plus, it's one of the only things that makes me feel connected to my mom. I don't remember much about her, but I see a little piece of her every time I look in the mirror.

Embarrassment and arousal still run hot inside me, and I can already hear Goldie in my head.

Have a little fun, Red. It doesn't hurt to try a few boys on for size.

But I'm definitely not up for another round of "Red's spectacularly unfulfilling one-night stands that make her feel like garbage after the fact." Goldie may not mind the bang and bye, but it's never settled well with me.

Besides, she doesn't know the full extent of how I turn into a woman possessed. And I have no plan on telling her about how it's almost that time of the month. If only I could down a bunch of Midol and hunker down with some ice cream, but no. This is my other monthly problem. This beast has a whole other set of needs that are difficult to satisfy.

Something nudges my shoulder. I turn to see the girl next to me holding out a box of mini muffins. A familiar blue-haired lady smiles at me from the box. Again, a spark of panic ignites in my chest before evaporating.

"Guys can be such dipshits," she says dryly. The girl is in similar trash troll mode. Her books are about anatomy, and I know she's got it even worse than me.

I manage a half smile. "No joke."

She gives the box a shake, still offering me one of the pre-packaged baked goods.

"I'm good, thanks," I beg off.

"Have you had this kind before?" she asks, not letting it go in the name of friendliness.

"Uh . . . "

Before I can answer, she goes on, pulling out a muffin for herself. "This is the newest kind of Magic Morsels. I love the mini brownies that make you feel like you've gotten a hug from grandma herself."

I keep it to myself that I've *actually* received real-life hugs from the grandma she speaks of. And the treats she offers have zero effect on me.

"But these are blueberry and make you more confident. It's a godsend when you're pre-med."

"Yeah . . . " I trail off. There are at least a dozen similar boxes littering the study tables. More than usual as we creep up on finals, which is probably what's got me so paranoid. I'm surrounded by my secret.

"I'm so glad we have Magic Morsels. Can you imagine being in college, away from home and feeling like a mess and not having a little magical pick me up?"

"Totally," I say, trying to seem pleasant, but I've got to get the hell out of here.

Thankfully, the girl finally pops the muffin into her mouth, ending the conversation.

Downing the last of my mocha, I grab my books and flee, chucking the cup in recycling along the way. I have to study, but my focus is shot.

If I don't pass Dr. Langley's class, I'll hurl myself into the ocean. I need this credit for my major. If I fail, I'll have to repeat the course, and the dragon is the only one who teaches Finance 201. I'm already three years older than the students in my class, and I feel behind as it is.

"Rogers," a voice calls out.

My head whips around. Speak of the damn devil herself.

"D-dr. Langley," I acknowledge with a stutter. Dammit. Why do I have to admire and fear her so much? Oh right, because Langley is a she-dragon powerhouse.

Students practically dive out of her way. Her dark brown skin is visibly moisturized, though I've never seen her crack a smile to threaten that implacable face with lines. Today's navy suit is perfectly pressed, and her thick, curly hair is pulled back into a tight poof. Heels click along the pavement like gunshots as she strides toward me.

Faefucks.

"I was going to email you, but this is fortuitous."

I force a polite smile. "Yeah . . . "

"I just got your last test scores, and I have to say, I'm disappointed."

My stomach drops out from under me. Am I going to throw up?

She licks her thumb and forefinger and sorts through the stack of papers she's holding until she pulls one out. I don't want to take it—the red marks on it make me positively ill. My sweaty fingers pinch the pages. The grade is written at the top, circled, highlighting my shame. D minus.

"I studied . . . " my words come out in a stammer. I want her to know I'm not a total loser.

"Smarter, not harder," she says in a clipped voice, then glances at her watch. I feel as though I'm an inconvenient road bump, keeping her from getting to the things that really matter. "You held such promise in the beginning, but you have shown a lack of focus."

Oh, I'm focused. I'm so focused my eyes are near bleeding and my brain wants to explode almost hourly. But all the hours I'm putting in just aren't helping.

"Perhaps if you spend a little less time at the Poison Apple, and a little more time studying, you'll stand a chance at passing my class."

I can't speak for the lump in my throat, but I mutely nod. How did she know I work at that bar? Even though I love working there, I suddenly feel like dirt in the dragon's presence.

My fingers curl into my palm to keep from nervously playing with my septum ring. I may be tatted and pierced up, but my makeshift armor isn't cutting it right now.

"I urge you not to waste the long weekend and put some actual effort into your studies. Or if that is too much for you, perhaps you need to consider another major more suitable to your lifestyle. Or maybe even another school."

My tongue is sandpaper. Before I can work up the nerve to say anything, she turns on her heel and marches away, gunshot heel clicks echoing through the quad.

The paper wrinkles in my hand. Does she know I flunked out of my last school?

Realizing I'm wrecking valuable feedback I desperately need, I try to smooth the paper along my thigh, then stash it in my backpack.

I readjust the hood to make sure it covers most of my hair again. I feel too exposed, too noticeable. I thought I'd gotten over this habit of retreating into my shell months ago, but the stress is getting to me. Between my shitty grades and those guys hassling me in the library, my jaw clenches so hard my ears hurt.

For a split second, I was worried those boys recognized me as the actual granddaughter of Grandma from 'Grandma's House,' the highest rated streaming show and lifestyle brand.

To me, she's just Gigi.

Eloise Rose Rogers became a worldwide celebrity when she launched Magic Morsels. The baked goods allow humans and non-magics to have a taste of magic, literally. Most every kid and professor on campus is packing Magic Morsels in their bag when they need a pick me up. Or if they want to have a little fun.

I'm the heiress to the biggest magical legacy this world has ever seen. But I want nothing to do with magic, and I don't want anyone to know where I come from. I simply want to live the little human life of obscurity I carved out for myself.

I overhear two girls chatting as they walk by. "I bet they

don't have to deal with this boring-ass shit in magic school. I wish we were levitating teacups instead of learning about another epically boring-ass war."

I resist the urge to chime in that magic students levitate teacups *while* reciting facts about boring-ass wars.

Over the summer, I transferred from the Fairy Fine Arts Academy to Boston University, a human college. And by the grace of the fae lords, I have yet to be recognized. I'd always kept a low profile and my grandma protected me from the media as best she could. But I still get a phantom icy drip down the back of my neck at the mere thought of my cover being blown.

Not even my best friends know the truth.

Before I could find a secluded corner to set up again, my phone vibrates.

When are you arriving?

Not, *are you still coming?* Not, *do you need to stay at school to study for finals?*

My Gigi knows I will use any excuse I can to avoid going home for the long weekend and phrased it so I can't worm my way out of it.

She was understanding enough when I wanted to leave the magic world and live life as a regular human. But she doesn't know *all* the reasons why I left.

I type a quick response, and then veer off course, heading toward my apartment.

Hot shame and sharp pain slices my heart as I think of one of the biggest reasons I left. My need to get something hard between my legs is only going to worsen over the next several days.

I can only pray to the sweet lords of fae that when I go home, *he* won't be there. Or I'm scared I won't be able to control myself.

CHAPTER 3
OVER THE RIVER AND THROUGH THE WOODS

RED

In two hours, I'm packed and on the train north.

Sinking into my seat and looking out at the passing woods, I've taken off my hoodie and even let down my hair in an attempt to relax. I turn up the volume on my music and try not to think. Not about my grades, not about the hot desire pressing inside me, and definitely not about a certain someone who broke my heart.

Something touches my bare arm. I jump nearly two feet off the seat. When I turn, the ticket inspector has his hands up and wears an apologetic smile.

I pop an earbud out and give him the once, no, twice over. He's kind of cute. A little old, but that wouldn't stop us from having a good time. The uniform does things for me I didn't expect.

"Sorry, I didn't mean to scare you," he says.

"You can scare me any day," I say in a way that suggests something else entirely, while I hold my ticket out for him to scan. I lick my lips and one of my shoulders pops up to make for a seductive pose.

"What?" A line of confusion forms between his brows.

Realizing what I'm doing, I quickly say, "Nothing, thanks." As soon as he's gone, I rush to put my oversized sweater back on and yank the hood up.

"Stupid, stupid," I whisper harshly as I smack my head against the window a couple of times. My head bounces off the glass and pain ripples through my forehead. Damn it. I rub at the ache.

Gah. I hate this time of the month, and I hate the effect it has on me. Embarrassment smothers the other feelings whipping about inside me. I can't tell if it's getting worse as I get older, or if Goldie is just having way too much of an influence on me.

Still, my body feels too hot and restless. Not even my music can drown out the sensations. My phone vibrates and I see Gigi has sent another text.

I may not be there to meet you, but someone from security will be there to let you in.

Cold drowns out the heat in my body. The thought of Hunter greeting me has me wanting to hurl myself right off the train and into the icy river we are passing over.

But he has done an excellent job of keeping his distance since I left. Ever since he learned I was a magic dud.

Straightening, I remind myself that I wanted nothing to do with magic, so it's just fine it wants nothing to do with me.

An open wound yawns inside me as I remember Hunter's shrewd blue eyes and perfect lips, and clean jawline. Lean and sharp, he always reminded me of a sculpture of Adonis. He is strong, pristine, and his strong sense of duty melted me into a puddle of hero worship.

14

Far from perfect myself, I almost return to smacking my head against the window. I turn up the music so loud it hurts my eardrums, but it distracts me for the rest of the trip.

When I step out at my stop, I inhale the sweet decay of dying orange leaves and thick humid air. The cold bites at my cheeks and nose, while mist clings to the tiny New Hampshire town. I'd have asked Gigi to pick me up at the station, but since the chance of Hunter showing up in her stead was too risky, I decide to walk.

Thirty minutes of tramping down the street until I find the worn lane leading to Grandma's house in the woods, and I'm still not sorry for my decision. My boots are slick and covered in mud, and I can't feel my toes, but forty-five minutes on foot is better than enduring a suffocating six-minute car ride with the likes of Hunter.

I swear if I even think about him for too long, my heart starts to bleed. And he could always scent weakness from a mile away. I may be a magic dud, but I'm done being weak.

At last, the massive glass house, surrounded by trees, comes into view. The modern mansion is one of Gigi's many homes, and I got her to agree to meet here for holidays. The mere idea of going to one of her places in a mage city makes my skin crawl.

I'm still grateful she agreed to my quiet exit from the world of magic, but even now, anxiety grips my throat.

Keying in the lock code, I open the front door and pull off my muddy boots. The whole place smells like fresh linens and sandalwood.

"Gigi, I'm here," I announce, in case she's here already. I didn't see any vehicles, but they'd be tucked away in the garage.

I pad my way along the hardwood floors in my socks.

Most grandmas are associated with soft pastel colors, flowers, and feminine touches, but the black framed windows and vaulted ceilings are modern and masculine.

The house is like a version of upscale camping, with trees lining every side of the glass house. Gigi has many sides but all of them are upscale luxury. Frankly, stepping outside it allows me to breathe for the first time.

Despite her promise that security would greet me, no one is here. Hunter isn't here. I let out a breath I'd been holding for hours.

I ascend the black floating staircase to check if she's upstairs. I wonder what she'll think of my new nose piercing and all the new stud earrings that line my ears. All of them are gold since I rash out with silver jewelry. My tattoos are hidden from view, not to mention a couple other piercings she will *never* see.

I don't want to shock her too much right away. But the style changes have reinvented me into a new woman. Well, mostly a new woman. Lately, I've been back to the neurotic mess I used to be.

My back straightens as I remember I don't have to be that anymore. I'm new, and I'm living my life on my terms.

A strange thrumming in my gut forces me to pause on the landing, and my body is overcome with restlessness.

Shaking off the feeling, I enter Gigi's bedroom. A rustling comes from the bathroom.

"Gigi, I'm here," I announce again, so I don't scare her. The rustling stops.

The thrumming in my body doubles, and I feel an uncharacteristic heat in my veins. I look at the trees outside; it's growing dark. I'm probably just hungry. We can whip something up from the fully stocked kitchen and I'll feel better.

I swallow and go on, "Like I said before, I can only stay through tomorrow. I need to get back and study for finals. I may need to do some studying here too."

She moves in the bathroom, but doesn't respond.

The furniture here is black and modern except for the massive four poster bed. At least twenty fluffy pillows cover the pristine white bedspread, and hand carved wood spirals toward the ceiling at each corner. I wrap my hands around one of the posts, my fingers tracing the designs.

Sweet fae lords, when was the last time I did my nails? They are chipped to hell.

"I hope you aren't upset I can't stay the whole weekend."

Still no answer. No movement either.

I frown. "You okay Gigi?" I take a step forward, but before I get any closer, a man steps out of the bathroom. He fills the door frame in a way my five-foot-two Gigi never could.

The thick knit sweater pulls against his muscular chest and shoulders down to the taper of his stomach. Fabric strands unravel into small holes here and there. Voluminous, silver hair, dark at the roots, falls just above his shoulders.

My breath hitches as I try to discern whether it's my insane hormones or if he actually is as gorgeous as I think he is.

Yeah, it's not just my hormones.

His beauty is layered in complexity. Four scars, long healed, run through one eye and split his eyebrow. The dark scruff on his strong jaw only adds to his air of masculine power and ruggedness.

The man is utterly magnetic and my body wobbles, wanting to find safe shore in those strong arms.

The dark gray orbs under his scars scan me up and down. They emanate danger, violence, and sex. If I didn't know any better, I'd say he looks like he wants to eat me up. And with the intense vibrations running through my body, I'm liable to let him. Instead, I state the obvious.

"You're not my Gigi."

CHAPTER 4
WHAT BIG FEET
YOU HAVE

BREXLEY

Magic smells. It's something only Weres know. Usually, it's not pleasant. It overpowers, it stings, and can even be rancid, which is why I normally steer clear of the magic cities. I prefer the clean scents of pine and rushing rivers.

But the stench is also part of what makes me so efficient. The moment I step into the radius of a mage city, I want to get gone. I don't dick around; I play to win.

I check out the old lady's bathroom trash bin for any clues about where she has gotten to. The damn trash is empty and the house is spotless. Remnants of Grandma's magic lingers in the air; violets and rubbing alcohol. However, the scent is faint, and the house was empty when I arrived. She hasn't been here in months.

While my sensitive nose is grateful for the respite, it means I'm far from finishing this job and going home.

The tip I got told me she'd be here already, but perhaps

I'm too early. I need to get out of here and hole up until Grandma arrives.

She couldn't have picked a more convenient spot, what with it being a house of glass. No one will notice me watching from the woods, just another wolf in the wild.

As I set the bin back down, something strange pulses under my skin, making my stomach flip flop with excitement. Like my body knows something big is about to happen before I do.

"Gigi, I'm here." A feminine voice with a slight rasp to it, announces herself.

I can hear whoever she is drawing near. There is no way I can slip out a window in time. Maybe it's one of Grandma's entourage, an assistant or someone who has information I can use on finding my target.

Or maybe it's something else that compels me to step out into the bedroom before I even think of a cover story for my presence.

I face a girl in her early twenties, pale eyes framed by long dark lashes, and a left eyebrow with a permanent skeptical arch to it. Her light skin has a sprinkle of freckles across a nose that has a defiant upward turn at the tip. An ornate gold septum piercing circles under her nose. Big chunks of long tendrils have fallen out of the unruly, oversized bun atop her head. Dark circles line her eyes, and she's wearing a Boston University sweater.

Maybe a college girl?

Pheromones and stress practically vibrate off her in visible waves.

Definitely a college girl.

She would look like every other pretty girl her age if it weren't for her fire engine red hair. Even more intriguing is,

I can't detect any hint of chemical dye most would use to get their hair that shade.

No, she smells fucking incredible. Like honey, cinnamon, and sex. It evokes a strange response in my body. I instantly want to tear off her rumpled clothes and bury myself in her.

I'd suspect her of being a witch, if it weren't for the fact she doesn't stink to high heaven.

The girl blinks. "You're not my Gigi."

"I'm not?" the words are out of my mouth before I even think about it. A muscle in my cheek jumps as I try to suppress a smile.

Her already skeptical eyebrow arches further, as she releases the bedpost she's been clutching. "Are you trying to tell me you are my Gigi, just gone through a few . . . changes?" The girl gives me a slow, pointed once over.

I follow her gaze down my body, as if trying to see what she sees.

My Gigi. The way this girl keeps saying it, she isn't using the old lady's moniker. She's the actual granddaughter of my target.

This wasn't in the dossier.

"I didn't think I raised my granddaughter to be so judgmental." I look at her from under the hair that's fallen over my forehead and into my eyes. I can't help the smirk that forms. Excitement and heat continues to race through me..

A cautious but curious sparkle enters her eyes. "Why grandma, I never noticed what big eyes you have."

I press my tongue against the back of my teeth. "All the better to see you with."

My eyes run up and down her body again, and I deliberately drink her in. Fae lords, why does she smell so delicious? The suddenly hard length in my jeans is cramped, at a painful angle. It begs me to let it free.

I take a step forward and she takes a step back, but she doesn't run.

I'm not one for games.

But right now, I am. I stalk her like she's prey and I'm the predator. I want to paw and bat her around before taking a bite out of her.

"And what big . . . " her eyes sweep over my shoulders down to my abdomen, "muscles you have, grandma." I see heat behind her gaze, as pheromones thicken in the air. My mouth waters.

I take another step forward, so she sidesteps. We are caught in some kind of dance, and I want to see where it ends.

"All the better to hug you with, my dear," I practically purr.

Her scent washes over me. There is something darker underneath her sweetness, like molasses. She's not magic but . . . my instincts are barrel rolling and somersaulting, trying to tell me something I can't decipher.

What is she? My senses hiss at me, demanding I find out. She smells like nothing I've encountered before, not mage, witch, or Were. Whatever it is, it is a siren to me. If I were less controlled, I'd tackle her on the bed and run my nose all over her body until I could make sense of this mystery.

The redhead pushes hair back from her face, as she squares her shoulders. "And grandma what big . . . shoes you have."

My tongue pokes out to lick the corner of my mouth as I look down at my boots, then back at her. Again, I can't fight the smile.

"All the better to—"

"So, you are the new security detail?" she interrupts my answer. It's more stated than asked.

I'm stuck between the unfinished, salacious comment hanging on my tongue and interpreting what she just said. *Security detail?*

"Do you know when my Gigi will be back?" She crosses to the window, and gazes out at the trees. She uses a lofty tone, as if she is a princess ordering a servant about.

"She didn't say," I answer slowly, watching the girl carefully. She's trying to act aloof, but I can sense the tension she's holding in her body, see it in her spine and shoulders. I can hear it in her voice, and I can smell it. There is no hiding from the wolf.

The redhead turns around, putting her back to the vast windows, and I find myself approaching her, encroaching on her personal space. I am nearly a foot taller, and she must crane her head to look up at me.

Her eyes go round as her tongue drags over her lips, wetting those rosy petals. My pants grow even tighter. That delicious scent of hers thickens.

Apparently, I've been a lone wolf too long. I should have indulged in some female company before pursuing this endeavor.

"So, what's your name?" she asks.

She is still attempting to act superior and unaffected. But her eyes flutter as if she is fighting something inside her. I wonder if it's the arousal permeating the air with intoxicating intensity.

I'm the Big Bad Wolf, and I'm going to eat you right up, little girl.

Instead of voicing my thoughts, I reply, "Brexley."

Why did I tell her my name?

"Do you have a last name, Brexley?" she asks, her eyes

23

dropping to my chest before traveling back up to meet my eyes.

I don't answer.

"Usually, the security detail has me address them by their last name," she says expectantly.

"Moon. Brexley Moon."

Under her delicious scent there is that something else. It's on the tip of my tongue, but I can't place it. What *is* it? Frustration mounts in me, in more ways than one. If I could get close enough, maybe I can figure it out.

She nods as if satisfied. "Call me Red, everyone does."

My hands land on the glass on either side of her head, effectively locking her in. A blush starts at her neck and travels up to her cheeks. She can't hide the shallow pants as she stares at me with lust shining in her eyes.

"Well little Red, what shall we do while we wait for your grandmother to get here?"

Energy thrums between us. It pounds in my ears and under my skin – like an ancient drumbeat I've somehow always known. It drowns out the reason why I'm here and puts all my focus on this girl.

Her loftiness evaporates and she whispers, "Don't touch me." Her focus bounces back and forth between my mouth and eyes.

The little girl says not to. But, oh fae lords, everything else about her is inviting. Begging me to come in.

"Why not?" I keep my voice low, like hers.

She wets her lips yet again. "Because . . . " she trails off, a little shudder going through her.

I want to suck on that full lower lip. Take it in my mouth to lick, suck, and nibble at it until she gasps.

But I built an existence on self-control and boundaries.

It's the only way I've lived this long. There is no breaking the foundation of my survival instincts.

As if completely disconnected from my brain, my hand moves to her face and my thumb brushes lightly against that lip that has me under its spell.

The moan that slips from her mouth is sin and sex. It morphs into a growl. She juts her arms out and I'm launched back.

I've never been caught off balance, until now. The backs of my knees hit the edge of Grandma's bed.

At first, I think the girl is angry. Red's face is arranged in a snarl, her eyes wild. But then she rips off her sweater and the shirt underneath in one fluid move, leaving her in the ugliest, nude bra I have ever seen in my life.

I blink and she is on top of me, smashing her hot, hungry mouth against mine. Red grinds desperately against my hard groin.

The control I cultivated for almost twenty years snaps like a brittle twig, and I grab her by that gorgeous fucking fire hair and release the beast inside.

CHAPTER 5
FOREST FIRE

RED

Inside, inside, I fucking need him inside me now.

My body was already a roiling mess of hormones, but when he touched me, it was like I became possessed. The weak, thready protest I had, burned away the second his thumb caressed my mouth.

Between my thighs is a pulsating slip and slide and I need, need, need . . .

Fae lords, I need release. No, not just release. I want to be filled, stretched, pounded into.

I force him on the bed, and now I'm mindlessly grinding and rubbing on him. Some small part at the back of my mind tries to warn me I'm out of control.

The protest disappears when Brexley reaches up and grabs both my aching breasts, his thumb roughly brushing through the material of my bra. The one I wear to ensure I keep my shirt on because it's so ugly. Stretched out in the wrong places, thin, and stained, it looks like it belongs to a bedraggled housewife with seven kids who never wants to be sexy again, to protect herself from having to push anything more between her legs.

The off-putting bra was getting fired because it did *not* do its job. It had ONE job. But the scarred sex god under me tweaks and plays with my aching tips through the hideous thing. I groan and rock harder against him, my nails cutting down his hard chest.

He's unleashed something inside of me.

Calm down. You are getting out of control. You don't want to freak him out.

I can't stop. It's difficult enough to try and tone myself down in normal circumstances. But there's something about Brexley, the energy thrumming between us that makes it almost impossible to hold back. The spicy, masculine smell that wraps around me and makes me wonder if his cock tastes as good as he smells.

A whisper of sensation against my back and the worn material releases from my chest. I sit up, still keeping my center flush against the promising hardness between his legs. Brexley rips the bra off and throws it, muttering, "You should burn that."

Violence and sex pulsate in me too strongly, and I slap him right across the face for the comment.

Everything in me freezes. *Did I just do that? Over a bra I absolutely should burn?*

Yep. My hand stings from the contact, and his cheek has an angry red glow.

He blinks up at me in surprise.

What the actual faefucks is wrong with me?

The reality of my violence cools my crazy impulses. Shame has me backing up off him.

Brexley's nostrils flare as his eyes darken dangerously, and there is a glimmer in them as if . . . as if he liked it. I'm yanked back as he grabs my wrist. "You want to act like a little brat? I'll treat you like one."

He searches my eyes, and I can only guess what he sees there. Excitement. Deep, bottomless lust. And a girl who wants a taste of the violence he promises.

This is exactly everything that's wrong with me. Yet, I see the same thrill mirrored in Brexley's expression. Eyes alight, lips parted, and tongue curled as if to suppress his fathomless hunger.

He flips us, laying me out. Rearing back on his knees, he rips off his sweater, revealing an unreal body.

Seriously, it has to be fake. Nobody has muscles sculpted like that. There are corners and ridges I instantly want to lick and grind against. A dark patch of hair travels suggestively down his taut abs, disappearing into his low-slung jeans. *Sweet witchtits*, he even has those deep divots defining his hips that make the most innocent of girls dumb and horny as hell. And I sure as hell am not innocent.

My desire explodes back into full flames at the sight of him looming over me.

I reach up, wanting to touch every bit of him at once. Before I can, he grabs me by the throat, slamming me down on the bed.

Fear and excitement spike in me, and I wriggle under-neath him. He shoves a jean-clad thigh between my legs, and I gratefully grind against it.

The sneer on his face is utterly lascivious as he peruses my half naked body. My hip tattoo starts at the bottom of my thigh but travels up my side until the ornate flowers just touch the bottom of my ribs.

His gaze follows the trail upward and then flickers as he reads the lines of text tattooed under my breast. "If you want to be free, give everything up that weighs you down."

29

I think it's appreciation in his expression, but I don't know him well enough to say for sure.

Brexley's sneer turns into a full-on leer when his eyes catch on my pierced nipples.

"Gold," he mutters with appreciation. He toys with one, then the other. I groan as liquid melts at my center. When he tugs slightly at one, I yelp and grind harder. The little pain spike only makes me wetter.

"Fuck me." My demand comes out hoarse.

His irises flash an eerie blueish-white color.

Whoa, what kind of mage is he? He has to be pretty powerful to be working security for Gigi.

My wonder is gone the moment his lips latch onto my nipple ring. His tongue expertly plays with the barbell, sending hot sparks straight to my core. He unzips my pants and pulls back enough to rip them down my legs, my panties going with them.

Before I can do or say anything, he buries his face between my legs.

I cry out. My knees try to bend up and out, but I'm restrained from the pants wrapped around my ankles. He laps at me like a goddamn starving animal. Hot shivers roll through me as I'm devoured. My hips can't stop bucking and I grab his thick hair, rubbing his face even harder against where I need it most. *I ache, I need, I need, I ache.*

He growls into me and the vibration, along with his scruff, drives me to the edge of madness.

I've disappeared into a fog of arousal and sex. There is nothing else but the firestorm raging inside of me, burning hard and fast as I race upward toward orgasm. Then it hits me and I'm screaming bloody murder as I hump Brexley's face, riding it like my life depends on it. My inner muscles clench and shiver, releasing tension I've built up for days.

Brexley has trapped my clit between his skilled lips and continues to suckle it as I ride him. Then as my body starts to relax, his fingers push their way into me and the penetration, so shocking, filling me, sends me right into another orgasm.

"Yes, yes, yes," I scream, my head thrown back.

Then he's gone, replaced by cold air, even as I continue to shudder through the tail end of release.

Blinking, I try to clear my foggy vision. Brexley's pants are unzipped and his thick cock juts out from them. No underwear. Fae lords, why is that so hot?

Even hotter, he pumps his hard dick with his hand while studying me with a gaze so scorching it could be mistaken for murderous rage. He licks my desire off the fingers of his other hand, while making sounds of satisfaction. Like he's tasting a delicious cream instead of the remnants of my orgasm.

Despite what I'm seeing, my brain doesn't compute. Guys don't like oral. They do it as a means to an end. Most of the one-nighters I'd had were lackluster at best, if they did it at all.

"So fucking good, I could eat you all day, little Red." He slides his middle finger all the way in his mouth before sucking it off with a loud noise of appreciation.

Well, fuck me.

The thing between his legs is a goddamn beast, so long and thick, it's as unreal to me as the rest of his body.

I whimper, pressing my legs together, feeling painfully empty.

Those irises flash icy white again, as if he knows. He shoves his pants down over his ass. At the same time, I kick my pants the rest of the way off.

I might have been somewhat sated. I might have gotten

my wits back after that last orgasm. But I'm a whimpering, horny mess at the sight of him naked.

My legs fall open.

He doesn't make me wait. Brexley drives his dick into me with a punishing force. My entire body jolts up along with the bed, which protests with a loud creak. When he slams in at the hilt, I let loose a breathless scream. Pain and pleasure war for dominance, but either way, I'm winning.

I'm stretched, filled to a near painful degree. But then he moves, and the friction is scalding and delicious. That cock drags back and forth inside me and my greedy inner muscles clench and tighten around him, not wanting to let go for even a second.

He slams into me over and over again. My legs wrap around him, heels digging into his lower back, while my nails cut into his shoulders.

Brexley buries his head into the crook of my neck as he fucks me like a beast. Every thrust pushes me up, up, up . . . until I tip over the edge. The last two orgasms were just a warm up, an appetizer to the Big One. This orgasm grips me, milking shudders from the marrow of my bones.

A hysterical animal screams from somewhere nearby.

Wait, that's me.

To stop the sound, my teeth clamp into Brexley's shoulder and I bite down.

He lets loose something akin to a roar and his hips double time. Then his pace stalls and stutters. I feel warmth flood my insides.

Before the reality of my having unprotected sex with a stranger can get its footing in my brains, the bedroom windows shatter in a violent explosion. Two boots hit the ground with a crunch.

CHAPTER 6
COOLING OFF

BREXLEY

P anting, out of breath from the most intense orgasm of my fucking life, my ire flares at the interruption. I may have gotten one bone shattering orgasm in, but I wasn't nearly done. I could fuck this girl until we both died, and then we would continue humping in hell.

But now I'm pissed. Pissed I've been interrupted while fucking the most delicious creature I've come into contact with. Pissed her scent is now dampened by the awful stink of magic.

Turning to look over my shoulder, I see who dares interrupt the best fuckfest of my goddamn life. The mage is dressed in black tactical gear up to the head mask.

A growl radiates from the center of my chest as I extract myself from Red with the greatest amount of willpower I've yet to harness. She shivers and whimpers when I leave her body. Then she scrambles back on the bed, while I square off against the uninvited guest. My dick is still hard, jutting out and glistening from Red's sweet desire.

"Where is it?" The intruder's voice comes out deep and distorted from a voice modifier. The question is directed at Red.

"Where is w-what?" Red stutters, pulling the blankets up to cover herself.

"The recipe."

Her face crumples in confusion. "What recipe?"

"You're coming with me," the robotic voice says instead of answering the question.

I'm already between the intruder and the naked, bewildered redhead, but I step forward as an intentional block.

"You didn't say the magic word," I say. Cold air sweeps in through the room from the open window, bathing me in the magic stink. Ugh. I fucking hate magic.

Behind me, Red scrambles to gather her clothes and get them back on.

The intruder doesn't appear armed, despite their tactical gear. Which means their magic is likely lethal.

"I only need the girl. Leave now, and you'll get to keep your life."

"I'm afraid that won't be happening," I say, rolling my neck and earning a couple sound cracks.

The masked figure tilts their head to the side. "Don't be a fool, enjoy your afterglow, and leave while you have the chance."

"Don't worry, I'll still likely need a cigarette when I'm done." I shoot the human condom a grin that communicates every bit of the violence I'm about to inflict.

My fangs elongate and I know my eyes are flashing white-blue in warning as I let my wolf rise to the surface.

Muscles and tendons bulge in my body as I get ready to shift.

"You're a Were," the intruder says in surprise.

I've given them pause. But I'm about to give them a hell of a lot more than that.

"Holy faefucks," Red breaths from behind me. She's dressed again. Her feet stumble until her back hits the far wall. Her arms wrap around her stomach, as if she needs to protect herself from me.

With anyone else, I would have encouraged the instinct. *Yes, beware the Big Bad Wolf. I might bite your head off.*

But seeing Red cower gives me a strange, twisty feeling in my stomach. I don't like it. I want to taste her again, but I want her pliant and willing, like she was before.

The harsh sting of hydrogen peroxide hits my senses like a sledgehammer. The temperature around us drops sharply, and the broken glass on the ground begins to frost over.

The human condom is an ice mage.

Well, fuck.

The mage winds their arms around with dramatic flair before shooting their palms forward. Rain blasts inward through the broken glass wall, turning into ice as it rails toward us.

The idiot wants to take Red captive but could hurt her in their attempt to take me out.

I turn and blur toward Red. My hands slamming protectively against the wall on either side of Red's head. My body crowds over hers. She bites her lip and is still protectively covering her torso with her arms.

Good, it makes her a smaller target under my large form. Her pale eyes search mine, and I see the panic rising in them. I give her a half smile to let her know everything is going to be alright.

Then the ice chunks slam into me like frozen fangs, their bites cutting my skin. Blood dribbles down my back, and I groan in pain. Thankfully, I'd begun the shift and my thick muscles protect me from any serious damage. But the human condom drew blood, and now I'm even more irate.

Red's hands press against my bare chest, something sparking in her eyes. Fear for her? Fear for me? No, she is trying to comfort me. And there is still something darker flickering in her gaze, like lust or anger. The girl is an enigma.

Again, the question continues to circle my brain. *What is she?*

But this time I answer.

Addictive.

For a millisecond, her touch moves every single emotion inside me, even the ones I thought long since atrophied and shriveled up.

I harden against the notion. I won't have feelings, even for doe-eyed girls who burn me with their touch.

"Get out of here, Red," I growl. I can't have her getting hurt. She's my only link to finding my target right now, and I can't afford to lose my lead if I want to wrap this little mission up and get back to my own life. Back to my solitude.

She continues to stare up at me, as if frozen to the spot.

"Get out, now," I roar, pushing her toward the door. She jerks back, nearly falling down. But she grabs the doorframe just in time to stay upright. Then she flies out of the room like the devil is on her heels.

She doesn't need to see what's about to happen. She doesn't need to see the beast I'm about to become.

The hairs in my nostrils shiver from the sting of rising magic again. I turn back to the masked intruder. They swing their arms a second time, gathering blue sparkling energy from the air. Magic shoots out from their hands with a boom. I charge right at them and leap. My skin morphs with a painful yet satisfying crack, white and silver fur sprouting from my skin as my muscles engorge and lengthen.

A biting, icy cold slams into me, but by then I'm fully wolf, crashing into the mage. My fur protects me from the worst of the freezing temperature. We both go down, until I'm standing on their chest, all two hundred fifty pounds of me.

The masked person grabs my muzzle and the air drops several more degrees around us. The cold burn of their magic's scent intensifies in my nostrils. A painful ice explosion rakes through my mouth and nose. I yank my face away, howling in pain.

I paw at my nose, desperate to unfreeze it.

My muzzle may be frozen, but my rage has been ignited. I go blind with it. Succumbing to the animal inside, I lose my logical mind to the violence.

BACK IN MY HUMAN FORM, I don't know how much time has passed. Night veils the windows now, so I can't see outside, but I'm on clear display for anyone who wishes to watch. Cold frosts my naked skin from the mage's attack, but I'm still running hot and it's melting fast. Blood covers my chest and arms.

Fuck.

I vaguely recall the gush of copper flooding my mouth and the satisfying crunch of the intruder's neck under my jaws. They lay on the ground now, like a broken, eviscerated doll.

I kick the body. "Why did you have to piss me off like that? You interrupted the best sex of my life, and now I can't even ask you any questions, you selfish fuck."

I find my ring on the ground nearby, and slide it back on my forefinger. Spinning the band calms me a fraction.

Then I crouch down and peel the mask off. A woman with brown skin and white eyes stares up sightlessly. Her hair is frost blue, and she looks to be in her mid-thirties. Blood from her ravaged throat dots her chin and cheek.

I did that. But I'm used to the sight. It's what I'm good at.

She was a formidable witch, professionally trained and likely a Level Four. Most Level Three mages are formidable in a fight, while Level Fours are lethal in combat. There are only a handful of Level Five rated mages, and I'd yet to meet one. The only Level Five mage I was aware of also happens to be Red's grandmother.

I underestimated the ice mage. Had I known she was above a Level Three, I wouldn't have fucked around.

But no, that's not what caused me to lose my footing. It was that little redhead. My senses were in overdrive as she drove me to distraction. She was the haze around my head and frankly, around my cock.

I drag a hand through my hair, not caring that I'm likely smearing the silver strands with blood. "Well, thanks to you, this mission is already a fucking disaster," I growl at the dead woman.

Never mind, I fucked the target's granddaughter. Never mind, I'm the one who lost control to get my dick wet.

Crouching down, I search the body for anything that can tell me why she was here.

Was the mage here to kill Grandma too? The old man wouldn't have called in anyone else other than me. It would muddy things up just like this.

No, they wanted the girl, and . . . a recipe?

Finding nothing, I stand and spin the titanium ring around my forefinger.

I don't know where Grandma is, but I need to find the little redhead. She's my best chance at getting to Grandma.

My tongue licks my fingers, and past the blood there she is again, her honey, cinnamon desire.

I need to kill Grandma. It's the only thing that matters to me.

But at the back of my mind, I wonder now that I've tasted Red, will once be enough?

CHAPTER 7
THE POISON APPLE

RED

After running like hell and grabbing the next train back to Boston with my tail tucked between my legs, I find myself pacing the apartment.

Unlike grandma's grand McMansion, I live in an apartment on the eighth floor, with no elevator and a questionable foundation. Strands of warm Christmas lights ribbon along the walls and ceiling, combating the cold dark of the New England night. My school books lie open, forgotten on the rickety dining table. I adopted the piece of furniture off the street where it'd been abandoned with a 'free' sign on it.

I'd tried to study to escape the feelings inside me, but I can't focus. I can't calm down. My studies usually completely absorb me, pulling me away from the insanity of life to a place where cold, hard numbers make sense of everything. But it has little to no effect on my racing thoughts.

What the fuck happened? And did I really just fuck a Were?

The sore satisfaction between my legs confirms that.

Were packs live way up in the icy northern territories but are so reclusive, they are never seen in civilization. In fact, they are so rarely spotted, rumors regularly surface that the Weres have all died out.

Maybe I should submit a statement to someplace official, sharing I got fucked by a species people claim is extinct. For posterity . . .

The usual shame of yet another random hookup grips me, except this was the first time I'd fucked someone on my grandmother's bed. I cover my face with my hands. I'm a fucking monster.

We hadn't even used a condom. While I'm on birth control, I went to the convenience store on my block to get a plan B pill.

Piling on my shame is a wash of fear and confusion. Some scary ninja demanded I give them a recipe, then tried to kidnap me. On top of that, I haven't been able to get a hold of Gigi.

I texted and called dozens of times with no response.

I don't know where she is, and I'd long ago given up trying to keep track of her schedule. During any given week she could be in as many as five of the major mage cities conducting business and signing cookbooks.

Dropping into my big, comfy red chair, I try to settle. But then I vault up again in less than two seconds, wringing my hands and pulling my hair.

If Brexley, Gigi's new security guy, hadn't been there, I would have been taken, blown away by those ice shards, or worse.

Why? Did the ninja take Gigi and now they want me?

Why me? I don't matter, and I sure as hell don't have anything to do with Grandma's House. Maybe the ninja thought I had recipes from an upcoming cookbook? Or maybe a recipe for Magic Morsels?

I wrack my brain to figure out what the big deal could be. Some of the Magic Morsels can allow a human to shoot water from their fingertips, or even get a sense of someone's emotional state for five to fifteen minutes. But that's still hardly worth hiring an ice mage to get. They are silly little nothing powers for any real mage.

Gigi does have some pretty ruthless competitors, but are they really willing to personally target me and my grandma over some mini muffins and magic parlor tricks?

Unable to untwist my thoughts, I text Goldie, looking for a distraction. She's dating someone new, and she's always ready to gush about the current beau, whether she is over the moon with them, or if they are on the outs cause there is something just not right about him.

For a moment, I think of telling her about the crazy shit I just went through, but I dismiss it before the idea even forms.

After fifteen minutes, there is still no response from Goldie.

Unlike me, where I formulate a response in my head but often forget to actually send the damn text—Goldie usually hits me back in less than two minutes.

It's midnight on a Friday night, and I know she is on shift with Cinder. I'd be there too, if I hadn't requested time off to go home for the weekend. But the Poison Apple must really be hopping tonight to keep Goldie's digits off the phone.

I shoot a message to both Goldie and Cinder that I'm on my way to work.

Changing out of my jeans and sweatshirt, I slide on dark red pleather pants that stretch over my rear. I don a black corset top that leaves my arms and shoulders exposed and snap a couple gold bands around my biceps. A dash of smoky eye makeup and lipgloss is all I need. Then I flip my mass of hair over and hit it with hair spray. Tossing it back, my already thick hair is now a voluminous, wild, red hot mane.

I blow a kiss to my two fur babies, having already plied them with parting bits of banana. I step out into the icy New England night, wearing a heavy black duster with the hood up.

The Poison Apple is only five blocks away and with the anxious energy zinging through my veins, the walk flies by. Even with the chilly fall temperatures, my skin is too hot under my coat as I think about Gigi not responding, and about the attack. About the scarred Were driving his thick cock into me, drowning me in his spicy, sexual scent, making me come so hard I can't think.

I smack myself in the head, hard. But it doesn't keep me from getting wet and achy again.

"Stop it," I mutter to myself. "You do not need more sex. You can be in control of your urges. You are better than this."

From my memory, Brexley's flashing eyes pierce me like two razor-sharp rapiers.

The need to turn around and go straight back to the apartment and pull out my helpful *friend* from the bedside drawer to work off some of this extra energy hits me, hard.

Seriously, what is wrong with me? Gigi is missing, someone tried to kidnap me, and I'm still thinking of getting railed by the security guard.

I rationalize that I'm compartmentalizing and trying to focus on the least terrifying bit of the day. Still, my skin thrums and aches when I think of him eating me out like his last meal.

I smack myself a second time, just to drive the point home. *I am in control.*

I'll probably never see Brexley again. Who knows if he even survived the ice mage? I try to ignore the sick lurch in my stomach. No. I don't believe that. He can clearly handle himself.

I just need to stay calm and in control until I hear from Gigi. So I'll work my shift and then go home—*alone*. It's a bulletproof plan.

Except for the part where my fast-rising arousal has other ideas. It doesn't matter that I had the ride of my life less than six hours ago. When it's that time of the month, I am insatiable.

I'll have to be extra careful not to let anyone touch me tonight. That's not so hard. Right?

CHAPTER 8
FAE CHIVALRY

RED

M ark, the hulking security guard, and I share a nod as he opens the door for me, letting me past the ridiculously long line of waiting humans. The Poison Apple is often crammed with people until closing, but tonight is extra busy.

As soon as I enter, I see why my best friend didn't respond. Goldie races back and forth, taking drink orders along with my other friend and co-worker, Cinder. People crowd in, shoulder to shoulder at the bar, vying for attention. I can't even get a glimpse of the ornate onyx and warm wood bar.

Gold and glass liquor shelves reach up three stories behind where Cinder and Goldie rush back and forth, slinging bottles, and sliding drinks to the thirsty crowd. A low golden light emanates off the display, casting everyone in a flattering, seductive glow. The glass ceiling is vaulted even higher to accommodate the massive oak tree growing inside the building. Long, majestic limbs spread out over numerous blood-red tufted couches and standing bar tables. Fairy lights and lamps decorate the tree, making for a romantic, magical effect, though this is a humans-only bar.

The second Goldie dragged me in here for an interview four months ago, I wanted to run right the fuck back out. I'd never had a job before and working in such a packed, grand space intimidated the unholy hell out of me. I tried to tell the new friend I'd met in my sociology class that I'd work at the library. But Goldie insisted I would love it and that it would be good for me.

After Goldie gushed to the owner, Rap, over how she would teach me everything, Rap agreed I fit the aesthetic and hired me on the spot. She waved us off to get started that very night.

After an embarrassing number of broken glasses, and several heart-wrenching cry fests in the stock closet, I did eventually learn. And Goldie had been there the entire time, assuring me that I needed to give myself time and that I was doing great. Cinder also came to my rescue on more than one occasion, with her quiet confidence and endless patience.

Slowly but surely, I broke out of my shell. The more people I served and talked to, the more confident I got. I dressed to match Goldie and Cinder's aesthetic, and we became known as the *lost girls*. While we work fluidly and effortlessly with each other, we are untouchable. Our reputation as the lost girls took such a hold that Goldie made us shirts. She insists our slogan is "unfuckablewith," but we came to agree that was still a work in progress.

The running joke we pretend not to hear from some of

the patrons is that we would make the ultimate threesome experience.

Watching my friends flow behind the bar, I take a moment to feel the deep appreciation I have for them. Where I come from, no one shows weakness. A mere drop of blood hits the water, and everyone usually rushes in to tear the meat off the bones.

Not these girls.

Dropping my stuff off in the back break room and clocking in, I slide in behind the bar and instantly start taking orders and slinging bottles.

Where my studies couldn't soothe me, I fall into the monotonous rhythm of work. At one point, two arms surround me from behind in a quick, grateful hug.

I tense, but I don't feel the usual rush of desire. Someone my body recognizes as a friend. Goldie.

Thank the fae lords, because getting aroused by my friends would make my already bizarre little life way harder to manage.

Goldie pulls me down several inches, so she can plant a kiss on my cheek. Her curly flaxen locks brush against my bare back, and I know she's left a kiss print on my cheek in Mistress Pink. Goldie's favorite lip shade matches her bubblegum pink and black outfit - the signature colors she wears even when she's not at work. Her full bosom is practically falling out of the halter top today. Goldie is a full figured, curvy girl with honey brown eyes, and gravity-defying confidence. She taught me that a skirt can always be shorter, and how to own a room when I walk into it.

I'd forgotten that today. But now that she's near, I remember who I am and my spine straightens.

I catch Cinder mouthing a 'thank you' at me as well.

Cinder's sleek dark hair is up into two high buns tonight, and she sports a grunge, goth look with fishnet traveling up her legs and arms. Sharp eyeliner wings dramatize the purple, monolid eyes she was blessed with through her Asian ancestry.

Before meeting them, I didn't have any friends, and now I have a whole place where I belong. They treat me like I'm normal, like I matter. Tears sting my eyes. I'm not sure what happened at Gigi's house, but the heavy stone sitting in my stomach tells me I may not have this for much longer. Something is coming, and I'm not sure exactly what it is, or how to stop it. But ice ninjas and knee-melting Weres are not part of my plan.

"You are a saint," Goldie nearly shouts so I can hear her. "But we are going to talk later about why you're helping us losers instead of going home for break like you said you were going to."

I wave her off and turn my attention to the guy requesting drinks with an overly bright smile. He's pretty and he knows it. A classic fuck boy.

This place is a hotbed for fuck boys who know girls swoon over the magic atmosphere of the Poison Apple. Having all these guys on the prowl is so not great for me when I aspire to go home, *alone*.

My stupid hormones rush up to the surface when he shoots me a flirtatious wink. As I turn around to grab the bottle and pour him a round of shots for his friends, a certain Were's scarred face swims in my mind's eye.

I can't forget that crazy gut reaction I had to Brexley. The Were is a sex god, but he might as well have red flags tattooed all over his body. Or I guess, slashed across his face in the form of giant claw-like scars.

When I turn back around with the round of shots, I nearly choke on my own tongue. I'm face to face with the very person I'm thinking of. Brexley casually leans against the counter. His intense gaze delivers a stab of arousal straight through my gut. People nearby can't help but steal glances at him. I wonder what they notice first, his scars or sex god energy?

A knowing smile plays at the corners of his lips, as if to say, "Hello, remember me? I've been inside you."

Images slam into my brain.

His head between my legs.

The feeling of him pounding into me.

His hand clamping my neck, squeezing just right until I saw stars.

Recovering from my misstep, I hand over the shots to the fuckboy who drops cash on the counter and disappears back into the crowd.

"You can't be in here," I yell over the din of the bar, not hiding my irritation. How the hell did he track me here? And why would he travel the three hours to come find me? A little part of me is impressed, which is dangerous. He's under my skin and I need him gone.

My hands brace against my side of the counter as I try to appear unaffected, but my nails dig into the wood.

"It's my job. I'm your security detail, remember?" he shouts to be heard, but still manages a teasing tone.

"Brexley, you need to go. Now." I try to look busy and unaffected, grabbing dirty glasses off the bar.

"I thought you called security by their last names?" he goads. He's not taking me seriously.

I set the glasses in the wash rack under the bar, avoiding his gaze. "Yeah, well, I call dudes I've screwed by their first name." With a quick glance around, I see no one is paying attention to our rather loud, intimate conversation.

And that wasn't true. I usually never saw or called my one-nighters again.

"We didn't even use a condom," I say in a hushed tone. He perks up, having heard me, despite the loud chatter and pulsating music.

"I'm clean if that's what you're worried about. As for the other thing . . . "

Pregnancy, he means pregnancy and it's a leading question. "I'm clean too. I'm also on the pill, and I took plan B just in case."

He immediately relaxes. Wish I could be so cavalier. *Men...*

I lean in, and he does the same until we are mere inches apart. "This is a humans-only bar, in a humans-only part of town. I can't serve fae," I say.

I can't serve mages either, but if he is a Were, he is a fae. Fae creatures are born into certain races like fairies, elves, and ogres. Each type of fae has their own brand of unique magic talents specific to their race. While mages are closer to humans, they possess an innate magic talent and can learn and grow their index of spells and abilities.

Brexley's dangerous, icy gaze drops to my lips as I speak before they lift back up to meet my gaze. "Good thing I'm here to service you."

The temperature of the bar raises at least sixty degrees, and sweat pops out on my brow and lower back.

Whoa, nelly! I don't need this.

My hormones had calmed down from our earlier tryst. But a simple phrase and a hot gaze and every needy impulse in me stands up and starts singing operatic, like a bunch of horny altar boys.

More, more, more. We must have more.

Heat rushes directly to my center. I casually reposition myself to press my thighs together as if it will keep the sudden rush of wetness at bay. I thought I had scratched this itch. But I want him again. Bad.

Are my episodes getting worse? Or does this silver-haired Were possess some extra special hold on me?

Brexley swipes his tongue out, touching the corner of his mouth in that positively lewd way again and sweeps his gaze up and down my body as if he knows the effect he has on me.

Fuckity fuck nutting nut nuts.

Internal muscles clench, making me feel oh so achy and empty. My body can't handle this. I'm too strung out. Like a heroin addict who can't wait to get their next dose. And if it weren't for the crowd I would have leapt over the counter and mounted him already.

I close my eyes and take a calming breath, reigning in my raging hormones. I calm a fraction enough for my irritation to rise again.

He doesn't know me. If it weren't for my bonkers hormones this wouldn't even be a thing.

Probably. Maybe.

Taking control of the mood, I ask him seriously, "What happened after I left?"

His expression immediately loses all flirtatious nature, and I'm facing a dark, foreboding man. No, a beast. It ripples there, just under the surface. Now that I've seen it, I can't unsee it.

"Don't worry, little Red, I took care of it." He says it in the patronizing tone I've heard all my life from people who work for Gigi. It's like he slammed a hand down on a big red button inside me and my arousal takes a back seat to watch the show.

"First off," I point one finger at him. "Don't call me that. And second, don't treat me like a child with some misguided notion you need to protect my delicate sensibilities."

Respect enters Brexley's eyes. "I shifted into my wolf form and killed her."

I work to keep my chin up and my face blank. *Killed her? Fucking killed her?*

"Who was she?"

"If I had to guess," he lowers his voice to a volume only I can hear, "I'd say a hired mercenary."

Ice fills my veins. "Why would someone hire a mercenary?"

Brexley runs his fingers along the countertop. "You heard her–for a recipe. So what secret recipe are you harboring that has got people ready to kidnap and kill over it?"

I bite my lip. "I don't have any recipes. I'm a nobody."

Brexley dips his head to look at me from under an arched eyebrow. "We both know that's not exactly true."

I flex and stretch my arms from where I'm braced against the bar, anxiety mounting in me. "I don't have anything to do with Gigi's business. Hell, I don't even know what she's working on half the time."

A pang of guilt goes through me at that. It's not that I don't support her empire, it's just that it makes me feel so small and powerless. I know what a disappointment I am, even if Gigi will never say it. In the human world, I'm still a nobody, but my little life feels important.

"You should be protecting Gigi. She's the one in danger," I tell him, loudly. My stomach lurches. Nothing has happened yet, as far as I know. But I feel like I'm falling hundreds of feet without any net to catch me. After my mom died in a car crash when I was four, Gigi became my only family. Even if we live very separate lives, I would be devastated if anything happened to her.

"Is she okay? Where is she?" I ask, realizing he would likely know since he works for her. Maybe he has some other means of contacting her. I hit up some of her entourage, but they are just as confused as me. She seems to have all but vanished.

Fae lords, I hope she's okay. She *has* to be okay.

"Hey, can I order yet or what?" A man next to Brexley asks.

I hold up a finger to the guy, still awaiting my answer.

Brexley doubles down. "I'm to stay close to you."

"Is she okay?" I ask again, fear turning my insides cold.

"Hey, flirt with scar-face some other time," the man interrupts again. "I need a drink, babe."

I shoot him a glare, but Brexley is already straightening and turning toward the guy. Coming to his full height, he has several inches and twice the cut brawn of the dude in a bright purple polo shirt with too much gel in his hair. And sweet fucking fae, the collar of Brexley's shirt is stretched wide, revealing the symmetrical, tight muscles wrapped around his shoulders and collarbone.

"You owe the lady an apology," Brexley says evenly.

I'm on the other side of the bar, and even I have the urge to take a step back. Danger laces his words.

A moment of trepidation crosses the man's face, but he wrinkles his nose and doubles down. "You are the one being rude, buddy. There are a lot of people here trying to get a drink. We waited out in the cold only to come in and find this chick screwing around instead of doing her job."

Brexley repeats his words slowly. "You owe her an apology." Then his fangs begin to elongate in his mouth, eyes flashing a bright ice blue.

The guy stumbles back, causing protests behind him that go silent when people see what has him tripping over himself.

My hand slides down my face. What in the witchtits did he not understand about the humans-only bar?

"Oh fuck, is that . . . is that a Were?" Goldie breathes behind me, her hands encircling my arm. "I thought they were all banished way north and live in packs in the freezing cold."

"They were, and they do," I say, having zero explanation as to why one followed me home.

"I—I'm sorry," the guy stutters in my direction.

"Like you mean it," Brexley says in a low rumble I find both soothing and scary as fuck. He gives the guy a pointed look at his pants.

The guy pulls out his wallet and slaps a twenty-dollar bill on the counter and stutters out another apology before making a hasty retreat. He keeps glancing over his shoulder as if terrified he'll be followed and torn to pieces.

By the time Brexley turns back to me, his wolf has receded except for the icy blue glint in his eyes. A smug grin curves his lips. Goldie clutches my arm harder. I turn to her. "Can you give us a minute?"

She searches my eyes to make sure I'm not secretly in distress before returning to her section. Even Cinder is shooting me concerned glances from the other end of the bar.

"You're an idiot, you know that?" I say, enunciating the words as if it will help him understand.

The icy glint disappears from his eyes, and the grin turns into a grimace. "Why's that?"

With a jerk of my head, I bring his attention to the many security guards winding their way through the crowd to get to him.

"Well, I can't say it's been fun," I say, picking up a bottle of whisky, ready to go back to serving.

"I'm not leaving," Brexley leans over the bar and growls.

I lower the bottle to stress my point, "Go find my grandma, and do your job."

Presumably, Brexley can report to homebase to find her.

You could too, a nasty voice whispers in my mind.

Hunter. I could call Hunter.

A cold sloshing rocks my gut.

Brexley's expression empties as he takes quick stock of the room. Mark, Rishi, and even Aki, the three muscular and very capable bouncers close in from every direction.

Then with a nod, Brexley disappears into the crowd. When I say disappears, I mean, disappears. Even security is left scratching their heads, trying to figure out where he went.

I try to swallow down the thick lump of anxiety that built in my throat, but it stays lodged there. Judging by the pointed looks I keep getting from Goldie and Cinder, there are about a hundred questions coming my way over what the hell just happened.

I lick my lips once, twice, three times. The old habit I worked so hard to break just resurfaced. A true indicator I've just been pushed past my limits. I bite my lower lip to keep from wetting them again.

There is still time to figure out a cover story. Because there is no way in hell I'm telling them who I really am. I've worked too hard to have a normal life with normal friends.

Them knowing about the attack, Brexley, and my grandma won't help any.

I was a reject in my last life, I won't be one in this life too. Magic needs to stay the hell out of my life, and I plan to keep it that way. And it starts with staying far away from Brexley Moon.

BLOW YOUR HOUSE DOWN

BREXLEY

When Red finally emerges from the Poison Apple, it's three am. Not only is she impossible to miss because of her hair, but also because my body grew excited mere moments before she exited onto the street.

Without knowing why at first, my blood ran hot and fast, my heart pounded in a frenzy. My palms even turned sweaty, how fucking ridiculous is that? I'm a professional killer. I stay cool and calm no matter what the situation.

Except, there is no denying when I spot the little redhead, I want to chase and pant after her like an excitable pup. It's as if life infuses me with a rush of dopamine, or a hit of ecstasy.

"On your way to Grandma's house, little Red?" I ask, falling into step next to her.

Red jerks, looking at me with bewildered fear for a moment. And then something else—something darker flashes in her eyes as she licks her lips. She shakes herself and resumes a quick pace down the street. "Don't call me that. What are you doing here?"

"Like I said, I'm to stay with you," I growl.

We continue to walk in the freezing night, silent now.

Being out in the cold for hours upon end has made me cranky. Desperately wanting to be near her again makes me utterly cantankerous. I couldn't stop thinking about the many sides of the girl I'd known for less than a day, and that is a problem. I can't be led around by my dick if I want to get the job done.

The instant I left the bar, I wanted back in. I needed to be near her.

To find Grandma. To kill Grandma, I insist to myself.

But I feel like a drug addict in withdrawal. I want to bury myself in her again. Make her scream and shudder until she passes out.

In any other circumstance, I would have turned and high-tailed it from such an intense attraction. I'd have fled from anything threatening to suck me in and tie me down.

But that's ridiculous. Some little redhead I just met can't have that kind of hold over me.

Not when she's in an oversized sweatshirt and messy bun, and not now when she's wearing impossibly provocative, form fitting clothing. Not when her hair is a luxurious thick mane released for every lustful eye to ogle in that bar.

No. I've just been hard up. While I can admit the girl is one hell of a lay, and that she is an intriguing enigma, it's not enough to get me to forget why I'm here.

My last marker needs to be cleared. More than anything I need to be free, truly free of any bonds.

I'm here to kill Grandma. That was the only reason I protected Red.

"You didn't have to do that, you know," Red says, and her brows gather as she grows pensive. Her voice is even raspier than normal, after yelling back and forth to patrons in the noisy bar.

Sweet fae lords, I remember how that voice sounds screaming in pleasure.

"Do what?" My hands fist in my coat pockets. My pants are suddenly too tight.

"Make that guy apologize. Dealing with rude jerks is kind of part of the job description. I can handle myself."

My hands relax.

The granddaughter of the most powerful witch is fiercely independent, and I can't help but respect that. I still don't know why she isn't cozy in some mage city penthouse, with her own entourage, doing designer drugs and practicing dangerous magics for thrills, but damned if part of me doesn't want to find out.

"I'm sure you can. But I can't abide rudeness."

Her eyes flick to me. "Wouldn't you say it's rude to keep following a girl around when she asks you to stop?"

"I have a duty to fulfill." It's not a lie. She simply doesn't know what duty I'm fulfilling.

"Is my grandma okay?" she asks again in a low voice as if afraid of the answer. Her shoulders tense and her hands push harder into the pockets of her coat.

I decide to go with the truth. "I don't know. But I need to stay close to you until she resurfaces."

Red swallows hard but doesn't say anything else as we continue to walk down the frozen streets. Dawn is still hours from breaking. I can't help but wonder how often she has done this trek by herself. It isn't safe for a human girl to traipse around Boston like this. Maybe if she had magic to defend herself, but I still haven't scented an iota of power on her.

Finally, we stop at an old, crumbling brick building. Red turns to me and sticks her chin up. "There, you walked me home. Are you satisfied? You can go now."

"I need to come in with you."

Fear flickers in her eyes before she can mask it.

That's right little girl, let the Big Bad Wolf in your house.

"That's not necessary," she says stiffly.

I resist reaching out to push some of her hair back over her shoulder. I know too well that it's soft as velvet. "I don't know who sent that mage, or why your grandma has gone underground. But it's likely you're not safe here."

Red shook her head. "No one will find me here."

"I did," I pointed out.

She bites her lip as she arches a brow. "Yes, how did you find me?"

I could tell her it's what I do. A wolf has hunting skills unlike any other. She didn't arrive at her grandma's in a car, and it wasn't hard to scent her to the train station then to Boston. But explaining that would make me seem like a creep.

Yes, little girl, I hunted you across state lines using your sweet scent.

I simply say, "I have a particular set of skills."

Acceptance enters her eyes at my explanation. Afterall, most humans and mages know very little about Weres. It's best to keep a shroud of mystery around all I can do. Fae abilities are usually kept to their own.

"You can't be my security, not after we . . . "

"Humped like animals?"

She flinches but her eyes darken with lust at the same

time. Little Red wants me again, but she won't admit it to herself.

"We got caught up in a moment," I say. "It won't happen again."

My cock screams at me for uttering such bullshit.

Red licks her lips.

There is a way to make this simple for her. Make her hate me. "I know you're young, but you can be an adult about this, right?" I make sure to use the most condescending tone possible.

Eyes the color of morning mist fly wide, and her cheeks flush bright cherry red. She looks as if I slapped her. "I'm not that young. I'm twenty-four. And what are you? An old man at twenty-six?"

"Twenty-nine, which makes me the more adult of the two of us."

"That's just stupid."

"You're the one who is catching feelings, though I hardly blame you. I am a good time in the sack." I waggle my eyebrows at her, but I know I come off more vicious than mirthful.

"I am not catching feelings," she shrieks.

"Good, then you'll have no problem with me continuing as your security detail."

Red glares at me, knowing she walked right into that. "I still doubt any mage is going to bother traveling into a human city to track me down."

I step into her space, forcing her to look up at me again. Why do I find it so satisfying? Is it because I enjoy feeling like the predator I am, dominating her space? Or is it the way her eyes go round, and her jaw slackens as if I've short circuited her brain?

"How do you know they won't follow you here?" I ask.

Then I pull the dirtiest lie of all to get what I want. "Don't you think it would add to your grandmother's troubles if you put yourself in danger?"

It's a low blow and I know it. Though I have no idea as to the kind of relationship Red has with her grandma, her concern for the old woman's safety has me betting they're pretty close.

Red continues to stare up at me, her eyes searching back and forth, internally debating what I've said.

The urge to dip down and kiss those lips grips me, but I hold steady. If I kiss her, she'll never let me up to her apartment.

"Fine, but there are rules," Red challenges.

"Do tell, college girl."

She rolls her eyes at my nickname before stating her terms. "No touching."

I don't respond. My brain immediately jerks back to all the touching I did earlier today. How much I want to do it again.

She holds a finger up. "I'm serious, no touching. Not a single accidental brush. You keep your hands off me at all times."

"I can do that," I say, trying to convince myself I can.

"And you sleep on the couch," she finally submits, turning sharply and stomping up the couple steps to unlock the building door.

I suppress a smile as I trail behind her. Little Red just let the Big Bad wolf into her house. Now all I have to do is keep from eating her up . . . again.

CHAPTER 10
OFF KILL-TER

BREXLEY

"Aren't you going to come in?" Red asks, sliding her coat off. She sets it down on a table that looks like it might collapse under the weight of all the open textbooks and her laptop.

I'm not surprised often, but she keeps managing the feat.

"You live here?" I say, hoping against hope this is some kind of sick joke.

Red furrows her brow in a full out scowl. "Yes," she snaps. "Now in or out, little doggie, and shut the door."

I'm too stunned to even respond to her insult.

Red disappears into the next room.

I begrudgingly shut and lock the door behind me with a *snickt*.

Still hovering at the entrance, I can't help but notice how one of my legs is bent while the other is completely straight. The floor is horribly tilted. I'm well aware old construction in New England has a tendency to shift and slip, but my senses are shouting at me *the whole damn building is going to come down and to get out now.*

When Red emerges, she's in black sweatpants and a soft-looking forest green University shirt. She wrestles with her massive locks, wrapping them up into a messy bun again, tendrils still managing to escape her wrangling. Big puffy slippers cover her feet as she pads *up* to the kitchenette where she begins to fill the kettle with water.

The small apartment has been painted tangerine and the kitchen cabinets are eggplant purple. I wrinkle my nose, wondering how many of the furniture items she got from a thrift store. I can smell the remnants of all the other families, the other houses, the history.

I'm not a fan of history, or the way it smells.

The scent of mildew wafts off the book-cluttered table. I'd bet my fluffy ass she likely plucked that piece of garbage right off the street.

A human is unlikely to smell the layers of what is assailing my nose, but I feel attacked in this small space. Not only my nose, but my equilibrium, because of the fucked-up floor.

"Want some tea?" Red asks without turning around, pulling down a box of tea from a mostly empty cabinet. "I always need a cup of chamomile to signal to my brain that it's time to sleep, otherwise I'll be up past dawn."

"Why—why do you live here?"

Red turns around, resting her hip against the counter. "Excuse me?" She raises an eyebrow.

I still refuse to move from the doorway. "You're right, that came out wrong. Why do you live *like this*?" I cast a look of disbelief at her place.

Fae lords, if I weren't so horrified by her living conditions, I'd be more affected by that pout.

"If you don't like it, you are more than welcome to leave," she says coldly.

I start to take a step forward, and I'm immediately disoriented by the floor and stop again. "Seriously, you're related to the most powerful witch, known for her lifestyle brand of throw pillows, cookie recipes, and comfort. Why in fae lords are you living in a dirty little hovel?"

In a second, she's across the room poking me in the chest. "First off, we don't say witch or warlock anymore. It's an outdated term. My Gigi is a mage. Secondly, my apartment is not dirty."

She may think I'm crass, but I'm far too much a gentleman to tell her about the smell coming from the magenta fabric she fashioned into makeshift curtains.

"Did she cut you off?" I lean in. "Because the way you talk about your grandma led me to believe you have a good relationship, but this. . .a person would only live like this if exiled to it."

Red's eyes flash, a blush building in her cheeks. She lets out a pissed off snort that reminds me of a bull.

"I'll have you know, I choose to live like this."

I'm not fast enough to mask the horror that crosses my face.

Red's eyes turn to slits. "Is this why you work for my grandma? You want the bougie lifestyle and sweet pay? I wouldn't have pegged you for one of her shallow servants who kiss ass to get the perks."

"I don't kiss anyone's ass, but I sure as hell have standards," I say, sweeping out an arm to indicate her lack of them.

"I have standards," her voice becomes shrill, and she fists her hands. "I choose to stand on my own two feet and earn my way."

"You just walked away from all the money and comfort to live like this?" My confusion deepens.

Red stomps back *up* to the kitchen to remove the whistling kettle.

"Forget it, you wouldn't understand," she mutters angrily.

I risk falling through the floor by crossing up to her. "Explain it to me," I say, stepping close until Red is forced to turn and tilt her head back to look at me. I tell myself it's necessary to be this close so I can breathe in her sweet scent instead of the barrage of odors from her furniture.

She still wears a defensive glower but says. "I'm a magic dud, okay?"

If she expects a reaction, she won't get one.

Apparently, my senses didn't mislead me. They usually don't, but it's still hard to believe the infamous Grandma would spawn a relative devoid of magic. Eloise Rogers was the first person to infuse foods with magic enough to share with humans. But more than that, she knows how to scale her businesses.

She developed her own brand of magic flours and baking spices, available in many markets. Eloise Rogers owns a number of farms with crops she has magically infused that return every season with the same powerful properties. Which means Grandma's House and Magic Morsels are brands that will long outlive her. But only Grandma's House has access to the certain ingredients that go into making Magic Morsels. She simultaneously created and cornered a market.

It isn't that crazy that a Level Five mage sired a Level Four daughter. The dossier stated Eloise Rogers's daughter, Samantha Rogers, died in a car crash some twenty years ago. No picture was attached, only a list of stats. Her talent involved helping develop other people's magic abilities. Most mages of her ilk usually end up as professors or managers. And she was in fact, studying to be a teacher.

But to have that much familial power dribble down to a dud of a grandchild? That's unusual. There was no mention of Red whatsoever, and even using my own sources, I could not find her background. And that means there is no record of a father or his race or breeding.

What could cancel out so much power?

"I flunked out of Fairy Fine Arts Academy, okay?" Red's hand grips the countertop as if bracing herself. "Everyone thought I would rise to the power of my grandmother, that I would be the most powerful legacy of all, but no matter what test I underwent, how much I tried, I have zero, zippo, zilch magic." Fury brims in her eyes but I can tell she only directs it at herself.

She sets her rear against the counter and crosses her arms. "Gigi didn't exile me. In fact, she was really nice about it." Red's hand disappears in her sweatshirt sleeve as she wipes at her eyes.

"It was everyone else who was fucking awful. Humans think that FFA is all milk, honey, and power. But it's a hellhole and I was glad to leave it. Those insufferable legacies who were born into billions of dollars and all the magic they could want have zero conscience, and I never want to be anything like them. So I left. I left it all behind to start a new life, one I built myself."

She glances at me before closing her eyes and rubbing her forehead with her still sleeve covered hand. "I don't know why I'm justifying this to you," she sighs.

When did my throat get so tight? I concentrate on the redhead next to me, resisting the intense urge to wrap my arms around her.

The pain she experienced at FFA, I want to know it, touch it. Because it might be similar to my own, and knowing we both . . .

I take a step back.

This is too much. I'm in danger of actually caring about this girl.

For witchtits' sake I met her mere hours ago, there is no accounting for this.

Okay, so I immediately fucked her on her grandma's bed. Maybe that's what has got my head all mixed up.

But I'm going to destroy her world, so I better stop being so interested in it. No more questions. I've never had a second thought before completing a kill, and I can't afford any sympathies.

I can't afford to brush that fallen hair from her bun back from her face as I tilt her chin up to kiss those pouty lips.

I take a second step back.

This is all irrelevant information that does not serve my goal. Knowing the tangy sweetness between her legs is irrelevant.

A rustling comes from behind me. Whipping around, I ready myself to fight off whatever presence has invaded. My fangs and claws emerge, ready to bite and slash at any threat.

How did I get so distracted that I didn't notice someone entering? Did they enter through the window?

"Please don't kill my rabbits," Red says dryly. After one last brush of her cheeks with her hand, she visibly pulls herself together then says in a baby voice, "Are my sweet fluff butts awake?"

She passes me to greet the two bunnies who twitch their noses and eagerly run up to the edge of a large pen and stand for her to pet their floppy ears. One is the color of cinnamon, and the other is a light gray. Red calls the brown one Bangs, a girl rabbit, while the other is a boy named Bombs. Red unhooks the latch, releasing two small fur-pedos who zoom out, badgering her every step.

"Mama's got you," Red coos while carefully making her way to the fridge. She pulls out a big bunch of cilantro. They give credence to their names, Bangs and Bombs, by the way they explode in a frenzy. The two rabbits go nuts, running in circles, leaping into the air, shaking their butts. They follow her back to their corner where there is a litter box, several tunnels and a doll's bed. She lays the greens in their bowl and they are soon crunching away at the thick stems. Their setup is nicer than Red's.

She starts to walk away from them, but then shooting me a wary glance, she latches the pen shut again. I get the impression she would let them stay out if it weren't for my presence.

"Litter box trained rabbits?" I ask.

Her voice sounds tired as she pours hot water into a mug already equipped with a bag of chamomile. "I'm not home enough for a dog, and I don't care for cats." Then she shoots me a warning glance. "If one whisker or hair is out of place on my rabbits in the morning, I will personally turn you into a winter coat, wolf form or not."

"How about that tea?" I say, noting she made only one cup.

She sniffs. "I read somewhere that tea is bad for dogs." Then she disappears into her bedroom, kicking the door shut behind her. I'm left with a tiny, lumpy couch set at a dramatic slant next to two happily munching rabbits.

How did my uncomplicated life come to this? I ease my way *up* to the couch and sit down. I can already tell it's going to be a long night.

CHAPTER 11

EVERYONE'S A BUZZ

BREXLEY

Red can't sleep. I know because I can't either.

I hear her toss and turn through the thin walls. I've been twisting the ring around my finger and pacing the nauseatingly uneven floor for an hour. If I weren't deliberately silent-footed about it, she'd likely hear me too.

Why does the floor have to slope down toward the bedroom, like gravity is pulling me toward her?

This little fire-haired girl has gotten under my skin. All I want is to break down her door and fuck her unconscious. I want to nuzzle that spot between her neck and shoulder before sinking my teeth into her, leaving a mark. Like she's my territory.

She's not mine. She's as good as the next female.

Not a single bit of my brain believes me. Not now that I know how Red tastes, how she feels under me. I could walk out into the night and find a willing girl to fuck in the shadows and slip back here in no time. But that's not what I want.

Again, I eye the door, considering how little effort it would take to destroy the barrier.

I teeter on the edge of control in a way I haven't felt for years. Even knowing the full moon is in a couple of days doesn't account for this.

I experienced plenty of this when I was younger. When I reached nineteen, and the moons grew full, I'd have to retreat and chain myself up. Otherwise, I risked going feral on the streets and hurting someone with my moon craze, or worse, accidentally mating with someone.

I'd rather die than mate with anyone.

But I haven't had to yank the leash on my restraint like this for years. Had I seriously been inside her only twelve hours ago? It seems like it has been forever.

A frustrated groan reaches my ears, and I hear wood slide against wood. Red's opening a drawer. Then a low buzz starts up.

It takes me less than a second to realize what she is doing. I find myself pressed against Red's door. My hands splay across the peeling paint.

Her honeyed arousal has surrounded me all day, but now it fully blooms even through a closed door. The tiniest whimper reaches my ears as the vibrating buzz oscillates. I imagine her rubbing her toy against those impatient lower lips, circling her overly sensitive bud. Needy little thing. She's been licked and fucked to orgasm already today, but it's not enough.

Her tense energy vibrates through the door and I know she's not even close to satisfied. I'm not either.

My fingers curl until my nails dig into the wood.

Fuck my life. I'm so hard I could drill a hole in this door with my dick.

No touching, that's the rule.

I do everything I can to diffuse my arousal. Everything but actually move away from the door.

Submitting to my need, I unfasten my pants and pull out my rock-hard cock with one hand. I stroke my length with an almost punishing grip while the nails on my other hand continue to dig into her door.

A low muffled groan has me wondering if she's using a pillow or her hand to dampen the sounds. The wavering of the buzzing increases. I'm almost positive whatever she has, she's driving it into her wet slit.

My hand slides up and down my cock at top speed. My arousal is so tight it gathers at my temples, the base of my spine, and in my balls.

Her gasps and moans can't be choked down, and I can tell she's coming.

Like with most women, I buried my face in Red's shoulder as I fucked her. I don't care to see my partner come, and I don't care for them to see me. It's an unnecessary intimacy. But suddenly I'm desperate to know what Red looks like as she shakes and melts around her toy.

Fuck. I want to know the part of her lips, the arch of her back. I want to wrap my hand around that elegant column of neck and force her to look right at me as I slam her body over the edge with mine again.

My hips jerk as I explode. Release sweeps me away, swirling images of Red in my mind.

When I return to my senses, some of the fire drained from my blood, I realize what a fucking mess I'm in.

Not just because I marked her door and need to clean that up as soon as possible. . .

When I look up, I realize my nails turned to claws at some point and I've scratched four long deep gashes into her door. It looks like an animal tried to claw their way in.

They mirror the deep scars on my face.

I might as well have carved my name into her door.

Stepping back, I barely register the buzzing has ceased. For the first time, I seriously consider cutting and running. Zipping up, I tell myself I could walk out the door and spare myself any further confusion, leaving her to find claw marks and a mess on her door.

Could I tell the old man he needs to find another way for me to repay him my debt? Or better yet, tell Jameson to fuck off and forget I owe him anything entirely.

An invisible noose tightens around my neck. The wolf in me is as much made of loyalty as it is of violence and wildness. And the tight collar around me for the rest of my life would only remind me of my unfulfilled duty, and of Red.

No. I need to stick this out. Finish my mission, and then when I leave, I never have to think about the ridiculous magicless witch who wants to live as a human in an apartment with a tilted floor.

I can control myself. I have to.

CHAPTER 12

MOCHAS & FRUSTRATION

RED

Come morning, I drag my ass out of bed to find an equally cranky Brexley already awake in the living room. I wrapped myself in a kimono, in case he was still here. I half expected him to flee in the night. But nope. There he lurks at my window, wearing nothing but low-slung jeans, and looking like he'll murder the next person who speaks to him.

He's as sexy as he is dangerous. I want to lick up those ridged abs.

Well, now I'm extra damn ornery.

"What the hell happened to my door?" Claw marks are slashed across it, and part of it, near the door handle, is shinier than the rest. Like someone spot cleaned there.

I go to the fridge to grab a big handful of parsley for my leaping bun babies. Bangs and Bombs descend on the treats as soon as I drop them in their pen. I'm glad to find them unharmed. Otherwise, I'd have to start my morning with murder. And I'm far too busy for that today.

"I had a nightmare," he growls.

"And apparently I haven't woken up from mine because you are still here," I mutter. Oh yeah, I need some caffeine stat. I should at the very least be nervous at how he defiled my door. But no, I'm just pissed off.

His eyes darken and his nostrils flare.

Oooh scary. Whatever.

Doing my best impression of an ice queen, I inform Brexley, "I'm going to the campus café. I need to study and take some practice tests."

"So kind of you to invite me," he practically snarls. Yep, definitely as cranky as me.

"I'm not, I just assume you'll follow me, like you followed me home, little doggie."

"Keep it up and I'll pee in your shoes."

"As long as you don't hump my leg." I say before disappearing back in my room to shower and change.

"You wish," I hear him mumble.

I do. I really do.

I barely slept a wink. Knowing Brexley was in the other room, fully capable of banging me until I passed the fuck out, made it even worse. I itched to open the door and mount him.

Though it wouldn't give me the same level of satisfaction; I pulled out my sex toy. Only after a couple of orgasms was I able to fully curb myself from making another huge mistake.

Brexley clearly doesn't like me, having all but called me immature and implied he can tolerate me while he completes his mission. But that doesn't seem to stop him from being okay with fucking me. Despite my rule, I know he wouldn't stop me from slipping into the living room and riding him until we both come.

But *I'm* not okay with it. So I stayed put.

It takes a minute to pull all my hair up in a sturdy clip before I step in the shower. The head only spits lukewarm water, despite cranking the heat all the way up. I'm careful not to get my hair wet because I'm not up for dealing with extra bowls of water from the sink to fully get all the soap out. Another day I'll be running on dry shampoo and fumes.

Scrubbing myself down, I do some math.

Only three days left until my hormones reach their frenzied peak, and then I'll even out. I've been through this enough times on my own to know the pattern. While I never felt comfortable telling Gigi about my urges, I once tried to talk about it with my doctor when I was seventeen. He brushed it off as hormones and that everyone my age goes through it.

Somehow his dismissive response never made me feel all that assured. Either I am a freak, or everyone else has massive amounts of self control compared to me. And right now, my self control feels pushed to the limit.

Three more days of feeling increasingly hot, empty, and aching with the sexiest beast I've ever seen nearby is a fresh level of hell for me.

At least my arousal is somewhat dulled by the fact I'm so tired and stressed, my brain can barely function.

Still no word from Gigi. I have to remind myself she is one of the most powerful mages in the world, and if something had happened, it couldn't stay hidden. I shoot off a quick prayer she is okay as I finish getting ready.

T HE B EAN and Book café already brims with holiday decorations and students who are also cramming for finals. The place is the definition of cozy with equal parts book-shelves, windows, and exposed brick walls. Plants cover nearly every surface and drip from the ceiling along with Edison bulbs.

I love that the coffee scent is so strong, I often come out smelling like dark roast after spending a few hours here.

"Damn," I say under my breath.

"What?" Brexley growls. His mood hasn't improved one bit.

"My favorite table is taken." I gesture to the favored spot. It's the only spot big enough to easily support my books, laptop, and the massive mugs they use here.

Without a word, Brexley stalks over to the table where a couple of girls are studying. They glance up at him. They do a double take as he continues to tower over them. I can see lust and fear fill their eyes in equal measure as he speaks to them. I can't make out what he says, but next thing I know they are grabbing their stuff and heading out. As they walk by, the girls shoot knowing glances at me.

My jaw drops, and I can't refasten it, not even as Brexley waves me over to my favorite spot.

"What did you say to them?" I ask as I drop my bag on the table.

"That if they don't leave, I'll huff and I'll puff and blow the table over."

"You're an idiot," I say, but I'm still stunned.

He casts me a wicked grin. "Now repay the favor and get me a big black coffee. Or I'll give the table away to someone who is nice to me."

I scoff but walk to the front counter.

The barista offers me their newest assortment of Magic

Morsels. My heart lurches in my chest. Sure enough, my grandma's face is on a big poster by the pile of baked goods. Damn. This was one of the last spots Gigi's franchise hadn't touched. Paranoia creeps into my bones again, and I mumble that I'll pass before making my usual order along with Brexley's coffee.

Soon, I'm cradling my cup of caffeine. I bring my face close to the steaming wide brim mug and inhale deeply. This mocha, loaded with extra espresso shots, is going to save my life today.

Exhaustion, stress, and horniness makes me a bit dramatic.

"You look like you are going to start licking from that thing like a cat with a bowl of cream," Brexley says, having already chugged half a mug of black coffee. He spins the ring around his forefinger.

I glare up at him. Goddammit why did that sound so sexual? It only pisses me off more.

"Do you come with a muzzle, or do I need to buy one?"

"Not a morning person, are we?" he taunts.

I position my middle finger on my cup especially for him. He smirks, but his eyes are still dull and tired. He's got a case of messy bedhead and his clothes are rumpled, but it doesn't detract from his appeal one bit. Damn him.

I'm back in trash troll mode, but I did manage to wash my face and brush my teeth. My campus hoodie is so big, I consider disappearing right into it, like a turtle. Then I'll resurface in two or three days.

The hot, chocolatey liquid hits my lips and I close my eyes and let out an involuntary moan. What I actually want to do is let out a sob of relief.

A growl escapes Brexley. But when I open my eyes, he is

chugging the rest of his coffee and looking anywhere but at me.

Glancing at the time on my laptop, I note it's already eleven AM. Panic wraps around my throat. My study time is siphoning away like sand in a sieve.

I pull out my laptop and get to work. Dr. Langley's comments have lodged themselves in my guts like hard marbles. I *have* to do better. I just need some dedicated study time.

My phone vibrates on the table, a text. I snatch it up, hoping against hope it's Gigi. My heart sinks into my stomach as I set it down. It vibrates again. I don't bother picking it up this time, moving my attention back to my laptop.

The phone continues to buzz as text after text comes in. Finally, Brexley picks it up and hands it to me. "Aren't you going to answer?"

I take it from him, careful not to touch his fingers. With a glance, I confirm it's still not Gigi. "It's my friends," I say.

"Has something so horrible befallen them that they need to text you every point five seconds?" His irritation is back in full force.

"No," I say, "I have."

His brows dip as he scowls, confused.

"You. *You* are the horrible thing that has befallen me. They want to know about you," I say in an accusing tone.

Brexley's face smooths as he leans back in his chair. "What are you going to tell them?"

"I don't know," I say, my tone clipped as I tap two fingers on the back of the phone. "That's why I'm not responding."

"You could tell them I'm your new study partner," he grins, but it comes out more like he's baring his teeth.

The look I shoot him could freeze water.

"They don't know who you are, do they?" he asks, propping an elbow on the table.

My crankiness jacks up another level. "No, and I don't plan on telling them. I worked really hard to cobble this little life together, and I'm not going to let some weird magic shit mess that up."

"So you're prejudiced against magic because you don't have any?" He toys with his mug, his tone indicating he already assumes it's true.

I wrinkle my nose. The way he says it makes me sound like a petty brat.

My laptop shuts with a click. "No, I'm prejudiced against magic because I hate the hierarchy bullshit it creates. The way mages think they are better than everyone else. The way everyone is judged by their ability and not their character."

"Sweetheart, that's the whole world you are describing," he says drolly.

My teeth grind and a low growl gathers in my throat. Brexley may be hot, but I realize he is as stuck up and condescending as all the mages I've grown up around.

"That's not true. Some people don't care about what you can or can't do for them. Leaving all the magic bullshit behind and living in a human city, I've made real friends. And speaking of which, they still want to know why a Were is in a human city. What should I tell them? Shall we start with where you were raised, move on to how many brothers and sisters you have, and finish with why you act like a possessive stalker?" I goad, my fingers now poised over the phone, as if prepared to type.

His scowl returns.

I set the phone down. "Hey dude, it's your own damn

fault. You outed yourself with your alphahole behavior last night and now everyone wants to know *all* about you."

"I was being chivalrous," he mutters. "A mistake I won't make again."

I bite back the urge to laugh.

Glancing at the phone, I rub a hand down my face. "But seriously, what in the hell am I going to tell them?" All the messages are from Cinder and Goldie, mainly Goldie.

Because I wasn't on the schedule last night, I split as soon as it slowed down, leaving them to close. And thusly skated by without having to answer any questions. But today is a new glorious morning and I don't need a forecast to know the barrage of questions aren't likely to let up.

"What in the faefucks do I tell them?" I ask out loud, not really expecting an answer.

He crosses his forearms on the table. "Well, I may be around for a while, so you probably need to tell them something."

"There's no way they are buying you as my study partner," I rub my forehead again, already planning to buy a second mocha. Maybe just a cup of espresso shots loaded with sugar . . .

"How about your tutor?" he suggests.

My hand closes around my remaining mocha.

No, I can't afford to throw what precious little I have left at his face, no matter how bad I want to.

Those blue-gray eyes catch the movement. He suppresses a smirk as if he knows exactly what I'm thinking.

"Well, you don't want to tell them I'm your bodyguard, and I need to stay close. I'm a fan of Occam's razor."

"Occam's razor?" I straighten.

"Yes, it's a principle that states the simplest explanation is the best one."

I wave a dismissive hand. "Yeah, I know what it is. But how does it relate to this situation?" I raise the cup to my lips, begrudgingly ready to take the last swallow.

"I need to stay close for the foreseeable future, and you say I act possessive. Tell them I'm your boyfriend."

I choke on that last sip. I fight for my life against the chocolate and coffee trying to flood my windpipe. The coughing fit is so violent I get looks from people at other tables. Brexley starts to get up as if he intends to pound on my back. I hold up a hand, silently signaling him to sit down.

When I get ahold of myself, I wipe away the tears that leaked from my eyes. "How the hell would they buy that you are my boyfriend when they have never heard me mention you before? And where would I even meet a Were?" Alarm bells clang all the way around. This is a bad idea.

His tongue presses against the inside of his cheek as he leans in, bracing his forearms on the table. "You can tell them you didn't want to say you had a werewolf boyfriend in Canada because you didn't think they would believe you."

"Is that where you're from? Canada?"

Brexley's face shutters as if he dislikes me asking him such a personal question. "No, but isn't that the deal? A long-distance boyfriend or girlfriend from Canada is fake ninety percent of the time?"

I edge back and look away, biting the inside of my cheek. How does he keep doing that? Infuriating me one minute and making me want to laugh the next.

"Fine," I say before my brain fully processes this. Then

my head snaps toward him. "But the no touching rule stands."

"That will be . . . difficult. To convince them that is."

I suspect he means it'll be difficult on more than one level. "You'll have to rely on your charm. Because there will be absolutely zero touching. It's that or I tell them you are a creepy stalker. Goldie will likely go after you with a stiletto and I've long suspected Cinder can shoot lasers from her eyes." I pop an eyebrow for dramatic effect.

Brexley rolls his eyes. "Fine. Fake boyfriend, zero touching."

I nod as if satisfied. But I'm not satisfied, not by a long shot. My legs cross and clench as I try to ignore the throbbing need there.

I want Brexely between my thighs. It's almost impossible to focus knowing how he feels inside me. How bone-meltingly satisfied I'd been, even if it was only for a brief time.

But I double down on my focus. Nothing is going to keep me from passing this class, graduating with my degree and protecting my low profile.

CHAPTER 13
ISSAC CLOUT - FAR KILLER AND HELPFUL DUDE

BREXLEY

I want to ask Red about what she is studying. The question swells and ebbs over and over inside me, like waves lapping the shore.

But I know if I ignore the impulse, it will go away. That's how I learned to live on my own. Cut off all ties, and simply ignore that gnawing hunger inside for companionship. Like any muscle, the urge atrophies over time.

I told Red I threatened those girls to get her favorite table, but the truth is I surreptitiously slid them a sizable amount of money and said they looked like they could use a lunch break and my girlfriend could really use this table. It's part of what fueled my ridiculous idea to tell Red's friends we are romantically involved.

If I turned my wolfish charm on those two girls, I likely wouldn't have needed to pay them off. But while I didn't go to college, I'm aware most students are just scraping by. I know how that feels firsthand.

Red's gobsmacked expression morphed into pure delight, as her body relaxed like she'd been given instant relief. Her reaction hit me in the gut like a sledgehammer. I liked the feeling far too much and made a point to myself not to do anything to evoke it again.

Red insists she needs all the study time she can get. I know it's partly a mechanism she is using to compartmentalize the fear she has for her grandmother, but the other part of her is possessed by something else. Ignoring the question at the tip of my tongue is harder to do when I can smell the panic and fear mounting the longer she sits.

Finally, I stand, telling her I need to stretch my legs. She waves me off without a second thought, so I walk out into the crisp, gray daylight.

The urge to shift and run, sprint through the city until I can't think, grips me. I want to get lost in my animal side, instead of thinking about the redhead inside the coffee shop. I spin the ring on my forefinger more furiously than before.

My phone vibrates with an unknown number. I hit the button but say nothing as I put it to my ear.

"Is it done?"

Impatient old bastard.

I turn my back to the café, not that Red could hear. "No. There's been a . . . complication."

"Complication," Jameson echoes, and I hear all his anger and impatience in the one word.

"Seems I'm not the only one after Grandma," I explain. "She's gone underground."

"I don't care. Get it done."

My hackles rise. "Of course, I'll get it done," I snap.

"I waited twenty-five years, I'm tired of waiting."

For a second I want to ask why. Why he wants Grandma dead. But no, that won't make a difference. I'm bound to the marker and it will be done whether I know why or not.

"Not my fault you're on the verge of death, old man," I taunt. "Now get off my back and let me do this my way." I end the call before he can respond. The cold bites at my cheeks and nose and I welcome it. It cools my fury and restores my logic.

Before I know it, I've walked a distance from the coffee shop into the midst of a campus field. On a sunnier day, the courtyard would be crawling with frisbee throwing idiots and study groups, but the clouds overhead threaten imminent rain or snow.

I'm still close enough to the café that I can keep an eye on Red, but I've gotten enough distance that I realize how much I've lost it. I'm here to kill that girl's grandma and I can't lose sight of that.

But she just texted her friends that I'm her boyfriend. I scrub my face with a hand, stopping to lean against the base of a statue. Why did I say such a thing?

It's fucking ridiculous, that's what it is.

I look up at the copper molded face of Issac Clout, the human conqueror of fae. His curly hair is etched in detail, and he holds up his sharp, fae-killing spear. Had he spotted me, he would be as ruthless with his weapon as I'll be toward Red's grandmother.

I straighten. The current situation is perfect for my purposes. I can remain as close as I want now. Doing whatever is necessary is what makes me the best hunter there is. I will sniff out Grandma, and Red will stay in her little human world. Not that I care where Red stays or goes.

I stride back toward the café. As I approach the table

where Red sits, I can tell she's agitated. Sliding into the seat across from her, I try to pretend I don't notice her continually squirming in her seat. While her pen taps against the table without any rhythm, her knee jiggles beneath the table. I'm tempted to say something when she sighs for the third time in five minutes, but I manage to resist.

Not my business.

Just when I think she's about to explode, Red pushes up from the table. "I need to get home and grab a book I forgot. And then I need to go to the library. I'll be able to think better there."

The empty mugs rattle on the table.

Our gazes lock in uncertainty.

Another slam of the ground and all the tables rattle violently. Red grabs her mug as we hear the crash of ceramic around us. Others look around, frantically trying to discern the cause of two earthquakes so close together.

A dark feeling fills me. Red's gaze slides from mine to over my shoulder, to the café window, rounding in horror as they go. "What the fuck is that doing here?"

I turn around. Two massive trunks in a gray, green hue lumber toward us. The pair of elephantine legs belong to an ogre, and it's headed right toward the café.

This isn't a coincidence. This is another attack.

"We need to get out of here."

"Holy hell, how is another fae here?" she breathes, while she remains sitting as if frozen by fear.

I reach out to grab her arm, but she jerks out of reach before I can.

No touching, right.

Instead, I grab her laptop and shove it in her open bag with her books, using it as bait. Now she is on her feet.

"Is there a back way out of here?" I yell to a slack jawed barista. She blinks twice before shaking her head no.

Faefucks. Knowing there is no other way, I charge toward the door, Red's bag slung over my shoulder. She's hot on my heels. *Good girl.*

Outside, the crisp air is now polluted by the ogre's hot, fetid breath. He stands over twenty-five feet, and his head flattens at the top where long, lateral wrinkles of flesh gather over his eyes. A mouth decorated with three rotted teeth opens and a grunt emerges. Worst of all, a mottled schwang hangs between his legs as he doesn't have a single stitch on.

"Yuck," I hear Red mutter, and know she's admiring the same appendage.

Two murky yellow eyes roll down toward us.

"Run," I snap.

We both take off, but the Ogre has a long reach. A ham fist closes around Red, and he plucks her off the ground.

The pained sound of distress that escapes her makes my blood boil and panic shoot off like fireworks in my head.

I drop the bag and rip off my shirt. I kick off my boots, then my pants and jump into action. My muscles swell and heat until they are almost on fire. Silver fur sprouts on my naked body and I change in a single leap. The Ogre turns, lumbering away with Red who yells curses and struggles futilely in his grip. Clumps of grass spin out from under my feet as I close the distance.

Leaping up, I land on the ogre's shoulder, biting down on the thick hide of his neck. It should be his most vulnerable part, but like the rest of his body he's protected by almost impenetrable skin. Still, I sink my teeth in harder. A roar escapes the ogre, and he opens his hand, dropping Red.

She hits the ground with an 'oof,' but she survives the

fall. The Ogre wraps a meaty hand around my torso and flings me across the field. A yelp escapes me as I fly through the air before smashing side first into the ground. I skid several more feet.

The ogre's hand closes around Red a second time, even as she tries to scramble away. I don't hesitate to dash across the field. I leap again and bite into the same spot on his neck, hoping I broke some of the skin so I can dig in. Trying to cut in deeper, I jerk my head back and forth. A sour, salty taste fills my mouth as I break through the tough hide, tasting the copper of blood. But my bite is too shallow. I'm not doing much more than annoying the ogre.

I'm swatted away like a fly, and slam into the ground again. Pain radiates through my ribs. They're bruised if not cracked. My focus outweighs any injury, and I turn to the lumbering Ogre again, already reassessing.

The damn thing is built like a tank, but ogres are notoriously slow, stupid, and easily confused. I doubt the fae will let me challenge him to a game of wits. Then my eyes alight on Issac Clout's statue. Maybe he can continue to serve his mission in death.

Dive bombing the ogre's feet, I nip and bark, weaving between his legs. The Ogre can't walk straight as I badger him. He groans and waves his free hand in an attempt to keep his balance.

I slowly herd the Ogre toward the statue. The Ogre grunts and whines in discontent as I continue to attack his feet. When he's close enough, I let the ogre's leg slam into my body. The blow knocks the wind out of me and definitely cracks a rib, but the fae creature loses his footing. Down he goes in a slow fall forward. The squish of the spear puncturing through his right eyeball accompanies a splash, and a hellish cry of pain from the fae. I ram into his other leg, pushing it out from under him. The Ogre sinks further onto the spear until he stills. All is quiet save for my panting breath.

I trot over to the left side of the Ogre and find Red trapped by a big flat hand. My heart leaps up to my throat at seeing her flattened. I can't help the half growl, half whimper that emerges from me.

The protective side of me riots inside. Is she hurt? Not that it matters. Red's health isn't pertinent to my mission. And yet, if Red even so much as has a bruise on her body, I'll have to kill the Ogre all over again.

An angry blush floods her cheeks as she struggles against the weight. I can't help her in my wolf form, so I focus until my bones crack and rearrange. Fur retracts, and in a few steps, I am a man again.

"Fuck nuggets," she mutters, still trying to get free. I realize she's more pissed than anything.

Red halts her struggle, turning her gaze up at me. Pupils dilate as she takes in my naked form. Her gaze stops between my legs. She's seen my dick before, but it's good to know it still gives her pause.

That's okay little Red. I can't touch you, but you are more than welcome to touch me.

As if realizing she's staring, she jerks her head away.

I lift the massive hand. My muscles strain against the dead weight.

As soon as Red crawls out, I ask, "Are you okay?"

She rubs her ribs, and mutters, "Yeah, I'm fine."

I wonder if they are bruised from the ogre's hold.

A crowd begins to form as people deem it safe enough to get a closer look. I cross to my pile of discarded clothes, pulling my pants back on. Patrons of the café stand outside, alternately surveying the dead Ogre and me with overt fascination.

I want to bare my teeth and snap at them. But I simply shove my feet into my boots. A soft coo comes from a college girl nearest me as I raise my arms to pull my sweater over my head. Then I grab Red's bag, ready to get the hell out of here.

Red waits nearby, but her glare is trained on the ogling girl who sighed over me.

"Let's go," I grumble, and Red doesn't fight me.

"Hey, wait," someone yells behind us. "The cops are on the way."

I pick up the pace. "We are not dealing with Five-O," I say, in case Red considers stopping.

"You think it was after me?" Red pants as she tries to keep up with me.

"The Ogre planned on taking you somewhere," I say. "After the ice mage, it's too much of a coincidence."

"I was still hoping. . ."

I cut her off. "Hope will get you killed."

Red frowns and I half expect her to start arguing with me about the merits of hope. Which would be a tremendously bad idea, since I'd be forced to rip her throat out on the spot.

Instead, she gently asks, "You okay?" Red gives me a worried up and down look.

Her concern softens me a little. She's not the one who tossed me like a bag of beans. "A couple cracked ribs. They'll heal in a few hours."

"Oh, good," she says, though her eyes and voice are vacant. "Okay, well let's get back to my place."

"Forget that. We are leaving town."

She stops and rears back. "What? No."

Irritation scratches at my insides as I'm forced to stop

and explain. "They found you not once, but twice. Whoever wants you won't stop."

And if Red gets nabbed, there goes my only connection to Grandma. It has absolutely nothing to do with wanting to keep the little redhead safe.

Nope. This is business, and she is my asset. Simple as that.

Red's expression cools. "You'll stop them."

"Oh, *now* you don't mind me hanging around?"

"I am not leaving. I refuse to be scared or bullied." There is a strange tremor in her voice. Whatever emotional response she is having, I don't care.

Her stance squares off as if preparing for a fight.

I drag a hand through my hair. "Why can't you just listen to me?"

She snatches her bag from me, still careful not to touch, then slings it over her shoulder. "Because I'm a person with thoughts, opinions, and free will. I can see how that would be so annoying."

"It is annoying when I'm trying to save your cute little ass."

She blinks. "You think my ass is cute?"

I close the space between us, adrenaline and annoyance getting the better of me. "I don't know. Turn around and let me see it again." I press my tongue against the inside of my cheek.

Red's eyes narrow as she looks up at me, our faces inches away. "You're a pig, Brexley." Then she stomps around me.

I take the opportunity to appraise her backside. Need and arousal grip me as I imagine those perfect globes bare and flushed after I've bent her over. I rub my chin.

Again, the beat of some ancient drum fills me,

compelling me to claim her. The girl has no idea how much she is tempting fate.

"I'm the Big Bad Wolf, baby," I correct her, but she is too far away to hear

CHAPTER 14
FLOATING PENS & MEET THE FRIENDS

RED

When we get back to the apartment, I'm only half surprised to find two figures draped on my couch. Goldie and Cinder have made themselves at home, holding steaming mugs of coffee, a box of Magic Morsels German chocolate cakes between them. Empty wrappers litter the couch and floor.

Why are there a bunch of pens on the ground, rolled to the side of my apartment?

Then I remember the Magic Morsels wedged between them give humans the power to levitate small items for a short period of time. Judging by the torn plastic sheaths, and the number of pens on the ground, they've been here a couple hours.

Fantastic. They've set up on my place to jump me and Brexley.

"Where did you get the coffee from?" I set my backpack

down on the table. The girls openly gape at Brexley who followed me in. He doesn't seem as perturbed by their presence as he does by the tilt of my apartment floor. He braces a hand against the wall by the door, but if he's hoping the posture makes him look at ease, he is failing miserably.

Goldie doesn't peel her greedy eyes from Brexley as she answers, "I brought it. Fresh bag in the top left cabinet."

Seeing the pot hasn't yet been drained, I grab a mug and finish it off. "Did you hear an Ogre wandered onto the campus?" Cinder says.

The pot clangs as I slam it back into its perch too hard. My hand shakes.

"That's crazy," I say.

That's crazy is the go-to phrase whenever you have to respond but want to say nothing at all.

"Why are your clothes all wrinkled and messed up?" Goldie asks.

Looking at my reflection in the microwave, I can see my hair is also wild and messy. "Because I'm a hot mess trying to prepare for this one final."

Not bothering to add sweetener, I inhale the hot coffee. My insides still feel wonky after being nearly whisked away by that Ogre. I feel so ungrounded, even I begin to wonder if my tilted floor isn't a bit much.

Goldie hums, unconvinced. "Apparently a werewolf showed up and killed it when it started to attack people. There was footage," Goldie adds, swinging her gaze back and forth between me and Brexley.

They know. They know it was Brexley. They might even know the Ogre tried to whisk me away if someone was filming with their phone.

"We saw. It's been a crazy morning," I say, still giving

them nothing. I'm holding my mug like it's a lifeline. "Good thing Brexley was there. Ogre seemed confused. Maybe he was on drugs or something. He acted totally weird."

"You okay?" Cinder asks. Her question is sincere, and she isn't pushing for details. I'm grateful for that.

I nod. "Yeah. I'm cool. Like I said, it's just been a crazy day."

How many times can I use the word crazy? The words coming out of my mouth are so lame, I'd shoot them and put them out of their misery if I could.

Tall and silent over there isn't helping back me up. He couldn't come up with a decent lie to embellish my story?

Maybe I should shoot him instead. Give him the Old Yeller treatment . . .

"So." Goldie turns her attention back to Brexley.

I launch right into deflection. "Oh my gosh Goldie, did you feed the buns? You didn't have to do that. I texted you I've got them since I'm staying in town."

Bangs and Bombs are snuggled together on the carpet rug, their little noses bopping up and down as they sleep. Usually they'd be jumping up and down for my attention the second I get home. I recognize the signs of a bunny treat coma. Cinder especially spoils them when she drops by.

"Oh, did you? I guess I forgot," Goldie says airily.

She didn't forget. She and Cinder are here to pry into my life, and I can't tell if I'm annoyed or honored they care enough.

"Aren't you going to introduce us?" Goldie asks, shooting me a pointed look.

"Yeah." Cinder leans over to lock eyes with me as well.

The words behind their expressions are completely clear. *What the actual fuck? You have a secret boyfriend?*

Then before I can say anything, Goldie is on her feet and across the room in front of Brexley. I take the opportunity to sink into the spot on the couch she vacated. I pull my legs up and try not to think about how I'm in a modified fetal position. It won't protect me from the cringe about to happen.

She shoots her hand out at Brexley with a friendly smile that might possibly drown him in sunshine. "Hi, I'm Goldie."

For a moment, I don't breathe as I wait for him to take her hand. Brexley's expression is inscrutable. His dark, fore-boding broodiness crammed in the same room as my friends feels like being inside a very small glass, filled with oil and water.

If Brexley wants to play the part of my boyfriend, he is going to have to play nice. Though maybe it's better if this whole thing blows up right now, so I have an excuse to send him away.

Finally, he takes Goldie's hand and flashes a quick, strained smile. "Brexley Moon. Pleasure."

Next to me, Cinder waves a hand at him. "I'm Cinder."

Brexley nods at her. "Hey there."

Is it possible to die of literal embarrassment?

As I rush to suddenly gather up the pens on the ground, a trashy reality show about sexy mages all stuck in a beach house together flickers on my TV. I've watched it with my friends before. The group starts with a million dollars, but every time someone uses their powers, money gets knocked off. At the end, the group splits whatever's leftover. But between their need to impress and bed other mages in the house, it's clear most of them are willing to screw the others over. Or just screw them.

I set the pens on the table and return to my coffee and saving grace.

They are all Level Two mages, and still come from money and prestige. But anyone below a Level Three is considered insignificant in the magic world. Level Twos are especially savage in their attempts to claw their way up in any way possible, which makes them perfect for reality television.

Had I stayed at FFA, I would have come out with a rating, but Level Zero isn't technically a rating.

Goldie sets a hand on her hip as she cocks her head. "How come we've never heard of you before, Brexley?"

I drop my head, resting my forehead against the warm ceramic. For faefucks sake.

A smile quirks the corner of his mouth for a moment. "You'd have to ask Red, over there."

In less than a heartbeat, I'm on my feet. I barely save my coffee from sloshing out of the mug. "Brexley, do you want some coffee? You look like you could use some. I'll make some more." I practically run to the kitchenette and pull out the bag of grounds.

"Why don't you come all the way in?" Goldie says, a cheeky dare in her tone. "Cinder and I don't bite."

I barely catch the hot glance Brexley sends my way.

"I do," he says.

Oh. My. Fae lords. He did not just say that.

Still, he crosses to my reading chair and sits on the edge, first pushing up the sleeves of his sweater before resting his forearms on his thighs. It reminds me of a crash position. While Goldie reclaims her spot by Cinder.

I pause and close my eyes. Here it comes . . .

"Where are you from, Brexley?"

"Canada."

"Where in Canada?"

"Jasper."

"How did you get those scars?"

She did not just ask that.

"A fight I didn't win. That was the last fight I didn't win."

He seems somewhat comfortable answering that one, but I suppose with massive scars like that, he gets asked the question fairly often.

"How did you meet Red?"

Brexley pauses. Oh crap, I did not prepare him for this interrogation, but I figured we'd have more time.

Still, he doesn't take too long to respond. "Red mistook me for someone else. So I played along for a little while, until she realized I wasn't who she thought I was."

I turn off the faucet from filling the coffee pot with water. The urge to laugh bubbles up despite my anxiety.

As if sensing my reaction, Brexley's eyes flick to me, emanating a smoldering heat in my direction that makes me want to grip the counter and cross my legs.

He's just doing it for show, Red, calm your damn self.

Still looking at me with blatant intensity, his lips twist at one corner, an almost smile. "It's become our little joke, and now we are inseparable."

Cinder asked the question this time. "Who did she think you were?"

"Do you all attend Boston University?" Brexley redirects the conversation like a pro, but I don't know how long he'll put off Goldie.

My friends nod. Goldie says, "I'm majoring in business, and Cinder is majoring in art with a minor in philosophy." She barrels ahead, taking control of the conversation again. "I didn't know any Weres live this far south."

He doesn't answer. I can almost feel the room cool several degrees.

"Does your pack live near here?"

A dark cloud rolls into the room with her question.

"No." His tone in the one word clearly a warning not to press.

Either Goldie doesn't catch his blatant red lights, or more likely she doesn't care. "I thought Weres couldn't stand to be far from their packs for long? I've heard all kinds of crazy theories about it being a social co-dependence thing. That Weres have a physical bond that doesn't allow them to stray too far from the pack or they will literally die." She laughs at the last bit. "Seems no one knows much about it."

My finger hovers over the brew button, as I've completely frozen. Asking a fae about the inner workings of their clan, pack, or whatever group they are a part of is considered rude. But Goldie doesn't care. She's going straight for the jugular, and fear grips me that he will go for hers. Maybe literally.

But underneath my fear is a burning curiosity to hear his answer.

"It's the second," Brexley says in a quiet voice. His forearms still rest on his thighs, but his hands grip together in a tight fist that causes taut muscle to pull along his exposed forearms.

"What's that?" Goldie says, taken aback.

"It's the second thing you said. The bond is a lifeline that gives strength to the pack. Should a Were be cut off or exiled from the pack, they usually die within a matter of months. As would most humans if they were plucked from all of humanity and set on a frozen tundra by themselves."

Don't ask it. For fae lords sake, don't ask the question, Goldie.

"Were you exiled from your pack, Brexley?"

As desperate as I am to know the answer myself, I can't let this go on. I hate when someone tries to dig into my past and from the look on Brexley's face it looks like he feels the exact same.

I smash the brew button and quickly cross to sit on the arm of the reading chair. I'm careful not to touch Brexley, but I give the appearance of the doting girlfriend at his side. "Since I'm staying in town after all, I'm going to work the weekend with you guys at the bar. I could use the money anyway."

What I *need* is time to study my ass off for my finals this upcoming week. But what I need even more right now is to stop this conversation. Maybe if they know they'll see me later tonight they will leave now.

I could handle the situation if it was just myself, but Brexley made everything . . . complicated. He won't be allowed back in the Poison Apple now that he'd outed himself.

On the television, I recognize Everett Silber, a tele-kinetic. He stares at the camera with earnest sincerity, not bothering to push away the stray golden hair that frames his handsome face.

My gut flops like a slimy fish out of water. I attended the academy with him. On the show, he's portrayed as one of the more sensitive personas, America's sweetheart. But all I remember is how Everett would rearrange my locker from the inside so all my books would collapse on my head when I opened it. And when I started carrying all my books around with me to avoid the prank, he'd put extra pressure on my backpack, making it so heavy it would force me to my knees. Then he would laugh with his buddies as they traipsed away.

I lick my lips and fiddle with my nose ring, reminding myself I'm not that girl anymore. Here, I'm not some loser dud who can't defend herself. But no matter that I got piercings, a wardrobe update and a tattoo on my upper thigh, even the sight of Silber makes me feel like that girl again.

I need my friends out of the apartment. *Now*. Before Brexley or I ruin everything.

Goldie frowns at my offer to help at work. "The bar is super busy, but you should—"

"—definitely help us out," Cinder finishes for her.

Goldie shoots her a glare, but Cinder is unphased.

Sitting on the arm of the chair, electricity and heat practically sizzles off Brexley's body, drilling into mine. After fighting an Ogre and shifting, his scent is more powerful than before. I wish I could say it was like wet dog or something equally off-putting, but no. The gall of this sonofabitch to engulf me in a masculine scent close to that of sex, along with an underlying pine and spice . . . I cross one leg over the other as heat and liquid race to my core. The temptation to reach out to him becomes almost painful.

"Perfect." I clap my hands together to keep from touching Brexley. "And like I said, Goldie, since I'm back, you don't have to watch the buns for me anymore. But you are an absolute saint for treating them and bringing coffee." And I mean it. Having true friends has been life-changing, and I never want to take that for granted.

She grumbles a 'you're welcome' but she clearly knows I'm shutting down the conversation and doesn't like it.

Cinder sets her empty cup on the coffee table and stands, "We'll see you tonight then." The look she gives

Goldie might as well be a dozen needle jabs to get her ass off the couch.

"Right," Goldie says, standing as well. Then her face brightens as she turns to Brexley. "I'll talk to Rap, our boss, and explain how you were defending Red from that douche pickle and make it okay for you to come hang out with us tonight. And then we can chat more." The hunger in her eyes is bottomless.

I love my friend, and how she throws herself into things and attacks everything with exuberance. But nothing could have prepared me for this level of protective meddling. If I weren't trying to keep so many secrets under wraps, I might be enjoying this kind of love and attention. But there is too much at stake. My new life suddenly feels set up on strands of delicate sugar that are oh so breakable. If I just gut through whatever this thing is for a little while longer, I'm sure it will all blow over. And I can just live my life how I want to.

Before I can answer that Brexley won't be coming tonight, he jumps in.

"Sounds good, I appreciate that."

In lieu of glaring at him, I grind my teeth.

Goldie blows us a kiss. "Fantastic. See you both tonight!"

With that, she and Cinder make their exit. As soon as the door shuts, I fall to the couch like a collapsing star. "That was intense."

I scrub my hands over my face, hoping I can wipe the intensity of this morning away. Maybe I should pour whiskey in my coffee? Too bad I don't have any in the apartment.

"I'd say they bought it," Brexley says, watching me closely.

I scowl at him. "You don't understand. Goldie is a heat seeking missile. That was only the beginning of the interrogation. Tonight will be even worse."

"While I don't love questions, I can handle her. And Goldie seems like a useful ally. Being able to stay near you in the bar is for the best. By the way, have you heard from your grandma yet?"

My brain started to spiral into the possibility of another Ogre attacking the bar, but I redirect to my phone, checking it for the hundredth time today. "Not yet."

I pick up the empty snack cake box with Gigi's smiling face on the front of it. My heart sinks into my stomach. Where is she? Why are mages and fae coming after me? Is this still over one of Gigi's recipes?

I thought we'd done a stellar job of keeping my relationship to her under wraps, but I guess showing up at one of her houses made me a target.

"Does it bother you?" Brexley asks, interrupting my thoughts.

"Hmm?"

"Seeing her face everywhere?"

The box is still in my hand, and I realize I've been staring at it. I shrug one shoulder. "I've always been proud of Gigi, but yeah. It's a constant reminder of what a disappointment I am."

"Your grandma told you that?"

I shake my head. "No, but I know it's true. Life as a mage is all about ability, family, honor, and legacy. Without power, you are nothing. And everyone will make sure you know exactly where you stand on the hierarchy. If you try to step out of line or work your way up, the smackdown is usually swift, and often violent. Though it doesn't stop mages from trying."

I gesture to the television where Everett Silber floats a bevy of red roses around an attractive black man who now has a seductive glint in his eye. Everett may achieve short-term celebrity, but no one above his station will see it as an impressive enough feat to mingle in their social circles. At most, he would be considered an amusing dog they'd invite to a party or two.

Setting the box aside, I sit up straighter. "And while I want nothing to do with those people, I feel I don't belong with my own flesh and blood and that just . . . sucks."

When I finally lock eyes with Brexley, he looks at me with such intensity I fear my skin is liable to catch fire.

"What?" the question comes out breathy. It's as if he's sucked out all the air in the room, his presence consuming my small apartment. I'm frozen to the seat, scared to move, scared to breathe.

"I know exactly what you mean," he says.

My sandpaper tongue tries to moisten my suddenly dry lips.

Were you exiled from your pack?

I saved him from answering the question, but I want to hear him answer the question now, even more than Goldie did.

Hunger, rage, and pain shine out from his face. Brexley knows exactly what I mean.

Suddenly I don't need him to answer. I know with absolute certainty that's what happened.

But now what I want to know even more is, if so few Weres survive the separation, how did he?

While Brexley's eyes share the answer to the first question, they forbid any further prying. I'm pinned to the spot on the couch. Though we're relating now, he's on the verge of the storm of disappointment and pain wrapped up in his past. I'm certain if I try to push him, he'll leap on me and tear out my jugular.

Honestly, I'm no different. I'd do anything to protect this life I built to keep it separate from my past, keep it separate from magic.

Needing to break the intensity, I clear my throat and retreat to my bedroom, closing the door behind me. Once it's closed, I rest my back against it, assuring myself of the physical barrier between us. When Brexley is near me, I feel so exposed, and far too connected to someone I only just met.

A flash of Brexley's naked body slams into the front of my brain like a sledgehammer. In high definition, there he is again, panting, his naked chest and shoulders heaving as he drills into me. Power and strength line every last bit of him as he drives me to places I've only dreamed of.

But then, like switching cameras, I remember when he found me trapped under the ogre's hand. Worry and concern lined his face, like he cared about me.

I'm an idiot. This is exactly how I got so fucked up with Hunter. Making stuff up, because it's what I want to see. I refuse to fall victim to my own delusions again. I close my eyes and give myself a little silent jolt.

It's the hormones, you idiot. Just gut through this for a little longer and it will pass.

The wolf flirts and toys with me, but I have no doubt it's all a joke to him. Something to amuse himself with, while he works yet another security detail.

With so much desire rioting inside me, I'm in serious danger of catching mushy feeling.

That cools the fire in me.

I don't catch feels. I use and lose boys when I need them. Brexley is no different. Just because he has to stick around after the fact, it doesn't mean there is anything more than a sexual attraction here.

Giving myself another shake, I refocus on what's important. I need to get to the library. If I get lost in my studies, I won't get lost in the mystery that is Brexley. Or those eyes that set me alight like wildfire.

CHAPTER 15
SNOGGING IN THE STACKS

RED

Three hours in the library and I'm ready to climb the walls. Need grips me until my legs are as clenched as my teeth. My books and laptop are spread on the oversized desk, but while it looks like I've made myself at home, I've hardly focused for more than five minutes together.

Normally, taking the edge off like I had last night would have given me relief during the day. But something, or *someone* has brought all my desires back to the surface.

I keep snapping at Brexley.

Stop hovering over me.

Can you go somewhere else?

You are breathing too loud.

Each time, his eyes go flat, and he withdraws and disappears into the stacks for a while, but inevitably he ends up seated next to me, spinning that stupid ring. His presence is as aggravating as it is distracting.

After sending Brexley away for the seventh time, I fail my third practice exam for the day. I'm near my limit.

What happens when my limit breaks, I have no idea. I might dissolve into tears, go nuts and start throwing books everywhere, or fuck the nearest willing body.

No, I'm better than all that. I just need to stay in control and keep forging ahead. I've decided I will do whatever it takes to pass this class, and I can control my body. I fall into a rhythm of deep inhales and exhales. It works after a few minutes, and I calm down.

Someone giggling captures my attention, my eyes catch on a guy pulling his girl into the stacks. They recede into the shadows of the dusty shelves, but they don't notice I have a clear angle on them. Tucked away from the rest of the library, he attacks her neck. She writhes under him, her nails scraping along his scalp.

My pulse beats loudly in my ears. Heat blooms between my legs and my cheeks burn. When he roughly palms her breast, my breathing turns ragged. She throws her head back in ecstasy.

I shouldn't watch them, but I can't tear my eyes away.

His hand slides down between them to rub at the front of her jeans and her leg raises to hook around his hip. She pulls up her shirt to show she's not wearing a bra, and he instantly latches his lips onto her nipple as he rubs faster between her legs.

It's a slip and slide in my panties, and my heartbeat has moved there too. My head feels heavy, but my body is zinging with need. I suddenly feel so empty and aching.

When his fingers disappear under the hem of her pants this time, her hips jerk as if she's had an electric shock.

Oh, fae lords. My own fingers tap on my upper thigh, dangerously close to where I want friction.

"How's it going?" Brexley interrupts.

I surge to my feet so abruptly, the chair tips back and hits the ground. I lose footing and smash right into Brexley's hard chest as I trip over my feet. Strong hands grab my bare arms to keep me from falling over my toppled seat.

Fire lances through me and spears between my legs, and I shudder as a loud groan escapes. His touch both satisfies and drives my need higher. The contact feels so good, but I need more, so much more.

"What is it?" Brexley asks, on high alert.

I shake him off, even as everything inside screams at me to take action.

Shove your pants down, lay over the desk and let him fuck you right here.

Unable to speak at first, lest the wrong thing escapes, I lick my lips. The couple makes a hasty retreat from the commotion I just caused.

"I—I need to get out of here. I can't focus. I need to blow off steam."

Did I really just say that?

Shoving my books and laptop back into my bag, I refuse to make eye contact as I half walk, half run out of the library, heading straight for my apartment. I don't check to see if he is following me.

I'm so aroused I can't think. Am I running to the safety of my place, or running away from Brexley?

The way he devoured my sex slams into my head like a freight train. How his eyes flash when he is beyond aroused or aggravated.

I clench my eyes against the onslaught. After what feels like the longest walk of my life, I ascend the eight stories to my apartment and slam the door behind me. I only have an hour before I need to start getting ready for work, but it's more than enough time.

I didn't sense Brexley climbing the stairs behind me, but I know he'll come. But maybe not before I do . . .

The bedroom door slams shut behind me. I'm not sure if I'm panting from the many stairs or my heated state. Everything is too tight, too hot, too rough on my skin. In an unceremonious yank, I have my coat and Uni shirt over my head and on the ground. I push my pants down, leaving me in my old, ratty bra once again.

I can't help it. I can't. I want to stop myself, but my hands are shaking and I can't think.

Grabbing my vibrator from the drawer, I get under the covers, hoping it will smother the sound as I kick off my panties and click on the vibration.

I hiss as it hits my sensitive parts. I'm so needy, but it's too much. Directing it off to the side, I let the vibrations travel in a more indirect way to where I need it most.

The door creaks open and I freeze. Need and panic are locked in a war for dominance inside me.

Brexley stands there, filling up my doorway. A fierce expression is on his face as he scans me from head to toe. I'm suddenly so glad I chose to get under the covers so he can't see my bare center or what I'm doing to it. Though there is no denying the buzzing sound or what is happening under the sheets.

Even if I knew what to say, it wouldn't get past my petrified throat.

That devilish tongue I can't stop thinking about curls behind his teeth. "Do you need help, pet?"

He shouldn't be in here, but oh fae lords it would take so few steps for him to lose his clothes and get into bed with me. I know the long hard length of his cock. How it hits the spot nothing else can when I'm like this.

But I don't want to want him.

As if sensing the war inside me, he only leans against the doorjamb. His smile turns wicked, and I know I'm screwed. "Or maybe just a little encouragement?"

CHAPTER 16

'IF YOU SHOW ME, I'LL SHOW YOU

RED

The sun has set, and the only light streams in from the living room behind Brexley. At least the moment is somewhat wrapped in shadows and darkness.

Brexley's gaze falls to where the toy is poised under the covers at my swollen clit, while his own hand slides down to cover the impressive bulge in his pants.

I should kick his smug ass out right now. But a gush of liquid between my legs tells me my body will do no such thing. Maybe if I don't do or say anything he will leave.

"Did that couple necking in the stacks get you hot, little Red?"

"Don't call me that," I sputter, but I know my eyes are wide as saucers.

"From over here I can call you whatever I want. As long as I don't touch you, right?" He raises the eyebrow cut by scars. "I bet if I called you some pretty little names, I can make you come from that alone."

A snort escapes me.

"Don't believe me? I bet calling you a little cum slut might get you going."

The strangled moan that escapes me should be the least embarrassing thing about this situation, but I immediately hate myself for letting it out.

"That's it, my little cum slut, rub that vibrator over your aching cunt."

His language is utterly shocking, and I should tear his ears right off.

Instead, the toy follows the trajectory he suggests. I grunt and my knees lift under the covers. Fuck it's half painful, half exactly what I need.

"Are you thinking of how that college boy fingered his girl in the stacks? How you wish it was you being filled? Being stretched and teased by a strong digit that knows exactly where you need it?"

I want to tell him to stop. I need to tell him to stop talking like this and leave. It's so wrong.

Instead, a low guttural moan escapes me as I rub my clit more vigorously with the vibrator. Hot sparks start in my lower back and it feels too good.

"That's it, pet, come for me," he urges, eyes flashing supernaturally.

I couldn't stop even if I wanted to. My knees hike up and my head jerks back into the pillow as my inner muscles clench and shudder out a release.

My breath comes short and fast, but it's not enough. It's not the orgasm that's going to leave me satisfied. It barely scrapes off the top layer of my agitation.

"Show me," he says, his voice husky. Black pupils nearly swallow his now glowing eyes.

Suddenly, I realize how affected he is. I thought he was

in complete control, and so far he's held to the no touching rule, staying on the other side of the room. But I can tell now, he's skating on a thin edge.

I use my feet to push away the sheets until I'm baring myself to him. Shame and embarrassment flood me, but I don't backtrack.

The first time we ended up naked together, it was a frenzy. This perusal is painfully slower, more probing and intimate.

The hunger in his eyes and on his face is staggering. He examines the tattoo wrapped around my right hip. Beautifully detailed flowers wind up and down my side, and in the midst of them a wolf face peeks out from them. The guy in the tattoo parlor insisted, and Cinder said to always take his suggestion.

"He's an artist, and it's the same thing as going with what the chef suggests at his own restaurant."

True to her word, it came out a masterpiece.

Though now, I feel ridiculous with the likeness tattooed on me when facing down an actual wolf shifter.

He drinks me in with his eyes, like he'd kill to keep staring at me poised like this. Excitement visibly flares in his irises with a supernatural glow. His rapt attention is utterly intoxicating and completely fucking terrifying. "Even in that hideous bra, you are fucking tantalizing, my pet."

It has to be the only thing keeping him on the other side of the room. Today, the bra is doing its job. But I'm not so sure I want it too.

"Now you," I say, suddenly emboldened.

His eyes flick up to meet mine, and for a moment, I see a flash of fear. A fear of losing control? Or of being vulnerable? The fae lords know I'm vulnerable enough for the two of us right now.

But this is a game. Just a game.

There can't be a body count if neither of us takes this seriously, right?

Brexley rips his shirt over his head, throwing it behind him, and suddenly I'm as serious as a heart attack.

Taut, cut muscles are revealed. His masculine form is almost too much for me to look at. When I saw him naked after shifting, I didn't allow my gaze to linger for long. But now, I study all of him without shying away. The scars on his face and along his body add to his magnetism. Danger and power lace his muscles, matching the same energy in his eyes. I want to reach out and touch the puckered skin running along his bicep, and what looks like a healed bullet wound on his left hip.

Though his silvery hair and steely eyes create an icy effect, there is no question Brexley has been forged in fire. He's been burned but then he took the flames and turned them into a cold fire that he alone can wield.

My musings come to an abrupt halt when he unfastens his jeans and pulls out his long, thick cock. I already know he doesn't bother with underwear, but I'm instantly affected again.

From embarrassment and uncertainty, I'm launched into lightheadedness and needy as hell. My skin itches, aching to rub against all of his bare flesh. I've never been so hungry in my life, and no morsel of food will sate me. I want to eat Brexley whole. And that certainly poses a challenge, considering his . . . size.

He is intimidatingly big at full mast. And the masculinity lining his calloused hand holding his cock, has me practically whimpering.

"My, what a big dick you have." The joke slips out before I can catch it. Echoing the first time we met.

"All the better to fuck you with, my dear," he assures me, barely restrained mirth sparkling in his eyes.

But he won't. The rule that he can't touch me stands, and I know he won't. Not unless I invite him over here.

Then all humor vanishes from his face. "Spread yourself for me," he commands in a hoarse voice.

I obey him, setting the vibrator aside to give him a better view. I feel more exposed than I ever have in my life and I'm not sure if this is exhilarating or if I'm on the verge of an anxiety attack.

Right now, I can't allow myself to examine why I'm baring myself to a werewolf who pushes my buttons.

His breath audibly catches in his throat, and he grips his cock with what looks like bruising force. "Fuck Red. I want to shove my dick in your sweet, little, wet hole so bad."

My inner muscles clench so hard I almost come again at that. He's still across the room, but I feel as arrested as if he tied me up.

"Touch yourself," he says in a low growl.

I swipe a finger up and down my slit, and instantly I'm dying to come again. I reach for the vibrator, but he cuts me off with a sharp command. "No, leave it."

The look I shoot him must be utterly pathetic, like a wounded puppy.

He only smirks. "I wasn't kidding about making you come myself. I can't touch you, but I can tell you what I'd do if I was over there. I would lick right up and down that delicious pussy again."

My finger rubs faster up and down, mimicking what he's describing.

"Then I'd latch onto that perfect, little clit that is begging me to suck on it."

My thumb rubs against it and I'm not responsible for the sounds coming out of me.

"But is that what you want, Red? You want me to suck on your little clit as I pump my fingers into you?"

I nod, even as I hope he knows I can't let him touch me.

Who am I kidding? Would I really stop him? I'm already out of control, how much worse could it get?

Much, much worse, my brain whispers with certainty.

"Or do you want me to push this big cock into your little pussy? Stretch you until you are screaming with pleasure, like the last time?" He curls his tongue behind his teeth again; the expression is purely sexual.

One of his hands grips the door jamb, like it's the only thing keeping him rooted to the spot. Then he spits into his other hand and slides it up and down that dick. It's vulgar, like his words. And it completely turns me on.

Oh fuck, my fingers rub my clit, and I know it won't be much longer.

His hot gaze flicks back and forth between my face and where I'm touching myself. "Maybe I'll flip you onto your hands and knees so I can fuck you, doggy-style. I'd slam into you so deep you'd feel me in your throat over and over. Then spank that perfect ass that's begging for some abuse."

Mmmm, the idea of a little roughhousing, some violence mixed in with my pleasure, just shot me to a new height.

I know it's not normal, it's not right, but fae lords, if I don't want him to bruise me a little while pushing me over the edge. I want him to punish me by ramming his massive dick down my throat until I'm crying and choking and creaming myself.

Yep. Definitely not normal.

He jerks himself off faster, his back slightly caving over as if he is struggling to stand. I want that thick length filling me. I want it so bad the empty ache inside me is driving me mad. My fingers move of their own accord, frantically thrusting inside my aching core. My need generously slips down my palm.

"That's it Red, good girl."

A wordless gasp escapes me as my inner muscles dissolve into harsh shudders that overtake my entire being. My thighs shake uncontrollably. My eyes clench shut, then I hear the sounds of an animal crying out. It takes a while to realize it's me.

The wooden doorframe groans under his grip. A half grunt, half growl from Brexley has me fighting to open my eyes. He's coming, shooting it onto his hand. It's the most sensual fucking thing. His is pure masculinity and ferocity even as he succumbs to desire.

The vibrations of my orgasm begin to fade away and suddenly I feel like me again. Naked, exposed, in a room with Brexley, who just got off in his hand.

Continuing to slowly pump his cock though he's done, Brexley gives me an inscrutable look.

The awkwardness of the situation creeps in. Brexley knows when I'm getting myself off and invited himself in this time and I didn't stop him. *Oh my fae lords, what the hell am I doing?* I should have kicked him out, not from my room, but from the whole damn apartment.

But my body finally feels somewhat sated. And I have a feeling it has to do with the fevered peak he pushed me up to just by standing across the room and reciting dirty things to me while jerking off.

I blink and he's gone. I don't check to see where, I just

scramble up in time to shut the door, my panties hanging around one ankle. Still stunned by what just happened, I don't move for several minutes, trying to collect myself.

A loud slam vibrates from the living room, and I realize he's left the apartment.

As if things weren't weird and tense between us before, I have no idea how it's going to be now.

But maybe he's gone for good. Maybe Brexley left to call whoever sent him and say he needs off my security detail, and to send someone else to take care of me. It would be the professional thing to do.

He would be gone, and I could pretend this never happened.

Hell, maybe my body is over its "episode" and I'm back to normal for another month.

Maybe I'm that lucky.

CHAPTER 17

THE ASSHOLE & THE ADVISOR

BREXLEY

Maybe I'm lucky and Grandma will text Red her exact location. Hell, maybe she'll show up and I can whack the old lady then split.

Maybe Red will decide not to go to work, and I can stay down here and patrol the street where she lives. Not that I feel the need to protect her from the unnamed threat trying to kidnap her.

No, I care that someone is going to steal my only lead to Grandma. That's it, nothing more.

Liar.

The door swings open, and there she is.

We stare at each other for a long stretch.

"Any word from your grandma?"

"Nope."

Yep, I'm not that lucky.

"You changed your clothes," she comments.

My heavy gray sweater fights off the cold, and I'm

wearing a fresh pair of jeans. I didn't bother with a coat because I run hot, and lately, hotter than usual. "I did."

She doesn't need to know more than is necessary, so I don't explain where I got my new attire.

Not pressing the subject further, Red descends the few steps and passes me without another word.

My kind of girl.

We walk in the frozen night, heading toward the Poison Apple. Red's long, fire-colored hair rolls down her back in waves that the icy wind occasionally picks up off her long jacket. Against the gray, dull Boston streets, the girl is a bright beacon of color and life. She strides on without a clue of the warmth she leaves in her wake.

What is she?

Like she said, Red doesn't have power, but still, she is something I've never encountered before. On top of her already natural, delicious cinnamon scent is that essence I want to run my nose along until it stays inside me. That way I can pick it apart and discern her truth.

Another question pops into my mind. The one plaguing me all day.

Don't do it, wolf. Don't ask anything about her life. You live in the silence that surrounds you right now. Do not break it like a clumsy hammer. Let it lie.

"What are you studying so hard anyway?"

Dammit.

Red tilts her head to look up at me. "It's my financial audit class. I'm studying to be a financial advisor."

"The granddaughter of the most powerful witch in the entire world, heir to the lifestyle brand pervading every major chain in the world and you . . . you want to be an accountant?"

Red grabs one bicep as if she is trying to keep herself from hitting me.

"A financial advisor," she corrects. "And what is wrong with that?"

I shrug. "It's just so . . . human."

A smile breaks on her face and she is suddenly beaming. "Thank you."

I shake my head. This girl is ridiculous.

Her smile wanes. "Where I come from, mages are constantly in competition, trying to exert their power over each other in one way or another. One way is with money. But if you have power over your money, you have power over your future."

"Says the girl who rejects one of the biggest fortunes known to man, mage, or fae." My tone is coarse and judgmental to my own ears, though I meant it as a point of fact.

Her lower lip juts out in a pout that makes my pants a little tighter. Her eyes turn serious, and a dark glint sparkles in them. "It's not my fortune."

"Your grandma cut you off then?"

A line forms between her eyebrows. "No, but in order to understand how to manage money, I need to learn how to work with what most of the world does. I'm learning to be like everyone else."

Now, I make sure to sound as condescending as possible. "You're a princess playing peasant."

Red rears on me, stopping us in the middle of the sidewalk. Anger vibrates through her body, as if she's gearing up to knock out my teeth. "No, I'm not, you judgmental prick."

Oh damn. Anger flashes in her eyes like the fire in her hair. Why do I like it? Why do I want to push her harder? Get her to hit me like she had before we fucked?

"Sure you are. If you acknowledge money is power, why are you rejecting it? Do you think being human means being powerless? Which really makes you the same as all those in the mage cities who think humans are plebs. You want to be a big fish in a small pond, even if they don't notice you lurking below them. Watching their pathetic lives like a voyeur."

The flush that started at the base of her neck explodes in her face. "No, of course I don't think that. I'm not an asshole. I'm not any better than a human."

I shove my hands in my pockets and begin to walk again, forcing her to follow. "Oh, so that's it. You have shitty self-esteem, and you feel you are even less than a human. So, it's like self-exile because this is all you deserve. Did mommy and daddy abandon you and now you have something to prove?"

Words came out in an incoherent sputter for several minutes. "My self-esteem is just fine, you narcissistic asshole. My father was a human who left my mother pregnant and alone, and she was loving and wonderful until she died when I was four. I have nothing to prove to either of them. And I don't have to accept this crap. The shit you're saying tells me about how *you* operate. Clearly, you are the one here who thinks you are better than any human."

I whirl on her, and she stumbles back a step to keep from running into me. "You're damn right I am. I'm better than any human, mage, or fae you'll ever meet. I'm a survivor, and that's the most important quality one can possess in a cruel, unforgiving world like ours."

Her pale eyes round as they search mine, as if she's looking for any evidence there is more to me. That I'm not an absolute asshole I'm acting the part of. But she won't find it. This is how I am, and I don't apologize. Not for anyone.

Resisting the urge to poke her in the shoulder, I fist my hands in my pockets. "I'm the only thing keeping you safe right now, which is why you need to listen to me and do what I say."

The conversation has spiraled out from under my control. I realize I'm angry. Angry at her, and I'm actively trying to push her away. Wrestling for any inch of freedom against this insistent need to ask her about her life, against the strong desire to run my thumb over those pouty lips. It juts out even more than before.

I don't care about her. She's just a red X that's going to bring me what I need before I get the hell out of this side of the country. Then I'll retreat back into my quiet, mountainside home.

Still, I draw closer.

"What the hell happened to make you so goddamn bitter and cynical?" The answer to that is long and ugly, but she doesn't wait for my response before pressing on. "I've learned how to stand on my own two feet. The only reason I'm allowing you to hang around is because my grandma sent you."

Guilt strikes me like a viper, drawing blood. So I treat it with gasoline, pouring it on the fire I'd already lit.

"More like tilting on two feet. I understand standing on your own, but denying yourself money is stupid – wealth enables independence. And you aren't independent. You're a rich chick in denial, and a walking target. If I hadn't been there the last couple days, you would have been kidnapped or worse."

"What do you expect me to do? I'm just a human."

"Better, I expect you to do better. You claim you want to

make it on your own? Well, survivors figure it the fuck out. They don't play little college girl, and hope everything will be okay."

Her fiery expression crumbles into dust. She covers her stomach with her arms, as she pulls into herself. But she can't protect herself from my words. "So, because I don't have magic to fight off ice mages or Ogres, I'm a useless little princess amusing herself with the games of humans."

It is what I've been saying, but it isn't true. Red is much more than that. But I need to shove as much distance between us while staying as physically close as possible.

The word grinds its way out between my teeth. "Bingo."

Red turns abruptly and falls into an even faster stride to the bar. But not before I catch sight of her glassy eyes. She raises the hood on her long coat, so I can't see her tears.

Instead of seeing if they fall, I hang back as we finish our journey in silence.

So what if I hurt her feelings? She's ridiculous. A financial advisor who rejects money.

But why do I bother critiquing her life choices? I only need her for one thing.

Still, a stone drops in my stomach, giving me a sick feeling inside.

Suddenly I want to shift, burst into fur and sink into my animal mind so I don't have to think about anything I just said to the teary-eyed girl with the hard set jaw.

This is how one survives as a lone wolf. By slashing and clawing at any threat of connection or bond. I lost my ability to bond socially a long time ago. If I want to survive, and I do, I'll make sure I never form an attachment of any kind again.

Catching sight of Red touching her face surreptitiously,

I pretend I don't know she's wiping wetness from her cheeks. I tighten my fists until my knuckles hurt.

That's right, Red. This is who I am. You should be more careful because the Big Bad Wolf will eat you alive. If only your grandmother had warned you about wolves like me.

CHAPTER 18

RAP IN THE HOOD

BREXLEY

R ap, short for Rapunzel, is the owner of Poison Apple. After Goldie leads me into Rap's small office tucked away at the back of the bar, she babbles on to her boss about how I was just trying to help Red with an unruly customer. That I may be fae, but I won't cause any problems. The bubbly blonde doesn't realize Rap and I stopped listening as soon as she started.

Emerald green eyes assess me keenly, but I am doing the same to her as we face off, while Goldie stands to the side of us. Rap's banana yellow hair is gelled up in a mohawk. Streaks of pastel colors create a rainbow effect. Rap is older than her employees, but this woman has yet to hit thirty. Lean and muscular, she wears deliberately tattered clothes, but the kind you pay a designer to rip up ahead of time.

Unlike the rest of the bar, that drips with luxury and

whimsical decor, her office is bare, simple, and neat. Her laptop sits open on a steel desk with only a lamp next to it. A generic calendar without pictures is tacked on the wall next to the massive whiteboard displaying the employee schedule.

I recognize the look in her eye almost immediately. She's a survivor, like me. Someone capable of gnawing off their own arm to escape a raw deal. Someone not willing to let anyone fuck with their present or future.

And judging by the way Rap studies me, she isn't likely to let me stay, as I'd endanger both.

Something tickles my nose. The bar owner smells human, but not entirely.

No. She wasn't always human. This woman used to have the talent for magic, but she doesn't anymore. I don't hide the realization from alighting in my eyes.

It's rare, and I've only smelled it once or twice before, and I realize I've stumbled onto her secret.

Fear flashes through her eyes, our silent communication revealing everything between us.

*I know your secre*t, my eyes say.

Hers narrow. *I could kill you with the snap of my fingers.*

My eyebrow lifts a fraction. *Are you so sure? It would stir up a lot of trouble.*

Are you here to stir up trouble?

I'm like you. I need to keep a low profile. I won't fuck with you, you don't fuck with me.

Rap interrupts the stream of explanations from her employee. "Goldie must have gotten her name because of that golden tongue of hers. Alright, you can hang out. But you step one furry paw out of line, and I'll not only throw you out on your ass, I'll neuter you. Got it, wolf?"

There are few humans I respect, but this woman immediately commands it. I don't fear her, but I have no doubt she will do what she says. I wonder if her employees have any idea how much she is hiding. I bet my balls she doesn't let anyone close enough to catch a clue.

I respect that too.

"Yes, ma'am," I say.

A flicker of a smile tells me calling her ma'am was the right move. She sits back down to her laptop, dismissing us from her office.

When Goldie and I return to the bar, the girls are still busy prepping for their shift.

I've learned Red is a different person behind the bar. Not the girl who shrinks into her sweater, hiding behind a shell. Or the sexy she-demon possessed by the need to get off.

At work, she is a woman who commands the space and people around her with ease. Red isn't afraid to flaunt her tattoos and piercings as she levels a steely gaze at the crowd demanding liquor and her attention. Watching her like that is. . . heady. I'm getting a taste for all the sides of her, and it only makes me hungrier.

"Rap said it's cool," Goldie pumps an excited fist.

Disappointment swells in Red's eyes. The poor girl thought she could escape me. But she can't. Not until I'm done.

"Great," Red musters a halfhearted smile, remembering she must play the role of doting girlfriend.

Cinder is in equally risqué goth wear, clearly raided from a Hot Topic store. I get a sense the prerequisite to work at this bar is the ability to dress like a walking felony.

Which is why I can barely even glance at Red for longer than a moment since she took off her duster coat. The girl is wearing a black leather bra, and a skirt that looks painted on her perfect ass. A gold chain wraps around her neck and falls down the front of her chest to where it hooks into her gold navel ring. With her voluptuous red hair falling down around her exposed shoulders, and bicep cuffs, she looks like a goddamn Amazonian woman—powerful, sensual, commanding. The churning arousal inside me turns dark and angry.

Little Red looks like cinnamon, spice, and every delicious sin I want to run my tongue along.

The girl is staunch about not letting anyone touch her, yet here she is, exposing swaths of creamy, lightly freckled skin. Soon this bar will be packed, and I know countless eyes will be glued to her. It makes me want to drag her to a cave where I can fuck her until she can't see straight.

Finance major. Fucking ridiculous.

Turning my back to the bar, I run an agitated hand through my hair.

Witchtits. I'm hard as a rock, and angry as hell. This is going to be a long night.

Goldie turns to me with a bright smile, though I see something devious lurking in her eyes.

"Since you are staying, why don't you help me with some heavy boxes we need from the back?"

She thinks she's a wolf leading a lamb to slaughter, but I'm the predator here. Still, I'd do anything to put a little distance between me and Red.

Once we are in the back storeroom, Goldie whirls on me.

I sigh, resisting the urge to roll my eyes. "So, it's that time, is it? Ready to give me the speech and all that?"

"You're damn right it is." Her softness evaporates, and she looks ready to strike me with venomous teeth if I make the wrong move. She reminds me of a vengeful plus-size

Barbie doll. Although Barbie wishes she possessed such a sultry face.

"I don't know why Red kept you a secret, and while it's clear she's into you—"

My brain notes that part a bit too prominently.

"—I am also here to protect her heart. If you do anything to hurt her, I'll do what Rap said and even worse. Especially after. . ." Goldie's mouth snaps shut quicker than a nun's legs.

My toe finds the door and shuts it behind us. I tower over the short blonde. "After what?"

Regret fills her eyes as she knows she's made a mistake. She bites a bright pink lip, and I can see her brain racing to find a way out of this situation.

"Tell me, Goldie. Who hurt Red?" I try to sound soothing, to talk to her in a coaxing croon. But underneath my charm, something boils. Anger. Someone hurt the girl out behind the bar, and it makes me want to fang out.

Goldie covers her eyes. "Eff. She would kill me if I told you."

Goldie is a good friend. Any man with an ounce of wolf blood in their system could recognize the fierce loyalty this girl has. Unfortunately for Goldie, her desire to share and protect overwhelms her ability to keep secrets.

Then I pull the lowest of low moves.

I gently pull her hand away from her face and say softly, "I don't want to hurt her, Goldie. Tell me what happened so I can protect her heart too."

Hope sparks in Goldie's eyes.

I'm a goddamned dirty bastard.

"When I met her. . . Red was . . . shattered."

Everything inside me stills.

"She won't talk about her past. Maybe she's shared

more with you than with us, but I know she's been beat down in her life. And the only part I know about is this one guy . . . "

My hackles rise. "What guy?" The words come out on edge. The moment feels like glass, and I'm in danger of breaking it and ruining my chances of hearing more.

"Hunter. I think that's his name." Her nose wrinkles as she frowns. "Red was heartbroken. I don't know what he did to her, but she was a ghost of the girl she is now."

Who in faefucks is Hunter? And after I shake out of him what the fuck he did to Red, I'll rip his head clear off.

Taking a step back, I let out a breath, cooling my temper.

The hell are you doing, wolf? You are here until Grandma contacts Red. That's it. This Hunter is of no concern. Red's life is of no concern.

"Which boxes do you need help with?" I ask, changing modes.

"Don't tell her I told you," Goldie pleads with her big brown eyes.

I shoot her a quick smile. "Of course not."

Her shoulders sag in relief.

Goldie simply points at a pile of boxes. I grab them and go.

Tonight, I need to stay professional, aloof. But all I can think is, who is this Hunter and when can I rip out his throat?

CHAPTER 19
POWDER KEG

RED

If I thought Friday was a shit storm, Saturday is absolutely bonkers. The place is wall to wall packed. Despite Rap opening the skylight windows to let in a winter breeze, it's sweltering. I've always run hot, so I wore an outfit to let much of my skin breathe, but I'm still sweating like crazy. It's half the running back and forth, slinging bottles and drinks, but the other half has everything to do with Brexley prowling the edges of the bar.

No, I tell myself. It's my hormones. Any seductive gaze in here could spark the same effect in my body.

I've been extra careful not to touch anyone tonight. The cocktail goes on the bar and the customer picks it up there. No need for a handoff. No need to chance brushing fingers while I'm a powder keg.

Wiping my forehead with my forearm, I try to ignore how his eyes shine through the crowd, piercing my skin and heating my blood. I didn't think I'd be the girl who went for the guy even after he negged her, but apparently my coochie doesn't care what self-esteem he wrecks, as long as he destroys her too.

Stupid hormones.

After a full day of studying, and attacks both physical and emotional, I'm grateful to move and respond to orders without thinking. Still, the dragon lives rent free in my head, whispering that if I don't get it together, I won't pass her class.

Goldie catches my attention as she plays coy with the guy at the bar. Must be the newest dude on the chopping block. His teeth are almost too straight, too white. He sports designer clothes like a second skin. He's handsome in that classic rich boy way, and Goldie always falls flat on her face for those guys. But their beauty masks their red flags up front, making it hard to tell how much scum lays under the veneer.

I turn away, reminding myself I shouldn't judge, because I'm sure as hell not an expert at picking prospects. Still, I hope a tear-stained Goldie doesn't end up on my doorstep a week from now.

Thankfully, the rest of the shift is uneventful apart from the usual hustle. When the last people filter out and I'm onto closing duties, Rap strides toward me. Brexley has disappeared, but it's too much to hope he took off.

"Red, were you serious about going over the books with me? We can put your major to work on setting up my retirement plan even if that's not for another hundred years."

My entire body lightens. "Yes, of course. If you want me to." This is it. This is the feeling I'm chasing. Helping and supporting people with their financial goals. Maybe this is what having magic would have felt like.

She gives a curt nod. "Good, we'll talk about it after your finals are done."

I bite my lower lip to keep from completely beaming. But before I can get too excited, the front door opens, and someone enters.

"We're closed," Goldie calls out as she throws a tray of dirty glasses into the dishwasher.

I connect with the newcomer's gaze, and the floor drops out from under me.

Intense brown eyes, and a clear complexion accompany a strong jaw. The man walks in with an expression as serious as the lines in his lean body.

"Hunter," I breathe.

Memories tumble in my mind, memories of us entangled in a broom closet at FFA. Of us meeting at midnight under a tree just to share a kiss while I held back my every instinct to mount him like an animal. To keep the violence and intensity at bay, so he would kiss me just once more.

My body turns molten and everything inside of me is on fire with desire, but every part of me aches with the pain of longing. The kind that gathers pain between your eyes and makes your breath inhospitable in your own body.

"Red," Hunter says, his jaw tightening, making his temples flex. "I've been trying to find you." He sounds so concerned.

Pangs of longing and grief explode somewhere in my heart.

"He's a mage," Rap mutters the fact with distaste.

"I'm sorry," I say, bowing my head. "I'll get him out of here."

"You causing trouble, Red?" Rap asks, making heat flood my cheeks.

I really love this job, and I hate that magic and my past keeps popping up, endangering that.

"Trouble keeps finding me," I confess. It sure as hell

isn't because I'm starting it. I just want to bartend with my friends and pass my finals.

Rap raises an eyebrow at him and purses her lips. "He can stay. Fifteen minutes, and then I'll be back to put him out on his ass." Then she disappears back to her office.

Numbly, I turn to Goldie and Cinder who are now at attention because they realize the guy here is the same one I once mentioned in a drunken stupor. "You got this for a minute?"

Cinder shoots me the thumbs up, while Goldie only studies Hunter with a line between her brows.

I round the bar and gesture for him to follow me to the far side of the bar. He follows to where the massive tree limbs hang over the lounge chairs. I can't bring myself to sit down, but I clutch the back of a chair, putting it firmly between us.

Hunter stays standing and scans me from head to toe. "You look . . . different."

I've changed considerably from the girl he knew. I'd grown up hiding in thick turtleneck sweaters, my hair always pulled up and away in a messy bun. In this moment, I realize how I even used to stand differently, rounding my shoulders forward as if I could disappear into myself. But now, my shoulders are rolled back as I stand straight as a rod.

I can't tell if Hunter likes what he sees or not, but suddenly I'm far too aware of my bare midriff and all the piercings and tattoos I have on display. My stomach burns with shame and arousal.

"Why are you here, Hunter?" I manage to get out through rubbery lips.

There. His face clears and he returns to a businesslike manner, his normal mode. No time for nonsense. He'd been so adult, even when we were kids. "I believe you are in danger."

My hands grip the chair harder. "Do you know where Gigi is?"

After graduating, Hunter immediately went back to work under his father, who is head of security for Grandma's House. Last I heard, his father was grooming Hunter to take his stead for when he retires in a couple years.

Hunter shakes his head. "She's gone underground. My father may know something, but he won't share with me." His expression darkens.

If he's so serious, it's because he wants to live up to his father's expectations. Gigi's head of security never cracks a smile.

"No one knows much of anything right now, but I had to come find you. Make sure you are ok."

Hearing him say words I once longed to hear, suddenly I don't know how to act, what to say, or how to feel. I'd been so preoccupied the last twenty-four hours, I forgot to pine over him. Considering that had been a solid forty percent of my personality the last four months, I wonder who I am anymore. Who I am around Brexley . . .

"I've b—been fine."

"Dahl has been going out of their mind," Hunter says, taking a step closer.

The corner of my mouth twitches.

Dahl is my grandmother's chief assistant, who is nonbinary. They are strung as tight as a rubber band stretched between two cities. I can't imagine the hysterics they are exhibiting in the absence of Gigi, not being able to commit her to interviews, news spotlights, or promotional junkets.

Hunter and I grew close initially from our dislike of Dahl's tyrannical hold on schedules, and dramatics when a sponsorship didn't work out. Even as kids, we recognized Dahl was over the top.

I can't suppress my chuckle. "I bet that's something to see."

"If it weren't for your grandma going dark, I think you'd quite enjoy it." A small, elusive smile appears on his face. He so rarely smiled; a sighting always took my breath away. But I'm already holding my breath, so it's hard to say if it has the same effect.

No, no, no, don't fall back into this. You know he doesn't want you. Stop falling back in love with him, right now, you little idiot.

Hunter closes the distance until he is inches away. He encircles a hand around my forearm before I can move away or stop him.

It takes everything in me not to roll my eyes in the back of my head as liquid heat sweeps through my body. I want his hand to touch every part of me at once.

Fuck, lick, bite. Mark him.

Hunter's eyes darken and his voice drops into a husky tone. "I think you should come with me, Red. So I can protect you."

Then another presence interrupts, and the only reason it penetrates my sex-drenched brain is because of its potency.

Brexley. He stands on the other side of me. That uniquely spicy masculine scent envelops me.

Hunter meets Brexley's gaze over my head. The wolf has several inches on Hunter, both vertically and in the broadness of his muscled shoulders. I can feel the warning emanating from his body directed at the boy on my right.

"Who's this?" Hunter asks, his hand slipping away.

I want to sob with relief and frustration. Instead, I cross

my arms, digging my nails into either bicep to get control of myself.

"You don't know him?" I ask, working to make sense of the present. How does he not know Brexley, if they both work security for Gigi?

"I'm her bodyguard," Brexley's words come out in a smooth low rumble, but I sense his dislike for Hunter instantly.

"Hunter," he introduces himself to Brexley before turning back to me. "I'm sorry I couldn't get here sooner, but I'm here to take care of you now." He reaches out as if to grasp my arm again.

Part of me practically salivates at the idea of being touched again. Being touched by Hunter. Being kissed by Hunter. Like we used to. Old sadness and longing mix with my raging hormones in a familiar cocktail.

Red, you don't have magic. This can never work.

His words boomerang back to slice me deep.

Before Hunter can lay a finger on me, two hands grasp my waist and pull me against a firm chest. A shockwave slams into my body as Brexley's touch sears me, sending my pulse racing so fast I'm afraid I'll start hyperventilating. An inferno of velvet heat curls through me like a boom of paint clouds in a glass of water. The intense feeling floods south faster than I can say faefucks. Hunter's touch had me wet, but now I'm on the verge of coming.

I bite my lip so hard I taste copper. I need to get control of myself. If only he would let me go.

As if to prove I'm not in charge, my ass pushes back up against his crotch.

Damn you, traitorous coochie.

"She's taken care of just fine," Brexley says to Hunter, and his voice rumbles through my back. I fight a violent shudder of arousal. His fingers massage my bare hips. I can't tell if it's because he needs an outlet for his agitation or if he's worried I might try to step away from him.

My thoughts fight each other like rabid dogs.

Bend me over. Take me right against this chair. Take me where everyone can see.

Don't come. Don't come.

My thighs tremble.

Hunter squares off his shoulders and sends a cutting look at Brexley. "I am head of security and I am here to take over."

"If you were so effective, her grandmother wouldn't have had to hire a private party to ensure Red's safety. I don't walk away from a job unless it's done. You may be head boy somewhere else, but right now you are in my territory, and I suggest you back off."

Hunter looks like he's just been slapped across the face. Outrage and anger simmer and swirl across his chiseled features.

Finally, he looks down at me. "Red . . . "

Then he starts forward as if he means to rip me from Brexley's hold. And strangely, I'm repelled by the prospect of letting Hunter lay a finger on me. Not while touching Brexley. It would be wrong.

Brexley pushes me behind him and out of Hunter's reach. Hunter's eyes go dark with power.

I suck in a deep cleansing breath. Still frustrated and aching, I can at least think much more clearly now. And I quickly realize if I don't do something, these two bone-heads are going to lunge at each other's throats.

Rap gave me some leeway, but she'd fire my ass in a second if they brawled in here.

"Go back to Dahl and wait for Gigi," I say to Hunter,

surprising myself. "She needs more help than I do. And I'll be safe with Brexley." I can't look either of them in the eye, but I catch something flashing across Brexley's face at the last thing I say. Maybe disbelief? Awe? Arousal?

That last guess is colored by my raging hormones, demanding I fuck anyone and everyone right now.

No. Not just anyone. Brexley.

I am in control. I am in control.

"Red, can I talk to you in private?" Hunter urges.

The old me wants to go with him, but I need distance. I need to get all my senses back online.

"No, I'm busy, and you have a job to do. Go home, Hunter." Then before anyone can stop me, I bolt for the bathroom. If I don't handle this situation right now, I'll definitely do something I'll regret.

Instead of heading for the public restroom, lined with stalls, I use the one in the back meant for employees. It's a single occupancy and has a lock on it. I smash the button, not sure if I'm locking everyone else out or locking me in.

Then before I can think, I lift my skirt with shaking hands. I lean back against the cool ceramic sink as I rub my aching bud almost viciously. Throwing my head back, I come almost instantly with a strangled, guttural moan.

It's not enough. Not nearly enough. I shove my fingers into my dripping entrance and pump with savage speed, desperate to get to the right spot while my palm still rubs against my clit. I come a second time before I can suck in a breath and begin to make sense of the world again.

I realize I'm still half braced, half sagged against the sink, my hand covered with my own arousal.

I shut my eyes so tight I see stars.

It's never been this bad before, and to calm my some-what cooling body, I try to rationalize why.

Because I have, no, *had*, feelings for Hunter. Because he touched me, then Brexley touched me and that was too much.

But then what was that slam of power I felt from Brexley when he touched me?

Normally my arousal is indiscriminate, and I would cry out the more the merrier. But I didn't want Hunter touching me while Brexley did. In that moment, the Were owned me whether he knew it or not.

Before I could chalk it all up to something logical, a soft but audible knock raps against the door.

"You okay?" a rough male voice asks through the door.

It's Brexley.

I turn around and face myself in the mirror. My face and chest are almost as red as my hair.

"I'm fine," I try to say as normally as possible.

There is a pause then, "Are you sure?"

I turn on the faucet and wash my hands, skirt still askew. "Yes," I say crisply, desperately wanting him to go away. Turning the water off, I shake my hands dry.

"If you let me in, I could help you, Red. Let me help you, Red."

I go completely still. The suggestion in his voice . . . like he knows exactly what I ran in here to do. Like he's offering to . . . no, that's not right.

Images of letting him in and him fucking me over the sink until I'm screaming out of my mind has my engines revving again, hard.

"Ooh, Red." His words come out half teasing taunt, half blatant need. "Let the Big Bad Wolf in and I'll take care of that aching little cunt."

Oh fuck. Can he hear my body?

No, there is no way he can sense my body through the door.

Still, I edge toward the door, my hand outstretched to the handle. I don't even have to open it. I only have to pop the lock and let him do the rest. And I have no doubt he'd do just that.

It'd be so easy. I'd know relief, but first pleasure and ecstasy. I bet he'd pump me with a punishing speed and could go for as long as I needed. My skin screams in frustration.

"No one has to know," he purrs.

I sober so fast, I'm back against the other side of the bathroom, hand curled into my body.

No one has to know.

I'd heard the same thing from Hunter countless times. I'm someone to kiss and fuck in the dark, but nothing more. The Big Bad Wolf, who thinks I'm a spoiled princess, would lower himself to give me a pity fuck because I need it. And because he wouldn't mind getting his rocks off. How much of that would be because he is a wolf and enjoys getting territorial around other males?

The thoughts, one after another, are finally sobering. I push my skirt back down.

"Go away, Brexley."

Though I don't hear anything, I sense he's left. Despite my heavy eyeliner, I throw several handfuls of icy water over my face.

Wiping away the black streaks now running down my cheeks, I use a stern tone with the girl in the mirror. "You are not that girl anymore. You choose the time, you choose the place. You control your body."

My resolve crystallizes, but my hands still shake. It takes several more minutes to calm myself before I slip out, grab my stuff from the back room and take the back exit out of the Poison Apple.

If it came to some unknown threat lurking on the streets versus Brexley, I'd rather the devil I don't know. Because the devil I do is drawing me in and I'd rather lose my life than my soul right now.

CHAPTER 20

A GLAMOROUS DISTRACTION

BREXLEY

The damn fool girl made a run for it. Doesn't she know it's not safe for her out there? I charge out into the night, chasing her scent. She's on her way home, and she only has a five-minute head start on me.

As I hurry down the lane, Red's scent suddenly intensifies. And she's aroused . . .

I break into a run and turn a corner to find her walking in a different direction from her apartment, with Hunter. And he's *fucking touching her.*

His hands are hidden under her coat. From the outline of his arm, he's likely touching the bare skin of her back.

My blood boils, my fangs elongate, and my muscles bulge as I prepare to rip his head off. Hunter knows she's got a weak spot for him, and he's using it to his advantage.

The stink of his magic is near suffocating. In the club it

was like standing next to a car emitting diesel fumes. But now it presses on me like rotten vegetables.

As I advance, I see Red staring up at him with doe eyes as she licks her lips. If I don't get his hands off her, she might start humping him right here.

"Where the fuck do you think you are going?" I demand as I rip Hunter's hands off Red. He spins and regards me with confusion.

Pulling Red away, I move her behind me. Having several inches on Hunter, I sneer down at him. He seems even smaller than before, the little worm. "She told you to leave. It seems like you have a hard time understanding, so let me make it clear."

"What the hell?" a familiar voice comes from behind me.

I turn and find myself facing a second Hunter, except this one smells like diesel.

Fuck. Of course. This Hunter is slightly shorter and smells different. It's a glamor mage.

Realizing his cover's blown, the fake Hunter whips out a knife. I easily smack his arm down before delivering a blow to his midsection that sends him reeling.

Before I can land another punch, the imposter rises off the ground and slams up against the building. He grunts at the impact, eyes wild with fear. The scent of diesel becomes sickeningly strong.

The real Hunter holds a hand out, magic crackles around him as he keeps the imposter up against the wall. He's a telekinetic, but he's not as powerful a mage as the one on the wall. I can smell it.

"Why are you posing as me?" Hunter demands.

The false Hunter shakes his head and tightens his lips.

With a glance over my shoulder, I notice Red hunched

in on herself. She looks deeply shaken. I want to go to her, but this is more important.

"Who sent you?" I ask.

The glamor mage shakes his head again.

"I'm asking the questions here," Hunter snaps at me.

"No, you're the one sticking his nose in where he doesn't belong. Run on home to daddy, boy."

Whatever button I pressed, I pressed too hard.

Hunter drops the glamor mage as his power slams into me.

I fly back along the street and hit the pavement hard. Like being kicked by a horse, the blow expels all the oxygen from my lungs. I'm left gasping.

"I can't see why Grandma would hire a lowly, dirty fae like you. Seems like I need to tell her that you can't do the one job you were sent to do," he spits at me. "I can take over now."

In the blink of an eye, I'm on my feet, ripping my sweater off. The animalistic roar that comes out of me echoes down the street. Hunter windmills his arms, gathering his power, readying another attack.

He thinks he can take me down? The little prick has another thing coming. I've got a trick he's never seen before.

I charge toward him at a blurring speed. Before I get close enough, he slams me with his power and I'm knocked into a brick wall like a rag doll. My ribs bruise on impact.

Instead of letting me down, he holds me up. With this much distance between us, he's got the upper hand. I can't get close enough to slash him or show him my special trick. What I need is for him to come closer. Then I'll teach him a lesson he'll never forget.

"Why don't you come say that to my face?" I taunt.

Hunter draws near.

"Hunter, stop it," Red hisses. Her arms still wrapped around herself, she's smart enough not to physically get in the middle of this.

"No, no, let him," I insist. "He's clearly pissed your grandma trusted me over him. He's only been training to take care of your legacy since, what, childhood? And he was passed over because he couldn't cut it." I may have done some digging after Goldie tipped me off about this wet blanket. While Red worked behind the bar, I got on the web and found more than enough.

Hunter's cool demeanor has a crack in it, and I intend to wrench it all the way open.

"You shut your filthy mouth," he warns, barely restrained rage flashing in his eyes. Perspiration breaks out on his forehead and neck in little beads.

"I bet they charge you with shit like watching the flour and sugar, rather than give you any real responsibility."

"I said, shut your filthy mouth," he repeats.

That's it, little boy. Come closer.

That's when Red steps between us. "Hunter, stop."

Dammit Red, get out of the way. I just need him half a foot closer.

Hunter continues to stare at me hatefully over her shoulder, but he's stopped moving.

"I'm better than him, Red," he says, voice tight. "I can do this job better than him. He shouldn't be here."

"The glamor mage got away," she points out.

I search the streets and realize he's had plenty of time to get away. Well, chain me up and call me Fido. This has been a massive fuck up.

"That's not my fault, it's his," Hunter insists, and I can tell he would be on me if she wasn't standing in the way.

"You're the reason I was almost taken," she says quietly, calmly.

Hunter's brown eyes jerk to her. His face pales, and his arm shakes as he works to keep me restrained.

"I thought that was you." Red points in the direction the glamor mage split. "I thought you wanted me. I was ready to follow you wherever you wanted to go. You, or the fake you, said we should try to work things out."

And she was ready to go with Hunter. I feel something sharp under my ribs. For a minute, I think Hunter is still using his power against me. But that's not what it is. Red's words are having that effect on me.

He's instantly flustered. "Red, you're . . . we can't . . . you're human and I'm . . . "

What the fuck did he just say? Did he just imply he can't be with her because she doesn't have magic? If I wasn't restrained, I'd tear out his jugular right now.

"I know," Reds says, her voice even quieter than before. "But you're a weak spot for me, and that's why you need to go. Unless . . . "

"Unless?"

"Unless you were following me here because there is something you want to tell me?" She sounds hopeful. "Unless you mean it this time, and we can be together for real."

Hunter takes a step back from her. The fucking idiot.

"Go home. Find Gigi," she repeats her wishes from earlier.

Hunter takes a long hard look at her, then he lets me go.

I bend my knees and fall silently into the drop, easily landing onto my feet.

More than ever, I'm tempted to rip off one of Hunter's limbs, but Red has taken control of the situation.

Hunter turns and leaves without another word. We watch him until he disappears.

Red turns to me and says with a smile too bright, "Commitment. Runs 'em away every time. Am I right?"

CHAPTER 21

SECRETS OUT OF THE CLOSET

RED

"So you and Hunter . . . he used to be your boyfriend?" Brexley asks as soon as we are walking down the street to my place.

I lick my lips and shake my head. "Not really, no."

Brexley stops abruptly, forcing me to as well. I shoot him a questioning gaze, but a hard accusation stares back at me.

"Don't lie to me, Red." After that fight, his patience is thin.

The truth is the fake Hunter's touch was not as effective. Normally everything would disappear but my need, but this time, it felt wrong. Not like Brexley's touch. Even the old Hunter's touch had been more rife with past pain and feeling. Still, I'd followed the false Hunter because I was curious to see what he had to say. Maybe he had info on Gigi he didn't want to share in front of Brexley.

I cross my arms to rub either bicep, feeling cold suddenly, if not a little embarrassed. "I'm not lying. We were never . . . he and I . . . it was always done in the dark. In a closet, or an empty classroom at FFA. I was . . . " I squeeze either arm now, embarrassed to confess but unable to stop myself. "I was in love with him. I had been since we were kids. His father works as head of security for my grandma; he's a Level Four telekinetic. Hunter was always destined to join the ranks, even though he tests out as a Level Two. By eleven I told myself I was in love with him. Then we both attended the Academy together. Two years older than me, he assumed the role of protector as if he were practicing for his future duties. I pursued him, took advantage of his protective nature. I couldn't help myself and he felt sorry for me, maybe?"

Brexley saunters to me, an intent expression on his face. "Why the hell would he feel sorry for you?"

"Because I . . . I pretty much threw myself at him. Like some desperate kid." My nails dig into my arms.

"Desperate is not a word I would use to describe you," he says with an eyebrow lift and quirk of his lips. "Determined, stubborn, and willful as hell, but never desperate."

"Oh good, so I was just persistent in forcing him to be with me."

It wasn't any better.

A storm enters Brexley's eyes as his lips turn down, and he closes the distance between us. But he holds off from touching me. "Stop abusing your arms before I make you," he threatens.

I'd no doubt he'd break my "no touching" rule again, so I drop my hands from their bruising grip.

"And that's not what I meant."

"It doesn't matter. I know how I acted, how I am. I'm a lot."

The storm in his eyes ices over until I feel cold looking into them. "What the fuck are you talking about?"

As much as I loved Hunter, I knew how strange I'd get during my monthly episodes. Intense, needy, and even aggressive at times.

Don't stare at me like that when we are in public.

You are my future employer's granddaughter. We shouldn't be doing this.

What's wrong with you? Do you want people to know?

You could ruin my chances of taking my dad's position.

Then when we were finally entangled and sweaty in the closet, I would want too much. My need to devour him and be devoured in every way unsettled him. Hunter would tell me I was being off-putting, or ruining the moment when I asked him to talk dirty to me or use his mouth on my most needy parts.

"I was out of line with him a lot. He was just trying to protect me, and I kept wanting more. He said I needed to learn to control myself. If I did, maybe we could have . . ." Made it? No. I still would have flunked out, a magic dud. And Hunter is too powerful to leave magic behind. He was meant for powerful, important things. And I'm making a nice little strange life for myself.

Brexley stills. He doesn't even seem to breathe.

Then he takes off walking again. No, he stalks forward, tension and anger lining his shoulders.

It takes a couple skipping steps to catch up to him. I swallow hard over the lump of shame in my throat.

Why did I just admit that? I should keep my dumb mouth shut.

We walk another block in silence as I stew in my shame. I've never before explained my pseudo relationship with Hunter. Not even with Goldie or Cinder. Around them, I became this new, empowered female. Keeping my dark past hidden away helped me move on.

"For fuck's sake," Brexley mutters after a span of silence.

Then a hand grasps my arm and tugs me off the sidewalk, into an alleyway. My coat protects me from the power of his touch, but my insides still purr at the pressure. Purple light splashes the streets from a nearby neon sign. Ozone thickens in the air. It's going to rain soon.

Brexley has me up against a wall, his ice-blue eyes glinting with power, a half snarl on his face.

"Let me get this straight, little Red. This sonofabitch would use you for pleasure, but then judge you for how you wanted it, while also keeping you hidden like you're something to be ashamed of?"

The urge to defend Hunter swells up with ferocity. "If anything, I used him. He's bound to protect my family, which put me as the one in power. Then I also get into these . . . moods, and I'd practically attack him. He was probably just being nice all along and I didn't read the signals." Brexley had seen it. For crying out loud, I slapped him and responded to the filthiest of suggestions laced with violence.

Brexley's eyes flash again as he scoffs. "You can't make that guy do anything he doesn't want to."

"You just met him. How the hell would you know?"

Brexley's eyeroll turns my blood to bubbling lava. "I know exactly what he's about," he goes on. "And you have nothing to be ashamed of."

I sputter, unable to voice all the ways he's wrong. "I made him uncomfortable. I should have taken the hint."

"What did you ask him to do anyways?" The ferocity

dims and something else sparks in his eye. Curiosity and arousal?

Uh oh. My senses snap on full alert. I'm on thin ice here.

"I can be a lot. And he has more traditional tastes."

Brexley leans a hand on the wall next to my head. Even under his sweater, his bicep flexes, sending a fluttering through my stomach. I staunchly resolve to ignore it. But then his eyes hotly travel up and down my body.

I try to keep my back straight and exude confidence, but inside I'm a mess.

Don't touch me, for faefucks sake, do not touch me again, one part of my brain screams.

The other side is panting, begging for him to do it. Because if he touches me right now, I'll crack in half and lose all sanity. Even the shame of all those times I went out of my mind with desire for Hunter won't stop me from jumping Brexley if he so much as brushes a finger against my hair.

"So the boy is vanilla as fuck then," Brexley says. "What did you ask for that he wasn't willing to give?" His voice drops to a gravelly tone that curls in my most intimate parts. "Did you ask him to say dirty filthy things to you?" Then he used a mocking deep voice, "that's inappropriate Red, I don't use words like that."

Cold shock hits me. That's almost verbatim what Hunter would say.

The other arm comes up, and I try to ignore the second flexing bicep as his spicy, masculine scent surrounds me. His voice drops further. My eyes automatically flutter closed.

"Did you ask him to lick you where you need it most? I'm sure the pretty boy can't be bothered. He wouldn't know how to properly lick the cream off a cone if it was his favorite flavor and it made him explode in his pants."

A violent shiver runs through my body. Heat and lust spiral through me. Brexley knows exactly how to lick a girl, and that fact mutes my anger.

Please, no.

Please, yes.

My thighs clench tight against each other. I can't take it anymore. If I stay here one second longer, I'm going to break and embarrass myself.

I turn to go but Brexley only lowers his arm, more effectively boxing me in. I rear back, avoiding his touch. I'm reminded of when we first met at my grandma's, how he moved to trap me just like this. Then, I'd found it a fun, intriguing game gone wild. But now? Forget ogres and ice mages, I'd never been in more danger than right now.

My breath is shallow and I try to focus on the dirty alley wall over his shoulder. His eyes practically rake down my body. My nipples tighten, my piercings add hot spikes of pain and pleasure that nearly drive me out of my mind.

"Did you know that Weres have extraordinary tongues, dexterous, wide, which is why we really know how to lap up something sweet?"

"You're disgusting," I say. I'm flailing, trying to do anything I can to make him stop. But now I'm remembering. Remembering the feel of his mouth against me.

"Is that disgust I smell?" He chuckles darkly.

My eyes snap to his. Is that how he reads me so well? He can smell my desire? Outrage cuts through the arousal.

I glare. "Are you attempting to mix business with pleasure again? Because I thought we both agreed it was a bad idea."

Some of the playfulness drains from his expression as

he looks thoughtful. "I've never done it in the past, but you are . . . something else."

It doesn't sound like a compliment.

"Yeah, I'm something you can't handle." The second it's out of my mouth, I recognize my fatal mistake.

Brexley curls his tongue behind his teeth, leaning in until he is mere inchesfrom me. His face twists in a snarl, eyes sparkling in dark delight. "Oh little Red, now I'm going to have to eat you up."

CHAPTER 22
KISS WITH A FIST

BREXLEY

F uck "no touching."

I grab her by the back of her head and haul her into a bruising kiss. My hand pushes its way past her coat, meeting bare flesh before roughly forcing up that fucking leather bra that I should burn for torturing me all goddamn night long. I'll put it in the fire with the hideous bra she keeps wearing. It would make for a strange kind of yin/yang catharsis.

My fingers catch on her nipple ring, and I tweak and twist at it mercilessly. She squeals and I don't fucking care who hears it.

I'm going to touch and mark every last bit to show her how wrong she is. About Hunter, about me, about everything.

Her mouth is hot, willing, and the most sinful thing I've tasted after her pussy. Red's hips roll against my body, and I know she's aroused past frustration. Fucking good, because she's been frustrating me for too long already.

I give her nipple ring a particularly punishing tweak. She yelps against my mouth before she growls. Then she bites at my lip, trying to draw blood, her teeth scraping against mine in a fight for dominance. Her sudden violence excites me, so I yank the hair at the base of her skull, forcing her to submit to me. I deepen the kiss, sweeping my tongue in her mouth. I revel in her taste, exploring her mouth exactly how I want. I give her other nipple ring a twist. My cock is so hard it makes me goddamn furious.

"You think I can't handle you? Pet, I'm the only one who can."

Hands slam into my chest, and I'm forced back a couple of steps. Red's fist connects with my cheek before I compute what's coming. Pain explodes along my cheek like fire. My finger gently pads the tender skin as I take in Red's state. Swollen lips, eyes feverish and glassy, her coat is open, and the leather bra is still askew. Tousled flame hair spills over her shoulders, and for a moment I think I'm standing before a mythical fury.

Red's expression is caught between animalistic fury and the last fraying strands of hesitance. Fear flickers in between the two states. Not of me, she's scared of herself. But I can fix that. Give her something else to target her violence at.

I lick the taste of copper from inside my cheek. "Hard to act like a human now isn't it, my pet?" I taunt.

She punches me in the face again and again while saying, "I am human. My father was human and so am I."

I welcome the smash of her fist, knowing she can't seriously hurt me.

That's it, little Red. The prude boy can't take it, but I can. I can take all of you.

My fangs elongate and I know my eyes are flashing. I taste more blood, but it only excites me.

I grab her and twist until she's restrained in an arm lock. My open palm smacks her butt cheek so hard my palm stings. The scent of her arousal thickens around me even as I let her go. She stumbles forward, off balance.

I mock her again. "You're not human, you are a magic dud. But you do so love to play pretend."

A mane of red hair flips up and away from her face as she straightens. Her eyes are bright with excitement. *Oh yeah, baby can take as good as she gives.*

She kicks me in the chest, sending me slamming into the alley wall. I choke out a laugh. "Is this what you really want, little Red? Because I think you're still holding back."

"You are a fucking asshole, you know that?" she pants.

"Yeah, but I'm the asshole you want to peg." I laugh harder at my own joke though my ribs hurt from her kick. The power of her blow surprises me, but I'm almost used to this little redhead giving me a run for my money.

She punches me in the gut over that one, and I laugh breathlessly.

Then she jumps on me, legs wrapping around my hips. I instantly catch the skirt-clad ass under her coat. The tips of my fingers are close to her center and I feel how wet she is.

Red's mouth descends on mine in a punishing fervor, sending even more blood flowing across my tongue. I've never been kissed so thoroughly in my life. She kisses like she wants to eat me whole, while her hips rock furiously against me. "Fuck me," she demands. "Fuck me, goddammit."

This. This is the animal I knew she had inside her. Someone who has so much passion that she can't control it. I know exactly how she feels. She thinks we've been fighting, but it's all been foreplay. But that time is over. I plan to leave her a melted puddle by the time I'm done with her.

I walk us further into the darkened alleyway and push her back against the brick wall. Icy rain droplets spit down on us. Unable to help myself, I pull the hood of her jacket up. To protect her from the rain, or in case anyone walks by and thinks to look down the alley. They don't get to see her like this. Only I do.

Unzipping my pants, I pull out a cock hard enough to hammer nails. Reaching under her skirt, I rip her panties off, making sure the angle grates across her dripping pussy. She gasps in pain, but her hips rock faster, needing me even more now.

"I said fuck me," she growls.

At the same time I shove her torn, wet panties in her mouth, I thrust up into her soaked entrance. Her eyes go wide. We simultaneously groan. Fuck she is so tight and wet, I'm in danger of losing control immediately. Red's hips jerk and rock as she immediately starts to ride me.

Fuck, fuck, no, it's too much. She's too goddamn delicious and our bout of violence already has my blood pumping too hot. I need to slow down, or I'm going to lose it too soon. I need to be in control enough to make this last. My fingers dig into her hips with bruising force in an attempt to still them, but she's relentlessly trying to hump me.

She could easily spit out her own panties, but they remain in her mouth, eyes closed in equal parts ecstasy and need. My dirty little Red, riding me like a girl possessed and tasting her own desire.

She slides up and down my cock twice more before she shouts through the fabric.

"Jesus, fuck, witchtits," I moan as she tightens and clamps around me.

Keep it together wolf, show her you can handle this.

Getting control of myself while she writhes and comes on my cock, I pull the panties from her mouth and shove them in my back pocket. I'll need those later.

As soon as she sags against me, that's when I get going. I slam my hips up into her with relentless force. I dip down and catch that exposed nipple ring in my mouth and tug at it with my teeth.

I've had to hold back my entire life with females, but with Red, I don't have too. If I didn't know any better, I'd think she was a werewolf herself. But I know that's not possible. Not with how she smells and what I know about her family.

In seconds, Red's shuddering and coming around me again. Warmth and pressure spike in my balls, and I know I'm moments from blowing.

I want to look at her face. Watch her come. But the shadow of her hood prevents me, her eyes covered in darkness. It's for the best.

Still, I hunger for it. I crave it.

No, you don't need her. You don't need that piece of her.

My hips slam into her one last time as I'm skyrocketed to another realm. There is nothing but me and Red, and the intense sensation of firing straight into her delectable warmth. It's heaven, but I'm too much of a sinner to deserve this.

The heat of the moment ebbs away, and we are left panting in the darkened alley. I still can't see most of Red's face, so I don't know what she's thinking. Slowly, she unwraps her legs from my waist and I set her down. The only sounds are a police siren in the distance, a dog barking, and the rustle of our clothing as we readjust them. Out of her warmth, I'm cold. Too cold. Something in my chest hurts.

Finally, she asks. "Do you feel better now?" There is an eerie calm to her voice, and I don't know what it means.

Do I feel better? She's the one who needed to get off so badly. I was simply helping.

Even as I construct the thought, it doesn't settle right.

"What do you mean?" I ask.

"You wanted to show me how vanilla Hunter is. You wanted to win in your pissing match against him. Do you feel better now that you've won?"

"That's not . . . that's not what this was." Not entirely. In fact, it's growing to be so much more of a problem than I anticipated. I want to gather her back in my arms, nuzzle her neck, and kiss her softly. Resisting the urge causes me physical pain.

"Really?" she asks, but the question is rhetorical. "Because we both know you are all about you. And while I can appreciate your masculine Were need to swing your dick around, I don't care to be in the stakes in claiming territory." She sounds so cold, so distant, it makes my chest hurt.

"What does that mean?"

"It means," she sighs heavily, "while I might have these intense sexual urges . . . I still have feelings. And if you keep this up, I might start to develop the same delusions I had about Hunter. And that would be bad for both of us."

With that, she walks off, heading home again. I hang back in the shadows. I should run to catch up with her. Make sure she isn't unattended, watch out for dangerous entities, ask her again if she has reached out to her grandma or maybe heard anything. I should brush off everything we just did and what she just said.

Instead, I stand here like an open wound.

I have to complete the mission. I need to kill her grandma.

But for the first time, I don't know if I can.

CHAPTER 23

IF YOU GIVE A FRIEND A COOKIE

RED

S tudying the coffee in the bag, I seriously consider dumping some of the grounds straight into my mouth and chewing on them.

With a side glance at Brexley, I find him still standing by the window, staring out at the morning light like a watchdog. He looks as rested as I feel. And I feel like a train wreck on fire. I'm sexually satisfied beyond anything I've experienced before. So much that my hormones haven't uttered a peep and it has been six hours since Brexley took out everything he had on me. But there's a hollowness in my heart that wasn't there before. By all accounts we both should have slept like the dead, but no dice.

I think better of chowing down on the grounds and instead pour them into my coffee filter.

We haven't spoken since I got up.

Not only did Hunter's surprise appearance sting like salt in a wound, but the way Brexley challenged me, baited

173

me into fighting and then fucking him. . . I'm more than a little confused. My heart squeezes and yearns to the point of pain, but I'm not sure what for.

Brexley, my brain whispers.

I shake my head to myself. I've tasted enough loneliness to know when someone isn't in this for me. I hate the sudden sting of tears at the backs of my eyes. I hate that I shared so many things that make me vulnerable, even in the heat of a fight. Brexley doesn't deserve my secret longings or my pain, yet it keeps unfurling in front of him anyway.

And now, I have all but revealed that I want him, and that I'm incapable of keeping my heart out of it.

Will I ever stop being so pathetic?

No amount of leather, tattoos, or piercings will amount to enough armor to deny my weakness.

Even if Brexley is attracted to me, he has no intention of being serious about me. Which is just fine, because there is zero room in my life for sadistic werewolves with filthy mouths.

Maybe I'd made a mistake sending Hunter away? At least with him, I got used to the score.

The very thought of letting Hunter back in gives my stomach a sick twist.

Could I get away with sending them all away?

Then I remember the ice mage, the Ogre, and the glamor mage. So my options are to suffer from sexual humiliation and negging by a dangerously sexy werewolf, or get taken?

I find myself still weighing the options when my front door unlocks and opens.

Brexley is at the door in a blink, while I grab the closest

makeshift weapon, an oversized mug with skull and cross-bones and a quote from my favorite vampire romance. "Bloodsucker in the streets, Vamp in the sheets."

Goldie first looks at Brexley and then at me, in our ready positions. "Wow. Guess I should have knocked first. I forgot y'all might be banging things out. Oh! Coffee!" Then she brushes past Brexley and plucks the mug out of my hand.

She's wearing pink sweatpants and a long sleeve black tee. As she pours for herself, I notice she is not only wearing last night's makeup, but her curls are thoroughly fucked, like someone ran their hands through them. And only because I've come to know her so well, do I notice the familiar bitterness lining her eyes and edges of her mouth. Coupled with her early appearance, I know she's feeling rough. Goldie comes over regularly, but never before ten am. With our late shifts, she considers any time before then ungodly.

"Is it that guy last night?" I ask.

Her honey brown eyes turn up to meet mine and it's stamped all over her face. "Why are guys such pricks?"

Her eyes turn glassy even as she tries to blink the wetness away, and I pull her into a hug. Goldie taught me her love language is physical touch, and frankly it's nice to touch someone who feels safe and doesn't set me off.

The front door creaks. Brexley is about to make his escape. "I can wait outside."

Goldie pulls away and runs a hand through her hair. "Don't be ridiculous. If you are going to be around for any amount of time, there is no hiding the shit show that is my love life."

I scoop some sugar and extra cream into Goldie's coffee, then hand it to her. "What happened?"

"Ugh, before we go into it, do you have any of the good stuff left over?" Hope gleams from her eyes.

Brexley finally shuts the door, deciding to stay.

I hold up a finger. "Don't tell Cinder, but I have one left."

Goldie pumps her free fist into the air. "Yessss. Can I have it? Because I'm really sad, and life is hard." She gives me her biggest puppy eyes.

I laugh as I pull out a step stool from my closet so I can reach my top kitchen cabinet where I keep my secret stash. I pull down a plastic container.

Somehow Goldie has managed to break the choking tension between Brexley and me, and I'm grateful. It's easier to focus on her than the swirling of my own mind right now. He seems far more at ease too.

With the utmost reverence I pass the stash over to Goldie who looks as honored as if I'd handed her a queen's crown.

"What is it?" Brexley asks, his brows drawn.

Goldie's eyes widen dramatically as she takes her coffee and cookie over to my couch and settles in. "You don't know about her Gigi's cookies?"

I shoot Brexley a warning glance.

"Your grandma sends you cookies?" he asks in a cheeky tone that Goldie completely misses.

"Oh my gawd, her grandma sends Red a tin every month and Cinder and I are like vultures, trying to snag as many as we can. This one is gingerbread and sea salt with caramel, and it's my absolute favorite."

"That's what you said about the last batch," I say while pouring two more mugs of coffee. I hand Brexley the mug with a cute painted bunny face on it that says "Some Bunny

Loves You." He narrows his eyes at me but sips off the steaming top.

"The last batch was oatmeal butterscotch.. That was also my favorite."

"And the one before that?" I ask, trying and failing to suppress a smile.

Goldie moans and throws her head back. "Oh fae lords, the peanut butter double fudge cookies." She lifts her head. "What was the first kind I tried? The ones in the cute little windmill shapes."

"Oh, those were Dutch cookies called speculaas. They're kind of half shortbread, half spice cookie."

"Since you've been singing their praises, do I get to try any of it?" Brexley asks Goldie.

She freezes, fingers wrapped around the container. The fear in her eye is downright comical.

Goldie looks to me for help.

I shrug. She's the one who dug herself into this hole, making such a big deal out of how delicious they are. The silence continues as Goldie hangs herself on it.

Finally, I take mercy on her. "Goldie has done enough sharing for one night, it seems. She gets to keep the whole cookie for herself."

With a sigh of relief, Goldie relaxes the container she'd protectively held to her stomach.

"Don't worry, B-dog," Goldie says cheerfully. I can tell Brexley instantly hates her new nickname for him. "Next time Red gets some Gigi cookies, I'm sure she'll share with you."

My stomach tightens. The impossible image of us curled up on my broken couch while I feed Brexley cookies springs to mind. It's domestic, sweet, and utterly impossible.

Goldie pops the lid and pulls out the last cookie. "This cookie can make up for all the injustices of the world."

Bangs and Bombs immediately leap onto the couch, thinking she is holding a treat for them. She automatically raises her arm to keep it out of reach, even as they paw at her arm and jump all over her lap.

Laughing, I scoot the bunnies off the couch and park my butt next to Goldie's. Brexley takes a seat at the table.

"What makes them so magical?" he asks.

I shoot Brexley another dark look of warning, but he only innocently sips from the bunny mug.

"They are made with love and lard," Goldie repeats dutifully. It's in every note my Gigi sends along with the cookies.

"So what did this one do?" I ask Goldie, even as she moans around her first bite.

Once she finishes chewing, she says, "I'll tell you what he did. He was perfect, and cute, and said all the right things. A real prince charming, ya know?"

They are always prince charmings in the beginning.

"But he never lets me come over to his place. It's just weird. How can I properly judge what kind of guy he is if I never see where or how he lives? So I cut it off. I don't need the weirdness. But then he showed up last night, as you saw. He brings me a single red rose like it's some kind of scene out of a romance movie. So . . . " She trails off, blushing.

"Soo, you went home with him, didn't you?"

"Well yeah. He lives on Broadway and Pike, so it was an hour by subway but his place was gorgeous like all that side of town. Then we got down to business, and things were going great. Well, they were okay. The chemistry was kind of meh, but it's not always the greatest at first. Everyone knows that."

Brexley sputters and coughs. His face is practically purple as he chokes. "Wrong pipe," he rasps out by way of explanation.

"So then what happened?" I ask, urging Goldie to continue.

"What happened? What happened is I drifted off to sleep in a pair of strong arms and woke up to a slap in the face from a woman I've never seen before. Turns out, the little fucker took me home to the apartment he shares with *his girlfriend*. She was out late working and came back to find us in her bed."

My hand flies to my mouth. "Oh shit."

Goldie has a hand over her face and misses the dangerous glow now emitting from Brexley's eyes. I suppress a shiver. Cold hate radiates out from them. For a moment I don't realize why, but then I turn back to my very embarrassed friend.

Is he upset on her behalf? The Big Bad Wolf cares about a girl's shitty boy situation?

Once I think I have him figured out, he completely throws me off again.

"So I had a very long ride this morning and I feel like absolute crap." Goldie angrily rolls her eyes heavenward. "I swear, I still can't tell if this is some kind of test I keep failing, picking the wrong guys. Or if I'm just destined to be alone. Maybe my standards are too high, but I swear either this guy is a liar, or that one doesn't have a job. Is it bad I want one just right for me?"

"Eat some more cookie," I say, lifting her wrist. She's still clutching the half-eaten treat.

When Goldie finishes it, she sighs and sinks further into the couch. I get up and lay a throw blanket over her lap then grab a small handful of oats from the container next to the rabbit pen. I sprinkle her lap with oats then make a chittering sound to get the buns back on the couch. Bangs and Bombs are up in a second, chowing down as Goldie pets them. After they finish, they are likely to sit with her.

Putting the tv remote in her reach I say, "I have to get to the library, but you can stay here as long as you want."

My friend throws a grateful smile at me as I head toward the bedroom. Her eyes catch on the fresh claw marks on the door. She shoots me a deliberate look that asks if everything is okay.

I give her a quick nod before disappearing to grab a sweater and my bag. A low voice penetrates the closed door.

"Want me to kill him for you?"

I can only imagine Goldie's reaction. There is too long of a pause.

"No, no, I don't need that," she says finally.

"You don't deserve that shit. And if you want, I'm happy to pay him a visit and teach him how one treats a lady."

"The only favor I need is for you to treat my friend well. I'm so glad she's got someone like you, Brexley. Someone who's nice to her."

A dark bark of a laugh escapes me. I clap a hand over my mouth, but I know it's too late. Goldie may not have heard it, but I know Brexley has.

After a pause, he says, "Don't worry, I give her exactly what she needs."

Any mirth in me dies as I replay how he did that last night. It was exactly what I needed, but I hate it. I hate that I needed it and I hate that I want it again.

After such an intense banging, I'm totally cured of my monthly "episode." A day early even!

I don't feel any arousal or need, especially not toward Brexley.

A little voice whispers in my head. *Liar.*

CHAPTER 24
A QUICK-IE STUDY BREAK

BREXLEY

R ed emits a growl of frustration and starts to slam her book around before massaging her temples.

Yet again, we're back in the dusty library. Red has taken two practice tests. I peeked at the scores, she's making passing grades, but apparently, it's not enough.

Tomorrow is Monday which not only means she has classes, she has two finals. One she is prepared for, but the other she's close to tearing her hair out over.

"Why are you so freaked out about this test? It's not like it's the end of the world if you don't do well."

She turns to me, her mist-colored eyes flashing like flint. "If I fail this class, I have to repeat it."

"So?"

"So?" she echoes in outrage. "I'm behind enough as it is after dropping out of FFA. I failed most of my classes there and I refuse to be the same loser I was."

"How can you blame yourself for failing a mage

academy when you have no magic? That's as ridiculous as it is unrealistic."

Red fiddles with her septum ring and mutters, "It wasn't all magic application. I flunked the magic theory and history classes as well."

That takes me aback. I've never seen someone so fanatical about their studies. Red is no dummy, so why did she do so poorly then?

I say the next part very carefully. "At the risk of being skinned alive, do you maybe have a learning disability or something?"

She drops her hand, as her mouth opens then closes like a fish out of water. "No, I don't have a learning disability. In my defense, this financial auditing class is one of the hardest. And the professor is nicknamed the dragon because she is so ruthless. And the FFA was difficult because there were," she halts as if afraid of revealing too much. She finally lands on the word she can live with, "distractions."

"Hunter?" I ask.

Instead of confirming or denying, she nervously licks her lips.

"Can you cut that out? You lick your lips more than any other person I've met, and it's annoying as hell."

It also makes me want to kiss you senseless, every faefucking time.

Her brows lift in surprise even as she tightens her lips. "Sorry, it's a habit I thought I'd broken."

Now I feel bad for making her self-conscious about it. What is this girl doing to me?

"Okay," I say, switching to business mode, "what's going to help you feel better about this test? Do you need a tutor or what?"

"No." She turns back to her laptop with a furrowed

brow. "I can do this. It's just . . . my focus is all over the place. I'm so freaked out by the idea of repeating the past. My anxiety keeps getting in the way until I can't even see straight."

Now *this,* I can handle.

"Well then number one, you need to lay off the caffeine." I close her laptop and slide her books into her bag.

Red scowls. "Bite me."

"And number two." I pull her to her feet.

"I said no touching," she says breathlessly, and I can tell she is getting worked up again.

I ignore her and lead her through the stacks. "I can help you with the anxiety."

Reaching the private study rooms in the back, I find one that's empty and push her inside, shutting the door behind us.

I don't turn on the lights, but light filters in through the thin strip of window along the door.

"What are you doing?" Red asks.

I set her bag down and hoist her up by her hips, setting her on the edge of a long table.

"Helping you relax."

Before Red can respond, I step between her legs, cup her jaw, and capture her lips in a kiss. Despite her ire at being directed in here, she immediately opens her mouth. Her tongue dances with mine. She sighs.

It's not the violent frenzy like before. The kiss is deep and searching. With one hand, I reach up and pull out the soft scrunchie holding up the mass of hair. It falls around her, and my pants get tighter.

The heat between her legs penetrates my jeans as she rubs on my fast-growing hardness.

"This isn't going to help," she murmurs between kisses.

"Trust me," I say.

"Never," she instantly shoots back.

My lips curve against hers as I tug at the hair at the base of her skull and deepen the kiss. A low guttural moan escapes her throat. It may be the sexiest noise I've ever heard. No, the sounds of her falling apart in orgasm have that honor.

If I'm being honest, the slight rasp in her voice when she says fucking anything feels like velvet to my ears. She could recite boring financial terms and I'd be panting for her in minutes.

Red's grinding grows more desperate as we rub through our clothes. I know what she needs. She whimpers when I step away.

"Take off your leggings," I instruct.

In the low lighting, I see her shoot a nervous glance to the window and door. There's no lock on the door, and I know she's thinking anyone can see or walk in at any moment. But I don't want her thinking.

"Do you want to pass your tests or what?" I ask, deliberately pressing the hot button on what she wants.

While she does what I ask, I grab a couple of the armed chairs and set them on either side of her at the table.

She only partially listened, leaving her panties on, and her nerves are palpable.

"Dammit Red," I growl. "I told you to stop licking those luscious faefucking lips."

I resume my place back between her legs and give her a punishing kiss. While torturing, and teasing her lips with nibbles and licks, I direct her legs so her feet are on either chair. The arms of the chairs keep her legs stretched apart, so she's bared to me.

When I let her up for air, she's gasping. I run a finger up and down the soft cleft of her lower lips through her panties. A needy moan slips from her. She shed her rock band sweater, leaving her in a thin tank top. She skipped the bra and the pert points of her piercings stick out.

"We are going to work off that tension and clear your mind," I inform her with all the authority of a professor telling the class about their upcoming syllabus.

I take a moment to lave my tongue against her left nipple, teasing the metal bar in it. "Do you have any idea how obsessed I am with your piercings? How convenient they aren't silver, so I don't scald myself on them."

Then I push up her tank, leaning over to nibble on her jeweled navel ring and press my tongue into the small, sensitive indent. Her hips roll. She's an innie, and I'm obsessed with filling every part of her.

I rub more insistently through the thin panties, feeling the wetness spreading under my touch. Fuck, I'm hard for her.

She lets out a mewl. "I'm allergic to silver."

Then I drop down to one knee, pulling her hips right to the edge of the table. I flatten my tongue against those panties and drag it up and down. Red's head drops back, arms bracing behind her.

"Oh fuck," she breathes.

"In a minute," I promise.

Hooking a finger in her panties and dragging them to the side, I lick up her bare, exposed sex and her hips jerk.

"What a coincidence. They also make me wonder if you've ever thought of piercing your delicious little clit." With that I wrap my lips around her bud and suckle it gently but persistently.

This time, her groan of pleasure is strangled. She's like

an instrument and I'm the musician. I'm learning what touch, lick, and suck produce which pitch and length of note. And once I've learned all the notes, I'm going to pound out a symphony from her.

Inserting a finger while I suckle her clit, I pump it in and out of her wet hole. It evokes a higher, tighter note from her. I add another finger and the timbre drops. I speed up my sucking and the pace of my probing fingers, now covered in her sweetness. And she is caught on a note, moaning it out in one long strand.

My music is cut off abruptly, and I catch her wide eyes trained on the window. With a quick glance, I see the back of someone examining the books on the shelf right outside the room. They could turn and see us at any second. I growl into Red's sweet pussy, discontent that the song I've been composing has been interrupted.

Her hands try to still my head, but I'm too busy with my concert to abide. I nip her swollen, sensitive bud and she gives a little yip. The browser finally moves away from the window and Red relaxes, but only a fraction.

Pumping even faster, I force her to pant and moan. It rises in pitch again and comes out in short, staccato bursts as she gets closer to release. Looking up at her, I'm instantly fucking enchanted. Eyes shut tight in concentration; I watch her pushing toward what she wants so badly. I instinctively eat her faster, and my pace turns punishing.

Her hips jerk and twist against me as she gasps over and over, fighting for breath. Her thighs tremble violently. I greedily lap at her desire as it rushes out. So sweet, so sinful, I could make a meal of her. I'd eat her out morning, noon, and night.

Once her hips and legs sag, I stand. I quickly take out

my hard cock and enter her dripping pussy. My favorite groan yet comes out as I push in.

Heaven wraps around me with scalding heat and I want to die right here.

"So fucking big," she whispers, and I can't help the self-satisfied grin that spreads on my face. Her thighs already tremble, but I want to make them shake like an earthquake hit her cunt. My fingers pluck and squeeze at her pierced nipples, making her squirm.

She's so tight, and I slam into her relentlessly until she can't think about her studies, about the past, or anything else but me driving into her.

Soon, she's coming around me with silent gasping cries as she milks me. But before I can join her in orgasm, she pushes me off and I fall into one of the chairs. Then Red is there on her knees before me, choking down my big cock.

It's as if this girl was made for me. Whether she's throwing a punch at me, diving into her work, vibrating with anxiety, or deep throating me, it's undeniable this girl is larger than life. It's why she feels too much, because she *is* too much. She's everything. The world can't contain all her ferocity, her intensity, and desire.

But I can. I want all of it so badly. I want her to overwhelm me with her fears, her feelings, and with her tongue, exactly like she's doing right now. I squirm under her as I forget how to breathe. *Fucking witchtits, how is she even doing that?*

My hands wrap up in her velvet hair of fire as I lose all sense of reality. There is only Red, my new gravity. She sucks me like a pro and I was already on the edge. "Oh fuck, I'm going to . . ."

I try to warn her, but she only takes me deeper down the back of her throat as I come. Her nails dig into my hips as they jerk erratically, releasing the intense buildup. It's so good, the marrow in my bones must have melted right out of me.

When I manage to crack an eye open, Red is dabbing the corner of her mouth with her thumb like she just finished an excellent meal.

Holy faefucks. I think I'm in love.

Oh fuck. Oh fuck, no.

I slam the doors down on my emotions. Emptying my face of any expression, I can't let her know something is up. I take my time zipping my pants back up to give myself a moment to fully gain control over myself.

I assist Red to her feet and help her get dressed quickly. "We don't want to get caught," I whisper. Only a few minutes ago, I wouldn't have cared if the whole of the librarian staff filed in. I still wouldn't have stopped. But now, I'm desperate to get out of this room, and away from the thought I released into it.

Red's eyes are glassy and dazed, but she is pliant to my directions. Emerging from the study room, acting as natural as one can, I get her set back up at the table she was at before. Her arms don't seem to work too well, so I open her laptop and tell her to start another practice test, and I'll be right back.

I pause too long to see her look up at me from under her long dark lashes. Those abused lips are puffy and her red hair is a voluminous mess that makes my heart squeeze.

I'm off like a shot. Still dizzy from coming so hard, I work on not stumbling. I take a lap of the library before grabbing a peppermint tea from the café and returning to Red.

When I get back to Red's spot, I set it down next to her, but she barely notices, so enrapt in the practice test. Once or twice, she sips from the tea, but her eyes remain on her screen.

I grab the Iliad off a nearby shelf and open it, trying to lose myself in words I've savored before.

"Any moment might be our last. Everything is more beautiful because we're doomed. You will never be lovelier than you are now. We will never be here again."

I snap the book shut, not wanting to read stupid romantic trash. Why couldn't I open it to a battle scene? Now I can't even bring myself to flip over to the Trojan war.

Twenty minutes later, Red turns to me with a triumphant smile. "I did it."

Looking at her screen, I see she got a 96%. I smile at her lazily. "Told you I could help you."

I can tell she's not sure how she feels about my methods, but her glowing response to the score is proof enough it was a great idea.

Even as I revel in the success of my idea, something in me hardens. I am a lone wolf. Attachments mean certain death. I am not in love. I can't be in love.

But to be sure, I start to shut my emotions down, one by one. Red's expression shutters into confusion, and I realize she can see I'm changing before her eyes.

"Drink your tea and go home, little Red. I'll meet you later to take you to work."

"Oh, okay," she says, seeming at a loss for the shift in tone.

With that, I bolt.

Staying so close to Red is no longer a viable plan. It's time I resort to other methods if I plan on finding Grandma.

CHAPTER 25

YOU DON'T LIKE ME? I DON'T LIKE YOU

RED

B ack at my apartment, I'm riding two waves. Wave number one is sexually satisfied, and psyched beyond measure I actually passed a practice test with relative ease. The second wave is one of confusion. The feelings I'm developing toward the Were are too tender. I'm too invested. Brexley must have seen the earnest feeling on my face because I watched him shut down and make a hasty retreat.

It was all too familiar a response I'd get from Hunter.

I might get away without repeating my academic mistakes, but it seems I'm doomed to repeat the romantic ones.

Screw Brexley. I warned him my feelings get wrapped up easily, and that I can be delusional. That should have been enough to send him running.

Brexley never returned, but hours later when I step out onto the darkened, icy streets, there he is. Brexley shuffles, emerging from the shadows where he leaned against the building. Yet again, he's changed into fresh clothes, but I never see him carry a bag. Bundled in my coat, I pull it closer around me as if I can cover up my vulnerabilities. Hopefully he just thinks I'm cold.

"I'm going to work," I announce when he doesn't say anything.

Instead of answering with a snarky response, he simply nods. We stand there another minute before I start down the sidewalk. He silently walks alongside me. This is getting to be a bad pattern.

He should say something.

I should say something.

But what the fuck does one say?

Hey, it was a really bad idea for us to have a quickie today. Or what we did last night, or. . .

I shake my head. There is no way to address what's happened without making things worse.

The walk passes by faster than normal as my brain races to fill the span, trying to construct something to say.

Before we enter the Poison Apple, I stop and turn to him. "Listen, we both know that yet again, it was a mistake. You don't even like me. So let's just pretend it never happened. I'm reinstating the no touching rule. Sound good? Good." I nod to myself, satisfied with the one-sided conversation and ready to get to work.

"You think I don't like you?" he says, stopping me in my tracks.

He stares at me so intently I want to back up a few steps. I manage to stand my ground.

"You've made that pretty clear," I say slowly.

Sure, he's nice to my friends, saved me from multiple attacks, and stares at me like I'm the only girl in the entire universe when he's fucking the life out of me. But I know exactly what he thinks of me.

He licks his top lip as if giving serious consideration to what he is going to say next. Then I realize I don't want to hear whatever it is, so I whirl around and practically flee into the bar.

Did it sound like I was trying to get him to say he liked me?

Ugh, Red, yet again we are coming off desperate. Hunter didn't want you, and Brexley sure as hell doesn't want you.

Then I consider it may be the bodyguard dynamic. Having someone in my business all the time makes things feel mixed up and confusing.

As soon as I slip behind the bar with Goldie and Cinder, there is no Brexley, or horribly embarrassing encounter. I'm in control of my hormones again, and everything will be fine.

Throughout the night, I occasionally look up for Brexley, but I don't find him. Still, I know he is around here, somewhere, watching. Even with his larger-than-life presence and striking scars, he melts into the crowd.

Heat pulsates in me. The quickie is already wearing off, and by my calculation, this is the last day of my episode. Which makes it the most intense.

Keep your head down, Red. You got this.

At the height of the evening, drinks flow, music pulsates seductively, and the usual hypnotic vibe emanates from the low fairy lights of the massive tree hanging over the tables and lounge chairs. I'm lost to the rhythm and wonder if feeling in flow like this is similar to wielding magic. To be able to feel the energy and wield it with effortless motion.

The front doors slam open with a crash and a rush of icy wind. Two willowy, almost deathly pale people stroll into the bar. A hush rolls over the room. Even the music turns down at the violent entrance.

The crowd parts so I can see who is causing a fuss.

"Oh faefucks," I whisper.

First heat, then cold washes over my body as my fight-or-flight instincts kick in. Every internal alarm bell goes off, blaring so loud I can't think.

This can't be happening. This has to be a nightmare. Because in no universe would my personal tormentors from Fairy Fine Arts show up in a human town, to the very bar where I work.

"Wait, is that who I think it is?" Goldie asks in an awed tone. She knows her mage celebrities, so I've no doubt Goldie is well aware who is standing before us.

I lick my suddenly parched lips and croak out their names. "Hansel and Gretel."

CHAPTER 26
AN UNPLEASANT PAIR

BREXLEY

Magic stink wafts off the two people who entered. One is a man and the other a woman, though frankly they look like one person who's been split in half. Twins, if I had to guess. Thin sheets of white-blonde hair frame their faces and dip past their knees. Something about their dark eyes is severe and cold as the arctic. The way they scan the room, I can tell they are more pleased with themselves than anything they see.

Their magic, whatever it is, is powerful and vile, definitely Level Four. They wear the deep royal purple leathers that match.

A security guard approaches the female, "Hey, this is a humans-only bar. You can't be in here." Her head snaps toward him and power arcs from her eyes like tiny strands of lightning. The man suddenly gasps and doubles over, clutching at his stomach.

"Looks as though you are *hungry* for a fight," she purrs in a breathy voice that gives me goosebumps. My nose wrinkles against the sharp spike in her magic. The scent of spoiled milk and rotting meat assaults my senses. I suppress the urge to gag. I want to flee this place to get a clear breath of air, but I hold steady.

The bouncer cries out, reaching toward her, seeking mercy, before clutching his stomach again with a moan.

Everyone else takes a step back.

The white-haired man doesn't even turn to look at his sister. The woman tilts her head at the writhing security guard, as if pondering how much she can play with her toy before it breaks. Her brother continues to scan the bar as if searching for something in particular.

His eyes settle and alight on Red.

I don't like one single fucking thing about this.

He strides toward her in long, lazy steps, and people split to make way for him. Fear and awe fill the air in a cloying stench.

This. This is why Weres live far from civilization. I'm practically choking on all the emotion, magic and pheromones in the room.

Still, I snake through the crowd, pacing the newcomer as he makes his way toward Red.

He stops six feet from her, and I finally catch sight of her. Her eyes are wild. Like a trapped animal, the scent of her terror cuts through the spoiled magic. It's acidic yet somehow still sweet.

Fear is different from terror. I've sensed Red's fear of being attacked, her fear for her grandmother, her fear of failure, but her terror is acute. Fear is usually about antici-pation of the bad thing, but terror is immediacy to danger in the moment. Red seems struck, though it is just a mage walking toward her.

"Red," the man says, his voice like silk. "It's been such a long time."

Red nervously glances about the room, licking her lips. "Not nearly long enough, Hansel. Tell your sister to let him go."

Goldie and Cinder look back and forth between Red and the male mage with confused expressions.

"That's all you have to say?" He spreads his thin arms out wide. "You don't miss your old schoolmates?"

A muscle jumps in Red's face, and her knuckles go white where she grips the edge of the bar.

I squelch the instinct to run up and put myself between them. If I hang back, I have an opportunity to learn why people have been coming after Red. Because something tells me it has everything to do with these two.

But the fear on Red's face makes my emotions surge to the surface, as my wolf demands I protect her.

So I can get to her grandma, I insist to myself, but it's no use. Lying to myself is nearly impossible now. My wolf wants Red in every way, and right now, it wants her safe.

The bouncer moans in pain again.

Fire sparks in Red's eyes, overcoming her terror. She clutches the edge of the counter even harder as she leans in. "Go fuck your sister, Hansel." Again, she licks her lips as if she can't wet them enough.

"Did you hear that, Gretel?" Hansel says in a bored, disaffected voice that makes me want to punch him in the face.

"I did, dear brother," Gretel replies, losing interest in the security guard. He slumps to the ground, moaning and gasping, but seemingly released from whatever acute pain she was inflicting on him.

"Living among talentless humans has made you crude, Red. Last we saw you . . . " Hansel's eyes trace the piercing at her nose and travels down her revealing outfit with a disgusted leer. " . . . you were as timid and useless as a field mouse. But it looks as though you've entered an adorable little rebellious phase. Regardless, that is no way to talk to your friends."

Tonight, Red wears severely torn up jeans over fishnet stockings, and a rock band tee-shirt that's been cut off to reveal the bottom swells of her breasts. Half her hair is pulled up into a high ponytail and the smoky makeup on her eyes makes her gray irises pop. She's a sultry rock goddess, but right now she's not acting like it.

Red licks her lips yet again, the reaction is a compulsion she can't seem to control around these two. She shoots a wary glance at Goldie and Cinder. I notice Rap has appeared in the crowd at some point, but like me, she takes in the scene as if gauging what move is best to make next.

"Friends," Red's echo of his word comes out as a humorless, dry laugh. Fury and terror are still fighting for dominance in her.

She doesn't notice Cinder and Goldie exchange a confused look behind her back.

"Of course," Hansel tries to use a soothing tone, but it holds too much menace. "Gretel and I thought we'd catch up. Maybe you could be a good little slop slinger and pour us a drink. You know how *thirsty* we get. Maybe you should have one too, you look a bit parched."

Red's shoulders stiffen and she has gone so still, I wonder if she is still breathing.

It's then that Rap steps up. "Hey, you heard it before. This is a humans-only bar."

Gretel bares her teeth at Rap in a way that makes her eyes shine like evil oil droplets.

Hansel reaches in his coat pocket and pulls out a thick wad of cash. "Here, this will be more than enough to buy us some time to bend the rules." Then he throws the wad at Rap. It hits her, exploding into flying bills before settling on the ground. She doesn't move an inch, except for the narrowing of her eyes. If Rap's eyes were knives, he'd be sliced to ribbons. But the bar owner is still assessing her opponent, as am I. This Hansel is dangerous, but I haven't figured out the extent of his danger.

One of the women near Rap tries to surreptitiously bend down to pick up some of the bills.

"Uh uh uh," Hansel tsks just before he raises a hand and his magic flares. The woman gasps and claws at her own throat.

"My dear, you look positively parched." Hansel grins evilly. Most people scuttle backwards as the woman continues to gasp and groan. Her lips shrivel and whiten.

"So thirsty for money that doesn't belong to you," he lightly scolds while flexing his fingers, playing with the effect on his victim. Gretel lets out a deranged, hyena laugh behind him, openly delighted by his display of power.

Suddenly I know why Red developed the maddening habit of licking her lips. Hansel's used his power on her. A lot.

Rage bubbles up in me.

"That's enough, Hansel," Red says, quiet and steady.

His dark gaze snaps back to her as if he's forgotten himself. "Yes, indeed. We have much to discuss. I think you have something you want to share with me."

Supposedly, this recipe the ice mage referenced.

As soon as Hansel's hand lowers, the girl gasps in relief, having been released from his hold. She scrambles away, but instead of fleeing for the exit, she runs to the bar and half croaks, half begs Cinder for water. Cinder hastily fills a glass and hands it over. The woman downs it with desperation, sloshing most of the liquid down her shirt. Cinder fills two more glasses and sets them on the counter in a line.

Then the bartender shoots such a venomous look at Hansel, I almost believe Red's earlier claim. That Cinder can shoot laser, death-rays from her dark irises and explode the mage into red dust.

Meanwhile, Goldie alternates clutching her own throat and covering her mouth. I'm not sure if she means to steady herself or keep herself from launching right at Hansel and Gretel.

When I get her to meet my eye I slowly shake my head at her in warning, in case it's the second. If she throws herself in the way of these two psychopaths, she wouldn't be helping anyone. She'd only make a target of herself and that would destroy Red. I can't allow that.

Thankfully, the situation is too tense for me to take the time to dissect that last, ridiculous thought.

Hansel rubs his fingernails against his chest "Now Red, why don't you come with us? We have much to discuss."

Gretel moves around from behind him, advancing toward Red with a menacing grin on her face.

I close the distance and step into Gretel's path.

"She won't be going anywhere with you," I inform her in a lazy tone.

"Brex, no," I hear a breathless whisper behind me.

Is Red concerned about my safety? And *Brex*? The nickname causes warmth to extend out from the center of my chest like sun rays. There is absolutely no way they are taking the redhead.

Out of the corner of my vision, I catch Goldie and Cinder move into flanking positions behind Red. Like me, they are ready to spring into action for their friend.

The slim mage girl looks up at me with the curiosity of a serial killer wondering how I would look with my skin peeled off. I bare my teeth at her in a half snarl.

"What are you . . . going to do about it?" Gretel paused halfway into her question before finishing it with a second.

The bouncer limps away as quickly as he can, released from her evil magic.

I let my power come to the surface and my eyes glow as my fangs and claws elongate. "Care to find out?"

Gretel half sneers, half smiles. The bitch is crazy and I recognize bloodlust when I see it. I growl back at her.

"Gretel," Hansel snaps in warning. She stiffens and narrows her eyes at me before wandering back to her brother. Circling around behind him, she then drapes herself over his shoulders. Her nose nuzzles the side of his neck while her glare remains pinned on me.

Red might not have been wrong about them fucking each other.

While Hansel's eyes remain flat, an amused smile plays at his lips. "A Were. I've never met one before. I thought you were all extinct." He exaggerates his pronunciation on the last word.

"There are plenty of us left. We just like to stay far away from dickheads like you."

Hansel's eyes narrow. He's used to people groveling in fear around him. I level my own gaze at him, letting him know I'm not scared of him or his psycho sister.

I'm not sure if it's because he believes me, or the

wailing sound of sirens from outside that inspire him, but after a long pause, Hansel removes Gretel's arm from his shoulder. "Time to go, poppet."

She pouts, reminding me of an evil gremlin.

"Don't worry, Red. We'll catch up. Soon." Hansel throws over his shoulder as he leaves, Gretel begrudgingly at his heels.

Once they've exited the Poison Apple, it's like a collective breath is let out from all the humans. Chatter starts at a dull buzz as if no one is sure what to do next. But Rap does.

She easily steps up on a stool then onto the bar. Poising two fingers in her mouth, she lets loose an ear-splitting whistle. Everyone quiets.

"Apologies for the interruption, folks. Let's get this night back on track with some free drinks, shall we?" Then Rap casts a terse nod at Cinder and Goldie who square their shoulders, preparing for the battlefield of liquor hungry freeloaders.

Then Rap jumps down and walks past me and Red toward her office but not before she orders in a steel tone, "Both of you, in my office, now."

CHAPTER 27

WARDING AGAINST DANGER

RED

Rap is going to fire me.

And then when I try to find another job, she won't give me a good reference. She'll tell all prospective employers that trouble follows me. And then I won't be able to pay for my tuition and I'll have to either drop out or go back to using magic money to support my human existence. I've been so happy, so safe here, I'm not ready to lose it all.

The long walk to Rap's office feels like a death sentence. I can't stop trembling. My brain races too hot and fast.

Not to mention, Goldie and Cinder are probably livid, trying to figure out how I'm connected to mages and why we went to the same school together.

"Hey," a low voice interrupts my doomsday spiral. I look up at Brexley who is staring at me with genuine concern. "Everything is going to be okay."

"Everything is ruined," I say, my words coming out in a pained whisper.

We are in Rap's office with the door closed behind us, before he can respond. We could sit in the two green fabric seats in front of her desk, but I remain standing. Brexley does the same.

Rap leans over to brace her hands on her desk, giving both of us the stink eye.

"What do they want from you?" Rap demands more than asks.

"I don't know," I shake my head. I slip my shaking hands in the pockets of my pants to make them steady.

"Look, it's better if you just tell me—"

"I'm telling you. I honestly don't know. I'm not exactly friends with the deathly hallows twins as you could see, so I have no idea why they want me."

"She's telling the truth," Brexley adds in a calm, even tone.

Rap heaves a deep sigh and pinches between her eyes.

Here it comes.

"This isn't going to work," Rap starts.

I absolutely hate that a hot tear slips out of my eye. Brexley raises a hand as if he wants to comfort me, but then doesn't. The no touching rule is still in place. The twins sucked away any arousal in my body as effectively as Hansel can drain me dry of liquids.

Rap goes on. "We are going to need to get some wards put on this place to keep those creepy fuckers out of here."

Wait, what?

"What?" I stutter out, not understanding why Rap hasn't had my ass thrown out on the curb already.

"Those creeps, the ones who came to harass you? They can't be allowed back on the premises. It's a disturbance to our patrons and clearly a danger to you. So I'm going to get someone to ward our place against magic users."

"I think warding against fae isn't a bad idea either," Brexley adds.

"I'd like to keep you nearby," Rap says. "You are an excellent deterrent for the weird shit my guys aren't prepared to handle."

"I suppose it's possible for a ward to be built with exceptions," he says thoughtfully. "Depends on the skill of the mage."

What in the faefucks is happening right now?

"I don't understand," I say, brushing away another tear that has slipped out. "Aren't you going to fire me? You have a strict no magic or fae rule and not only did I bring him," I jerk my head at Brexley, "I'm the reason the twins showed up. I didn't warn you it might happen. I fucked everything up."

Rapunzel's normally hard ass expression softens. "Red, you think I'd let someone work here without knowing everything about them? I know where you come from, and I could see you came here for a fresh start." Her face toughens up again as she straightens to run a hand through her banana-rainbow colored mohawk. "I have a hard time denying anyone a fresh start, especially someone who works as hard as you do."

I slump into one of the chairs. Oh fae lords, now I'm really in danger of bursting into tears.

Something about the way she says it, tells me she has personal experience with running and cutting from the past.

"Take some time in here to calm down. I'm going to go make some calls, and maybe it's not a bad idea to get your apartment warded too." Rap rounds her desk but slows as she passes to squeeze my shoulder. "When you feel up to it,

I'm sure Cinder and Goldie would love your help out there. But take your time."

The door shuts quietly behind my boss.

Brexley kneels before me, holding the arms of the chair on either side of me. "Hey, hey, it's okay," he says in a low, soothing tone.

I don't realize what his reaction is for until I touch my face and find tears streaming down my cheeks in a torrent. A sob I try to suppress rocks my shoulders as I hold it in my chest.

"I'm not going to let them take you," he says.

I lick my lips and close my eyes, trying to block out the memories from FFA. How I worked so hard to never be caught alone in a corner with those two, but not always managing it. The consequences were . . . no, I couldn't think about it, or I'd really fall apart.

"Do you think they have something to do with the attacks?" I ask, though my voice is shaking.

"I do," he nods.

"There is nothing they could want from me. I don't understand."

"Take a breath. This isn't about you, right? This is about a recipe, about your grandma's business. You are a means to an end." Something strange flickers in his eyes before it vanishes.

I shut my eyes, wrap my arms around myself and try to bring clarity to my thoughts. "After they graduated, the twins went to work for their family. Their grandmother was one of Gigi's competitors, the Gingerbread Witch."

"Who is that?"

I open my eyes to see if he's mocking me. Most everyone follows mage culture, but I can see from Brexley's blank expression, he really doesn't know. He doesn't swallow the mage rags full of gossip like most humans. As it is, I would happily stay in the dark if Goldie and Cinder weren't into the stuff.

"The Gingerbread Witch has a popular baking show and also has a line of nationally distributed snacks under the Gumdrop moniker."

He nods as some recognition sparks in his eyes. The Gumdrop baked goods are extra delicious because of the Gingerbread Witch's methods, but there is no competition to what my grandma can do. No one had been able to bestow such power to humans before her.

"The twins went to work for her, but within a month, she died in a horrible factory accident. She somehow fell and got locked in one of the ovens. Then Hansel and Gretel inherited the business from her."

Brexley's eyes turn flat. "I'm guessing it wasn't an accident."

"The official reports say they have video that shows she was unsteady on her feet, but I wonder if maybe she wasn't overcome by a severe hunger or thirst that made her that way." My brain churns, filling in the blank spots. "And now, they're in competition with Grandma's House and maybe they think they can get to Gigi and her secret recipes through me. I remember in school they would talk about how humans didn't deserve the scraps of magic my grandmother shared with them. If she was smart, she'd retool and use her recipes to make mages even more powerful instead."

"So you think they want whatever recipe your grandma uses for Magic Morsels?"

I shrug. "It's a guess. Their magic is of similar nature to Gigi's. I suppose it's feasible they could figure out how to do what she does. But the only way to know is to talk to them about it further." I suppress a shudder knowing they rarely just 'talk' if they want something.

If they cornered me now, there would be no Hunter to step from the shadows to intimidate them off, like back in school. It was as if he'd been practicing on me to take his father's place. Oh fae lords, that's why they sent a glamor mage in Hunter's image. While we were discreet, the twins knew Hunter could lure me where they wanted me.

A hand covers mine, blanketing my anxiety with an electric, hot zing. My eyes jerk up to meet Brexley's. "I won't let them get you," he repeats.

Liquid heat gathers between my legs, but it's more than my usual biological reaction. Pressure crowds into my chest until it fills my throat, making me feel vulnerable but taken care of. I believe him.

Brexley stares at me with utmost conviction under his scars.

"Do you trust me?" he asks.

I stare down at his hands holding mine. "Never." Though it's not true. It's more like I don't trust myself.

Then he grins that wolfish smile. "Good."

FACING Cinder and Goldie at the end of the shift is almost as hard as facing Rap. I expected them to throw accusations and hate me for keeping secrets, but to their credit they kept neutral faces as they asked me only about a hundred questions.

Yes, I attended FFA.

No, I don't have any magic.

Yes, I come from a magic family.

Yes, I really am a finance student, and chose that major on purpose.

No, I'm not an undercover mage with hidden cameras using them for some reality show.

"Is he really your boyfriend?" Cinder asks me, while shooting a suspicious glance at Brexley.

"Yes," both Brexley and Goldie answer at the same time.

I know why Brexley needs to keep up the charade, but to have Goldie vouch. . .

I don't correct anyone.

"Did you not tell us about your past because you didn't think you could trust us?" Cinder asks, subtle accusation in the question.

Thankfully, Brexley stepped away to give us some space after the initial interrogation.

Goldie's mouth thins into a tight line as she studies me with patient intensity. She also wants an answer. I've hurt them both.

I rush to explain. "No, oh no. It's more like I love you guys and I love it here. I wanted to get as far away from my old life as possible. With you guys, it doesn't feel real. The past is like a nightmare I woke up from, and I didn't want to ruin this dream I'm living now."

Goldie's brows furrow. "You *want* to get away from a life of magic and wealth and—"

I cut Goldie off with a serious tone. "As you can see from the party crashers today, it's not all glamorous. Those people may have money and power, but most of them are bankrupt on the inside. I don't want to be anything like that. I just want to be plain ol' Red."

Goldie gathers me into a hug when she sees me getting emotional, and I let her.

"Well, you're not." Cinder says, her voice cold and cutting.

Goldie pulls back as we both look at Cinder, stunned.

"Cinder," Goldie chides.

"Well she's not," Cinder insists. "You aren't *just plain ol' anything*. You matter to us and we've seen you struggle to break from the old. You are so much more than those twins from *The Shining*, and we aren't going to let anything happen to you and nothing will make us stop caring about you."

Both Goldie and I blink. My mouth hangs open and then closes as a stinging begins at the back of my eyes. Something has lodged its way into my throat, and I've lost my ability to speak. Goldie's blinking begins to double time, like the gears in her head stopped working and steam is liable to escape her ears any minute. Cinder is normally reserved with her words, but that little speech practically moved me to tears.

At that, she joins in our group hug.

Rap breaks us up to pull me off to the side to let me know her friend went to my address to ward the apartment from intruders, and that she'll take a cut from my next pay to cover the service. Rap is being super supportive, but the woman does have a business to run. I don't begrudge her that.

But what the hell? She knew about me this whole time? I guess Rap did have access to everything when I submitted my employment info.

My boss has always been a mystery to me. And now, the woman adamant about running a humans-only bar has connections to mages who can ward her business?

When I ask about it, she gives me a tight-lipped smile and squeezes my shoulder. "Don't worry about me. All you need to know is, I take care of my lost girls."

For once, I wonder if Rap isn't a lost girl herself. Cinder, Goldie, and I are all here trying to make fresh, independent starts in one way or another. Did we come to Rap, or did she collect us? The thought makes my heart swell until it's almost too large for my ribcage to contain the mushy, engorged organ. But before I even think of digging any further, Rap is off, running the Poison Apple and being a general badass.

I sigh. If I end up even a fraction of the woman she is, I'll know I did good in this life. But first, I need to get a couple sadistic mages off my back and find my grandma. I pick up my cell and call her ten times in a row, hoping to get anything other than her voicemail this time.

My phone chimes with a text halfway through my tenth call. My heart flies right out of my chest. It's from Gigi.

Don't worry, she's safe. We'll be in touch.

Just as fast, my heart plummets to the ground where it goes splat. I scrub a hand over my face. I recognize the efficient, overprotective voice of Hunter's dad even in a text.

I need her to call me, I text back.

That won't be possible for a while. Not while she's in danger.

Ugh! I throw my hands in the air.

She's not the only one in danger, you complete Gigi-blocking A-hole!

My thumb hits delete repeatedly, dropping the insult. Theodore Dunkin does not respond to threats. He'll shut down completely and I'll get nothing. The head of security closes things up tighter than Fort Knox, which is what makes him so good at his job. It's also what makes him so infuriating.

I used to feel bad for Hunter, thinking he was starved for affection and love since his uptight, near militant father wouldn't give it to him. But the further I've gotten from Hunter, the more I realize he is almost exactly like his dad. I'd made up this fantasy of wanting to give Hunter everything he never wanted. My adoration doesn't count for shit. Only his father's approval matters, which is why I was always pushed to the back burner. And there I sat, waiting for him, patiently on fire until he'd pick me up to give me a modicum of relief. A crumb of affection.

Realizing I'm playing with my nose ring, I drop my hand.

I type a response.

She's not the only one in danger. Tell me what's going on.

Your grandmother and I believe it's best you don't know more than you have to. For both your safety.

More than I have to? I don't know anything. Other than her world is crushing mine. I love Gigi, but this is why I left. And for the first time, I couldn't help but feel a dark pit of disappointment open up inside my chest. I know she cares for me, but right now it doesn't feel like it at all. She left me with her mess, and it's tearing me apart.

My fingers hovered, ready to type all of that out. Then they relax. Unleashing all my upset in a text that would go through Dunkin, is not what I want. I want to talk to Gigi, look her in the eye, and demand she tell me why everyone is coming after me. What is she up to that would cause all this?

For a moment I consider asking him to take me to her. Surely, he could arrange for me to go into hiding with Gigi.

Every instinct inside me balks against that.

I have finals, I have friends, I have a life I already told Brexley I refused to run from. I don't trust that if I left, I wouldn't come back to cooled ash where my life used to be, having missed the wildfire that burned it down. If I'm here, I can keep trying to put the fires out. Maybe it's dumb, maybe it's an overinflated sense of ego, or perhaps it's just plain fear. In any case, I can't ask Dunkin for that. Not yet.

The phone chimes again. *I sent protection for you. Do whatever he tells you. He'll keep you safe. We'll be in touch.*

I bite my lip.

I wonder what Dunkin would think of his security detail telling me, "That's it pet, come for me."

A hot shudder sweeps away all my fears and disappointments.

Not knowing how else to convince Theodore Dunkin to let me talk to Gigi, I drop the phone.

Brexley magically falls into step with me when I start for home again.

"Your boss is holding my Gigi captive."

The Were stops cold, forcing me to stop. "What?" he asks.

"Theodore Dunkin. Hunter's father says Gigi is safe, but that I can't talk to her. Not while she's in so much danger." I can't help the disgust lacing my words. I know Brexley only works for him, but I can't help but be irritated by him too. He's one more thing standing in my way of Gigi.

Brexley slides his hands into his pockets, and we commence walking again. "Did he say when you could?"

I shook my head. "He said they would be in touch. But I doubt he'll even tell Gigi that I called. He wouldn't want to worry his number one asset."

"They'll be in touch," Brexley repeats absently.

I slam a fist into my palm and rub it in. "If they still haven't come round after finals, I'm going to personally track Dunkin down and shake that man until he tells me where she is."

Brexley is oddly silent. Like his mind is a million miles away. After a while, he says, "Your grandma doesn't seem to care what happens to you. Maybe she's not the nice old lady everyone thinks."

"Hey." I push his shoulder. The brick wall of a man doesn't yield even an inch. "That's my Gigi you're talking about." And no one gets to bad mouth her except me. "Of course, she cares about me. It's still likely she doesn't even know what's going on with me. Her entourage is so efficient, they circle their wagons around her for her own protection," I make air quotes around those last words, "until not even a speck of daylight or reality can get through. And since I forfeited that treatment, they've locked me out. But I know once she figures it out, Gigi will blast their asses out of the way to get to me."

As I say it out loud, the disappointment darkening my soul began to lighten. I speak the truth. It's Gigi's life, not the woman herself who causes the problems. "She loves me more than anything."

Again, Brexley's expression turns indecipherable. This time it's almost like he swallowed a bee and is trying to pretend he hadn't.

"You realize your friends think you come from some poor little no-name magic family. You didn't tell them about your grandmother, about your lineage." His abrupt change in topic throws me.

I push my hair back from my face. "It's better this way."

"They are your pack. You shouldn't lie to your pack." There is almost anger in his voice, but before I can respond, he picks up the pace. I huff and puff trying to keep up until I eventually slow and continue at my own rate. His tactic to keep me from questioning him about his pack is effective.

Though I find I'm more desperate than ever to know about what happened with his past. Almost as desperate as I am to feel his skin on mine again. I want to know what his scars are from, all of his secrets, and I want to make him feel as safe as he makes me feel.

I realize how hopeless I've become. If I know what's best for both of us, I'd send him away, but I crave him. I crave him on every level and I don't think I can let him go even if I tried.

A hollowness opens inside my chest, and dread pours in. Because I have absolutely no doubt that Brexley is going to leave me once the craziness ends and he's given another assignment. And I know he won't look back.

CHAPTER 28
THUMPER AND BANGS

BREXLEY

I can't get comfortable on Red's damn lumpy couch.

They'll be in touch.

The thing about tracking someone down that most people don't understand, is that it takes time. Stake-outs are laborious, boring, and a whole lot of nothing before you get the target in your sights. Even the old man fails to see the patience it takes to hunt another being. I'd been content to settle in for the long haul, betting on the sure thing. Inevitably, Gigi will come for Red.

But now the inevitability is waving right at my face. The particulars of what I'm here to do keep slipping away like powdered sugar in a sieve, only leaving the spicy taste of Red.

Telling her to strengthen her pack was my effort to guard her against the loss I'm going to bring down on her. If she has Goldie, Cinder, and Rap, she might survive the blow. The killing blow I was going to deliver.

But I'm finding it difficult to even imagine myself going through with my mission.

Shifting yet again, I'm convinced I'm going to need weeks of chiropractic adjustments to undo the damage of Red's sofa.

Maybe I could slip into her room, lie on the bed next to her.

No. Bad wolf.

All too soon, raw sexual energy builds back up inside me as I know it does in Red. It doesn't help that I'm hours from the full moon. I can control the moon craze, but it still drives me to a more wild, uninhibited state. The wolf in me wants to run, hunt, and fuck.

The need to fuck her right in front of Hunter was overwhelming. Let him see the pleasure on her face, hear her scream my name as I pound the letters into her sweet little pussy. Until it's undeniably mine.

The urge came so hard and forceful, that it almost threw me off balance.

Almost.

My attempt to expedite things led to nothing. After satisfying Red in the library, I took off to pursue some other means of tracking Grandma. The contacts I have in computer hacking and surveillance confirm Red's grandma hasn't touched her credit cards or any electronic since Friday morning when she was traveling to New Hampshire from New Mage City. She simply blipped out of existence.

They did manage to discover her email had already been hacked. My contact shared what had been looked at by the remote party. A lot of it was correspondence over Grandma's next big release. There were disagreements about the recipe being too much for humans. Some of her investors warned her of playing a dangerous game, while other employees in her organization were concerned about it getting passed by the FDA.

There was a message from the old lady to her assistant a week ago that grabbed my interest. It asked to send a package along to Red and to make sure to include the recipe with it. But Red hasn't received any packages since I've been here. I've even taken time to search the apartment for anything resembling this mysterious recipe and found zilch.

I bet my fluffy ass the twins were the hackers, and this was why they were targeting Red.

My thoughts are yanked back to how sweet her kisses are. Dammit, my focus is ruined again.

Tucking my hands behind my head, I justify my attraction to Red in a purely logical manner.

Why shouldn't I want her? She's gorgeous. I can admit that now. I'm enthralled by her fiery hair, the way she sucks me off, the way her eyes tighten when she's worried . . .

I drop my arms. Fuck. That isn't just raw attraction. Affection and something far worse are nastily weaving their way into my depraved fantasies about Red again.

Back on my feet, I return to pacing.

My fantasies of her aren't contained to me fucking her over a hard surface. Intermixed is Red in her soft university tee, biting her lip as she studies her laptop. The way her eyes light up when she talks about her plans of being a financial planner. Of her cooing to her rabbits as she picks one up and kisses their soft head, expressing an open moment of tenderness. Of her laughing at something Goldie says at the bar while she twirls a bottle of whiskey.

I catch myself giving head scratches to Bangs and Bombs in their pen, who curiously bop their nose at me.

A wolf petting rabbits. *Ridiculous.*

When I finally fall into a fitful sleep, I'm right where I want to be, pounding between Red's legs. Biting her shoulder, marking her as mine. I dream of her face as she comes. So vulnerable, so completely open as she succumbs to her pleasure. I want to see it again and again. Like a science experiment, I want to make her orgasm repeatedly, so I can study all the tiny inflections of her face. The ways she fights to stay in control before she accepts everything I have to give her.

I pound into her with an audible thump.

Her eyes are the color of a misty morning, and the slight rasp in her voice drives me to distraction. I can taste the smokiness when I kiss her mouth and play with her tongue.

Another audible thump as I bury myself into her.

I wake up with my cock in my hand and realize the smokiness isn't confined to my dreams.

Another thump.

The sound is from Red's rabbits. I catch one thumping its back foot. His eyes are wild and ears are tilted forward while the other one scrambles about in a panic.

A curse slips from me as I zip myself back up and jump to my feet. Smoky fumes grow more powerful. Opening the front door, heat sandblasts me in the face. A blaze of fire rages on the stairs. It's massive, but the paint is only just starting to melt off the walls and ceiling as if it was fine only mere seconds ago. I slam the door shut against the heat and smoke, my eyes blurry and burning from the conflagration. My throat is already raw, and panic flares in me. We're trapped.

Only then does the fire alarm for the building go off. The blare is enough to make my eardrums bleed.

Running into Red's room, I find her sitting up in bed,

hands covering her ears. She's only wearing a black sports bra and a pair of men's black boxers dotted with little red hearts. She squints as if in pain against the audible onslaught.

"Let's go, now," I bellow. I reach for her arm, but she jerks away. Apparently, the no touching rule is back in force. But I know how to get her moving. I grab her empty backpack off the ground then run to the main room and sweep my arm across the rickety table. Pushing all the textbooks and her laptop into the bag, I then sling it over my shoulder. Red emerges from her bedroom, hopping on one foot as she attempts to pull her second combat boot on.

"Out the window," I yell to her. "Fire escape."

Not wasting time, I throw the living room window up and gesture for her to go through.

But Red races over to her two bunnies who are scrambling in their pen. They continue to thump their feet and repeatedly jump out of her reach. Red grasps Bangs even as the female rabbit tries to wiggle out of her arms. As Red dives to pick up Bombs, I realize she's about to lose hold on the first one.

"Red," I bark. "Go," I point to the open window.

The crackle of wood grows louder and the front door is engulfed in flames. Smoke scrapes against my eyes and throat, overwhelming my senses. I cough, unable to see more than the vague outline of Red.

She is even more frantic to pick up Bombs. Unable to wait any longer, I drag Red to the window.

"I can't leave him!" she cries out in panic.

"I got him. Go." I yell.

She wastes precious seconds to search my face, as if she is trying to find the lie. Red openly says she won't trust me, but right now, she doesn't have a choice. I shove her out the window onto the fire escape ladder.

We have to get out of here or we are all going to be bones and ash.

Only when she's out, do I run to the pen and scoop the terrified rabbit into my arms. I tuck Bombs under my arm, securing him before I go through the open window.

A wolf shifter putting himself in danger to save a rabbit's life. Ridiculous.

As soon as I'm clear, fire explodes into the living room and I duck on instinct as flames shoot out of the window. The rabbit struggles against my bare torso, but I clamp him fast while being careful of his delicate ribs.

"Steady," I say to him in what I hope is a soothing tone.

One flight down, Red is holding Bangs tight to her chest. Black soot smears her sweating face. Her oversized, messy bun has even more tendrils falling out than normal. Even in her dirty, fear-stricken state, she's devastatingly beautiful.

"I got him." I assure her.

Red closes her eyes as if in relief. Then she makes her way slowly but steadily down the fire escape and I follow.

On the street, a number of people have gathered, having either exited the apartments or emerged from adjacent buildings to watch the blaze. The firefighters wasted no time unfurling their hoses and charging inside.

We watch the flurry of activity in awe of the flames and hustle of emergency services. They charge in and out, while others spray the building with a powerful hose. But the fire went up so powerful, so fast, it's taking time to get under control.

Some of the saved residents sit on the back of the

ambulances with blankets about their shoulders and oxygen masks on their faces. I even force Red to use the mask for a little while when a paramedic comes by to check on us. My lungs have already expelled all the nastiness.

Two bodies are now zipped up in bags on gurneys. People who didn't get out in time.

Tears clean tracks down Red's sooty face. Her eyes are riveted on the body bags before they scan back up to her apartment. She thinks this is somehow her fault.

I want to wrap my arms around her. Let those hot tears fall on my bare chest and tell her she can let go of what she's holding inside. She can give it all to me. She could never be too much. If she is the storm, I am the immovable rock who will be there from start to finish.

A lump forms in my throat.

Instead, I say, "I mean, I did say you should burn that ugly bra."

Red twists to face me, her jaw falls so hard it nearly scrapes the ground. A murderous rage sparks in her pupils, even as she clutches her rabbit. The only sign she hasn't gone totally apoplectic is her twitching eyelid.

I ignore her gobsmacked reaction and tell her what I've deduced. "It was a mage who set the fire."

"What? How do you know that?" Her voice is even rougher than usual because of the smoke.

"It started too big, too fast, and right outside your door. When I saw it, the fire was several feet high, and the paint had only just begun to char. If it started from a smaller source and grew, like an electrical fire, the paint would have already been yellowed, if not blackened or bubbled." The more I say, the more I crane my neck to watch for anyone dangerous lurking around.

"Rap had the place warded," she protests.

"Fire mages don't need to be in the building to start the fire. Whoever they are, they started it from outside. They wanted to drive us out into the open."

We are a conspicuous target. Me, barefoot, wearing only a pair of jeans with a backpack on one shoulder and a rabbit under the other, next to the sad, gorgeous girl wearing barely anything and nuzzling a bunny to her tear-stained face.

"We need to get out of here. Get cleaned up and get some rest," I say. Even Bangs, the dark brown rabbit, has turned a darker hue. I looked down at Bombs and find his light silver fur is now a dull lead color.

The only thing we have on our side is the mass of people lingering around. But I sense eyes on us, someone waiting in the shadows, waiting for their moment to pounce.

The twins are trying to get to Red again, but I won't let them.

Thankfully my phone remains in my back pocket. I pull it out and call a car service to pick us up. The black sedan shows up in no time. Per my instructions, they drive right to where we stand on the sidewalk, forcing people to move.

A young driver pops out in a uniform that doesn't quite fit his bony frame right. For a kid his age, his dark brown skin is exceedingly smooth. I'd half expect him to be riddled in pimples. Last time I saw him, he still wore braces.

The kid can't hide his surprise at the spectacle of both the burning building and his passengers. Still, he helps load Red into the car, even as he gives the tiny fluff bomb in her arms a dubious look.

"I tip well," I say, clapping him on the shoulder with my free hand.

The driver eases his stance but eyes the bunny in my arms before meeting my gaze. "I'm aware, sir. Glad to see you again."

"Thanks. . . " I search my smoke charred mind to find the name. ". . . Tom. Tom Thumb, right?"

He gives me the thumbs up with a grin then shuts the door after me.

"Sir?" Red asks in disbelief.

I ignore her prodding. We let the rabbits sit on our laps as Tom pulls away from the curb.

Tom already knows the way to our destination. During the day, it would take twenty minutes with traffic. But in the dead of night, it will only be a blessed ten. We are both in desperate need of a shower and water. But until we get to the safe house, my every cell is alert, on the lookout for danger.

Red's head drops off to the side as she dozes. I'm not sure if it's the smoke inhalation or her adrenaline wearing off, but the girl is exhausted. Her test is today, and this isn't going to help her concentration. At least her finals aren't until the afternoon. She might stand a chance of recovery.

The car jerks to a halt after only a couple of minutes. My hackles rise, and my fangs elongate. I'm careful to keep my claws in with the rabbit in my lap.

"Uh, sir?" the kid says. I look over his shoulder to see a car pulled out in the road, blocking the path. A short, heavyset man stands in front of it. Against his walnut-colored skin, his eyes glow red.

"Stay here," I order everyone, gently setting Bombs on the seat.

Before Red can get her protest out, I slam the door shut on them.

The fire mage looks like he should be at home, after a

day at the office, eating the dinner his wife made for him and ignoring her needs. The bottom button on his plaid shirt looks ready to shoot off his generous belly. His khakis are held on his hips by a tightly cinched belt only further exaggerating his rotund top to the straight line of his legs.

Hansel and Gretel sent him. I can smell the incompetence of a paid hand, now that I have a nose for it. His magic smells like burning death and that offends me even more.

"It is not a good night to fuck with me," I announce to the man without any preamble as I unfasten my jeans and shove them down my legs, baring myself. I have no patience left in me right now. "Your idiocy killed two people."

"Give me the girl and you can go," the fire mage announces in a thick Indian accent, not even acknowledging the damage he caused. Fire lights up in both of his palms.

I don't wait for another invitation. I charge at him, my bones cracking and rearranging. Fur sprouts along my body mid-leap as my clawed paws reach for him.

The man throws a firebolt just before his eyes widen in fear, realizing his fate. I'm too fast, and his fireball goes wide at the last second. But I have no problem hitting my mark. I land on his chest. His eyes blaze as he prepares to unleash more fire on me, but I activate the talent I so very much wanted to use on Hunter when he had me pinned against the wall.

I release the ball of force inside me. For a second, everything goes quiet, as if someone hit the mute button.

The fire dies in the man's eyes, leaving them muddy and bloodshot. The acidity of his panic spikes in my nose, but the smell of death has dissipated. I nulled his magic like an electromagnetic blast takes out any nearby electronic. It doesn't work on other fae creatures, but I can nullify any mage's magic if they are in close range.

Yet another secret of my fae race that keeps us safe from outside forces.

My powerful jaws clamp onto the mage's neck. Blood spurts into my mouth as I take my rage and aggression out on this stupid man.

How dare he? How dare he put Red in danger? The imbecile's incompetence is dangerous. He killed innocent people to lure her out into the open.

I wriggle and flop his body until I'm satisfied. The stench of magic is gone. After I'm done, I trot to the car, blood matting the fur on my face and chest.

Tom scrambles out of the driver seat but pauses before opening the door for me.

"Sir, I, uh, I don't think the rabbits will like a bloody wolf in the seat with them," he says breathlessly, as if afraid I'll rip his throat out for suggesting it.

I give him a nod before lowering my head. Slowly but surely, I relax into my human form. Tom is right there again, holding out my jeans. I take my time, putting them on gingerly. My muscles ache from the transformation. Usually, I let myself run longer in my wolf form before shifting back. Unable to keep the slight limp out of my walk, I feel like my body has been through a meat tenderizer.

Shifting is the equivalent of an intense weight-lifting workout, where you work to muscle failure. While I'm used to being pushed past my limits when shifting, I'm not used to doing it so fast. I'll need lots of water and protein to recover, or I'll wake up with one hell of a cramp in my calves, or worse, my ass.

A wry smile pulls across my face. Maybe I could ask Red to help massage the knots out of my glutes.

Tom gets the door and I slide inside. He even hands me a couple wet wipes, and I quickly clean off the blood staining my neck and chest.

Instead of being terrified, the little rabbit returns to my lap. My arm loosely encircles Bombs as Tom drives around the parked car and carcass of the fire mage.

The rabbit's tiny tongue is both rough and soft as he begins to lick my arm in earnest.

"He likes you," Red says.

Under the sooty streaks, her face is bloodless. I recognize the strange distance in her voice. She's numb, likely in shock. In the middle of the night, her apartment burned down, and she just watched me kill a man. It's a lot to process, which is why I doubt she's processing at all. It's all on hold, teetering on the edge of a cliff.

Where we are going, I can give her a safe space and a soft landing.

Yet under all that I smell something else. Fear. Red's afraid of *me*.

Even as I put my attention on the rabbit in my arms, something in me cracks. It leaves a deep fathomless fissure in its wake. *I'd never hurt her.*

But as soon as I think that, I remember why we are together at all.

My mission is to destroy her only family.

Never once in my career did I doubt myself. But Red has me doubting absolutely everything.

While Bombs continues to lick my arm, I carefully smooth back his soft ears. "If it weren't for your little pets here, I might not have woken up in time. They sensed the danger before me."

A ghost of a smile touches her mouth before disappearing just as fast. "Where are we going?"

"Isn't it obvious? To my place."

CHAPTER 29

A MODERN CASTLE

BREXLEY

Tom offers to help us take the rabbits up, but I wave him off. The doorman at the Sky Woods complex gives me a nod as he unlocks and pulls open the glass doors to the lobby.

I can tell if Red had more hands she'd attempt to cover up her current state of undress. A true professional, he doesn't even blink at our appearance. Good, I pay them enough not to bat an eye.

Red's brows are drawn as we cross the jade floor to the elevators. We head up to the fourteenth floor and I lead her to an apartment on the far corner of the building. It takes my fingerprint to unlock the door, then I invite Red to enter before me.

"Lights on," I say.

"Lights on," a robotic voice repeats. Suddenly the apartment is awash in warm light.

Red gasps softly.

My two-level condo is primarily dark stone and warm

wood tones. The living and kitchen area make up a large, open space. A dark metal staircase ascends to the second level that leads to the master bedroom and an office. The walkway is open and looks directly down into the main living area. A chandelier of glass globes the size of basketballs drips down over the living room.

"Shoes off," I say, while toeing mine off. Then I add as an afterthought, "please."

Bending over, I set Bombs onto the floor. "Make yourself at home," I say to both him and Red. She pauses to remove her boots before following suit, setting her rabbit down as well. They cautiously bob their heads and practically army crawl across the floor, scoping out the new territory.

I go straight to the kitchen and fill two big glasses of filtered ice water from the fridge. The high-tech appliances gleam like new. They've barely been touched since I bought this place.

I hand Red one of the waters. "Here, you need this."

The fire and smoke made my throat sore and parched, so I know hers must be too.

We both greedily drain the glasses.

After a thought, I retrieve a small ceramic ramekin and fill it with water then go set it near the rabbits who have taken refuge under my coffee table.

Rabbits in a wolf's home. Ridiculous.

I return to the kitchen to refill my glass and gulp down another.

After several long minutes of Red's gaze bouncing from her glass to the rest of the apartment, I say, "What is it?"

"What?" she asks, with wide eyes.

"You clearly want to ask me something. What is it?"

Her nails tap her glass, and my gaze momentarily slides

to her bare torso. What I wouldn't give to nuzzle up to that bare expanse of creamy skin right now. To lick her warm flesh and move further south until I lose myself in her. . .

"How much is Gigi paying you?" She sets the glass down and runs a finger around the rim as if agitated. The shock from the attacks is wearing off, but I'm not sure I like where this is going.

My surprised laugh comes out as a dry cough. "That's not a polite question, little Red."

I grab her glass and refill it before handing it back.

She blushes. "Sorry, I just. . .you seem so rugged and rough? I didn't expect you to live like this. I kind of expected some remote, run down cabin with a stone fireplace. Not GQ penthouse."

I shrug and glance at the modern gas fireplace in the living room. "Unlike you, I embrace wealth."

She blinks.

Then I concede, "To your credit, I do in fact own a cabin like you describe. That's where I reside most of the time, though it's not run down. This is only one of my abodes."

And the fact I've brought her here at all proves I must be suffering from temporary insanity. I own a number of houses and condos across the country and even a few abroad.

"My grandma doesn't pay you for this," she says matter-of-factly.

For a minute my heart stops in my chest, and my brain is too sluggish to figure out how she has finally concluded I'm sticking around to kill her kin.

"I mean, she doesn't pay you *this* much," she throws a hand at my apartment. "You told Hunter you work as a subcontractor. I just didn't realize how *well employed* you are. Is this all from private security?"

My heart starts beating again. "Yes." I lie.

She worries her lower lip. "You do more than private security."

It's like she is able to peel back my layers to see what's underneath, and I don't like anyone under my skin.

I start toward the back of the apartment, expecting her to follow. "I'll call a service to get some supplies for your pets, so they don't piddle on my nice wood floors." My words drip with disdain.

But the truth is, between the effective warning from the rabbits, along with the affection I received in the car, my insides have gone a little soft for the fluffy creatures.

Fucking ridiculous.

"You're a mercenary, aren't you?" Red asks, still right behind me.

I don't slow as I lead her up the stairs. "You can sleep in the master bedroom and use the master bath to clean up."

"The way you killed that fire mage. It was so efficient. Was that how you took care of the ice mage?"

Irritation slips into my tone as I continue to ignore her questions. "The place should be stocked with soaps and extra clothes you are more than welcome to. I'm going to grab some myself, and then sleep downstairs."

Red sticks to my heels right into the master bedroom. The king-sized bed is the definition of luxury, with a fluffy white comforter and big plush pillows I'd love to sink into right now.

I would love to sleep in here, especially after breaking my back on Red's lumpy little sofa. But it's better I lock her in a room away from any danger, and from me. I don't have guest bedrooms, they've all been converted into other spaces. But the couch will more than suffice.

I open some drawers and grab a pair of clean, loose

pants I can sleep in. When I turn to go, Red bars my way. Her chin is set, letting me know she refuses to move unless I answer her questions.

My eyebrow arches. "You know I can just pick you up and throw you on the bed?"

Fear and desire sparks in her eyes as she glances at the bed, then back to me.

Regaining her confidence, she sets her hands on her hips in a determined pose. "I'll just follow you and bother you all night." Her voice is still extra raspy despite the water. Her eyes are bloodshot, and she practically sags with exhaustion. Still, I have no doubt she'll make good on her promise.

"Fine," I say, discarding the pants on the bed. "I'm a mercenary killer. Is that what you want to hear? I even track people or items down for people if they've got enough cash. Rarely do I take private security jobs because I can't stand the scent of magic. It stinks to high heaven, and being forced to stay near any kind of mage for long is repellent."

Red jerks as though she's been slapped.

"I stink?" Glancing down at her body, her gaze softens as she realizes she's filthy.

Anger rips through me in a flash. I'm tired, irritated at being attacked, and I don't care for Red seeing through me. It makes me want to lash out.

"No, in point of fact, you don't. As you'll remember, you aren't magic, correct?" I tug my hair, feeling like a mad man. The ire fuels me until I don't know what is spilling out of me anymore. "Though something about you is fucking deviously enchanting. You smell like fucking heaven and honey. I want to lick you every second of the day until you are screaming incoherently for me to stop and continue at the same time."

The full moon only fuels my exasperation.

We are back to not touching, but I advance on her, steering her around so she is herded toward the bed. It's my favorite pastime, stalking Red, herding her like the innocent lamb she is.

Her pale eyes go wide as her knees hit the bed. There is barely an inch between us now. Her breath puffs against my neck, evoking goose flesh along my arms and torso.

"You're right to cling to your little rules, Red. Because if you didn't keep trying to put me at arm's length, I'd constantly bury myself in you. You'd never sleep or eat, you'd be too busy falling apart around me day and night for the rest of our lives."

"You don't even like me," she whispers while narrowing her eyes.

I bark a laugh. "Where the fuck did you get that idea?"

Did I just admit to liking her? I must be really losing it.

"You—you called me a princess who is slumming it."

My voice drops some of its razor edge. "I don't agree that you need to reject wealth in order to create a new life. I get that you don't want to end up like the bastard mages you know, but you're only denying yourself resources to make that new life. I see through your martyr act. You are punishing yourself. I don't know what for exactly, maybe because you feel you must repent for groveling at that loser, Hunter's feet for an ounce of attention? Or because you are a magic dud and ashamed of it? But either way, depriving yourself of money doesn't make those parts of your past go away."

Her mouth opens, and a tiny squeak emerges.

My hands are dangerously close to grabbing her hips and throwing her on the bed and making her forget her past in heart pounding, bone melting ways.

Desire vibrates off her in electric waves. I'm frustrated and hard, despite how exhausted I am.

"You, Red, are fucking ridiculous. No one else in your position would work half as hard to build a human life. Who else in your position would want to become an accountant of all fucking things? Who thinks that numbers are the way to secure other people's futures? Who worries so much about her grades and her friends and those two little rabbits downstairs?" I point back toward the door. I'm ranting but I barely know what about. All I know is I'm gripped in the full moon's spell, or maybe it's Red's spell. "But who cares about what some prudish, uptight little sonofabitch thinks about the fact you like sex? Hunter can go fuck himself, but I figure he can't even manage that. You care too much about everything and everyone."

Knowing I'm on the verge of doing something I'll regret, I turn and leave, stomping down the stairs and to the bar at the edge of the living room. Glass bottles clink against each other as I slam them around, looking for what I want. Picking up an old favorite, I tip a heavy pour of whiskey into a glass.

As I gulp down several burning swallows, the moon craze still threatens to take hold of me. I can't let it. No matter how fucking tempting she is. I'm already in too deep and I need to draw a line in the sand. This has to stop now. I can't fuck her and have feelings for her. My fingers itch as they half form into claws, scratching against the glass.

Red flies down the stairs. Her face is flushed in an annoyingly appealing way. "You can't just say all that shit and run away. You haven't heard what I think of you. You don't care about anything or anyone but yourself." She sweeps a hand out to the apartment. "Maybe money, but it's all about you, isn't it Brexley? You were hurt by your pack." Her eyes trace the lines of my scars. I find myself baring my teeth at her, but she goes on, the idiot girl. "And so you plan to never let anyone hurt you again. Which justifies you being a massive dick."

"You don't know a fucking thing about me, little girl," I say, slamming my glass down on the bar so hard everything shakes and rattles on it.

"Little girl?" she repeats. She blusters incoherently for a few minutes while I down the rest of my whiskey. "Why do you insist on treating me like I'm some naïve kid whenever it suits you?"

The alcohol burn churns with my moon craze and I realize I may have made a mistake with the drink. It's like I poured gasoline on the flames. Or maybe that's just from the flush of outrage on Red's cheeks.

"And anyways, you're wrong," she finally articulates. "I don't care about everything, and everyone. I don't care about *you*."

"Oh baby, you don't mean that," I say dryly.

Red raises her hand as if she's about to slap me. Her fingers curl into a fist and she stomps a few feet away. But I'm emboldened by the drink. In a flash, I'm in her face again.

"You don't care about me? Is that why you keep trying to get me to stop touching you?"

"What?" A puff of air explodes from her nostrils as she waves her arms about. "I don't want anyone to touch me. Don't give yourself so much credit."

"You let Goldie and Cinder touch you. But when I touch you, I know what happens." My eyes slowly rake down her body, pausing at her heaving breasts. Her piercings poke through her sports bra. I continue my perusal until my gaze rests at the apex of her thighs. I bet she's already slick. I curl my tongue behind my teeth in that way I know galls the shit out of her.

"Stop," she says breathlessly, as if the fight has gone out of her. Her arousal pulses off her, intertwining with mine. I know exactly what it takes to make those thighs tremble.

"You like it too much to keep me away for good." I taunt, angry at myself for wanting her so badly my mouth has gone completely dry.

She closes her eyes and the atmosphere changes. The anger transforms into an added dose of pheromones and the magnetism between us. It's fucking near painful, like skating along a razor's edge.

"Yes," she whispers, closing her eyes.

My voice drops to a low croon. "Does little Red want me to touch her? Make all this tension go away?"

Oh fae lords, say yes, let me do it.

She keeps her eyes closed tight, as if afraid she'll crumble if she opens them. "Why aren't you put off? I'm never satisfied. I always want more." The shame and pain intermixed in those words . . .

The growl that rolls through my chest and escapes my throat is pure masculine need. This is that dickhead, Hunter's fault. Making her think she's "too much" for wanting him. The dumb fucker didn't know what he had.

But I do. I know exactly what to do with a female this revved up. Fuck her into oblivion. Make her orgasm so hard and so often, she feels her brains might leak out of her ears.

"It must be hard, being so sexually repressed all these years." I bring my nose within mere centimeters of her neck, knowing my hot breath is why she shivers violently. I want to press my bare chest against hers, but I maintain the smallest amount of distance possible. My words come out husky. "He couldn't give you what you need, but do you

241

want me to prove to you again just how big my appetite is?"

When I pull back, Red's eyes are still closed and she's panting like she ran five miles.

When they open, her misty eyes emanate an unnatural white glow for less than a second before it dies off.

Shock hits me like a brick. I step back.

No. It can't be.

"It's not that I'm repressed, or a total nympho. Well not entirely. There's something you should know," she says, licking her lips. Red's resolve is melting fast, she's ready to give into me.

The wolf in me howls in grief and frustration.

Because I know better than to touch her now. She might as well be radioactive.

All this time, I've been addicted to the mystery of what Red is, and it took less than a moment for clarity to shred through the paper-thin covering. How did I miss it?

She nervously plays with the bottom of her bra band. "It happens every month where I get this insatiable urge. It started when I was sixteen and it's only gotten more intense as I've gotten older."

But she doesn't realize. She doesn't know.

Her dad was a human who left before she was born? *My fluffy white ass . . .*

"And tonight?"

"Tonight, my episode is. . . I'm nearly ready to crawl out of my skin," she confesses. Her eyes flash again.

Then she's on me, legs wrapped around my waist, kissing me, nipping my lips. The violence and the sex are unleashed as she claws at me. My dick begs to be let in, to join her like we did in the alleyway. Unhinged and out of control. She returns to her feet to rip my jeans open and pull my cock out.

She lunges and grabs my dick, before I can stop her. Wrapping her mouth around me, she takes me all the way in. A bone-shaking roar rips out of me.

My hands tangle into the hair at the back of her skull, and I rip her head back. She releases my cock with a sound pop. "Mmm," she gives a contented sigh as her eyes shut. "You taste so fucking good."

Wild and unhinged, she's a complete animal even if she doesn't shift. Only her primal side is in control, and it would do anything to get satisfaction. I know the feeling.

I grab her breast, giving it a punishing squeeze.

"More," she begs. "I need more. I need you in me, Brex."

I can't. I can't let this happen.

"Wolfie," she goads.

"Oh Christ," I mutter.

"My, what a big dick you have," she prompts me. It's our game.

I bite back the words. *All the better to fuck you with, my dear.*

"Don't you want to stick that hard cock inside me? Pound into me until you explode?" she purrs. Her entire body glows with pulsating sexual energy.

Keep it together, wolf.

It takes all my willpower to remove her from my body and set her on the couch.

I smile but it feels plastic and unnatural on my face. "Let's have a drink first, shall we? And then I'll take care of you, pet."

Pupils dilate as she sucks on her own fingers. Then she trails them down her bare, taut stomach. I see it so clearly now, the moon craze shining in her eyes.

I return to the bar and pour her a glass of whiskey as well. I remove the top from a small jar, revealing a shimmery white powder. I got it from a fairy on the black market. I already hate myself for what I'm about to do, but I have to.

My hand shakes as I pinch a bit of powder into her glass and swirl it inside. Then I top off my glass and walk back to Red.

She's tugged the hair tie out and her beautiful red mane falls around her shoulder. Red is splayed on my couch, fully naked, playing with herself.

Fuck. I may have to powder my own drink to keep myself from making the worst mistake of my life.

Almost as soon I hand Red the glass, she practically drains it. I sip on mine. She sets the glass down on the end table. "Don't you want to play with me?"

I don't bother lying. "Yes." But I continue to sit at the other end of the couch and sip my drink as I watch her fingers slide in and out of her channel.

Then Red is on my lap, eyes flashing white as she grinds her supple body against me. "Fae lords, I've never felt like this before. I've been intense with other guys in the past," her words begin to slur, but she hasn't noticed. "But you make me want to fuck you until we both die." Her head droops as her words trail off. "You make me want to. . . " Her body sags against me. She's out cold.

I throw back the rest of my drink. I'm a fucking bastard.

"Mate," I finish for her.

CHAPTER 30

FULL MOON RISING

RED

I wake slowly from a deep dream. Whatever the dream is, it leaves me empty and wanting. My legs clench each other. So painfully empty.

Cold reality cuts through some of my scalding desire when I try to move. Alarm snakes through me at the clanking sound along the heavy, cold weight around my neck. My fingers touch the iron collar and the alarm explodes into full-blown panic.

Still, I'm possessed by the energy of my episode. It's always sucked, but I'm practically out of my mind with lust. Molten lava flows through my veins. The ache between my legs throbs so intensely, I fear my body is going to cave in on itself. The need to be filled is so overwhelming, I'm dizzy. Energy zings through me, unfocused yet demanding to be channeled, taken out on something or someone. If I don't fuck or fight someone right now, my sanity is going to explode out the top of my head.

I focus on breathing, even as my fear and libido are

barrel rolling in a frenzy. Trying to access my senses, I find myself in a barren room with only a skylight and a couple dimmed canned lights. The collar is attached to the ground, and I can only get up to my hands and knees before it pulls me back down.

How the fuck did I get kidnapped? I don't remember.

Oh fae lords, did Hansel and Gretel find a way to nab me? Is Brexley okay?

Then my eyes lift, and I see Brexley standing next to a small table. In the time I've been out, he's clearly showered and changed into a fresh pair of jeans, but he didn't bother putting on a shirt. He looks far too calm, and there is a coldness about him that wasn't there before.

"What the faefucks is this?" I ask angrily. It masks the fear quaking through me. I gave my consent, but not for this. Is he more than a killer? Is he a psycho rapist?

Rage ripples through me, but against my will, my desire to jump him and fuck him only intensifies.

The chains jangle as I struggle against them. I growl.

"You were becoming . . . unmanageable," he says in a flat tone.

"Fuck you. Unchain me, and I'll show you how unmanageable I can be."

He stops in front of me, and I try to get up, but the chains jerk me back to my hands and knees at his feet. I'm livid and aroused like I've never been before in my life. Another growl escapes me.

"How long have I been out?"

"Not long," he assures me. Damp hair falls over his forehead, and he smells delectable.

I'm naked and clean. How did I get naked?

A vague memory of me stripping down and rubbing on Brexley's fully clothed body comes back to me.

"I have my finals today, I don't have time for this." That's right, let me out so I can go to school. But not before I mercilessly ride your dick.

"No one told you," he says quietly, almost to himself.

Something softens in his eyes. I wasn't sure if it was fear or shame, but either way it made something inside my chest twist in anticipation. Whatever he is going to tell me, I know I'm not going to like it.

"Told me what?"

Lick, suck, bite, fuck. Grab him and drag him here and use him.

It's so faefucking hard to focus. Desire ripples through me in intense, hateful waves.

"I wasn't sure what you were before. You smell like nothing and no one I've encountered before."

"I'm pissed off. That's what I am. Let me the fuck out."

His eyes drop to my chest, and I follow his gaze to my breasts. He can't know how they are begging to be touched, pinched, fuck, anything, just as long as they are touched.

"I can't do that, pet."

"Why the fuck not?"

"Because I can never tie myself down to another person." He snarls that last bit through his teeth as he pushes himself away from the small table. "Commitment means death."

"This is how you fuck someone casually?" I ask, incredulous.

"No, my pet, this is how I keep you from fucking me or anyone else in your current state."

"Brexley, let me out. You've gone insane. All you had to do was say no." Even as I say it, I close my eyes and pant as my thighs rub against each other and I rock back and forth. It's so, so hard to think. I just want to feel.

He crouches down into a squat, so he is eye level. "Believe me, I'm protecting you."

"You'll have to excuse me if I don't agree with you."

"You, my delicious pet —"

My pet. Before, I found the nickname kind of hot, when he wasn't irritating me. But now that I'm chained up like a dog? Har har. He won't have jokes after I neuter him.

"— are in heat because you have werewolf blood in you."

"Don't be ridiculous," I spit back, barely hearing him, too intent on the idea of chopping his balls off.

"Look up," he says gently. Then he stands again and walks back to the small table.

First, I shoot him a scathing glare before I turn my gaze upward to the sky light. Through it, the full moon is perfectly framed. My body shudders, and my hips buck as desire and violence fill me.

An unnatural growl rips from my throat. My head jerks back to Brexley as he returns, holding a mirror. He shows it to me and in it, I'm almost unrecognizable. My eyes glow an unnatural white.

What in the fae fuckity fuck fucks?

He continues in a quiet voice. "I don't believe you will change beyond this since you're only part wolf, but that's just a guess. There is next to no documentation on my kind, much less hybrids. I left my pack when I was nine, so I'm lacking a fair bit of knowledge myself."

"What's happening to me? Why do I feel like this?"

"You mentioned having episodes like this? Every thirty days? It's connected to the full moon. The three to five days leading up to it can really rev you up."

I snort. Fucking understatement. I'm half considering

grinding myself against the metal hook on the ground I'm chained to for some release.

He leans in until our lips almost touch. The strong sensation to lean forward and claim his lips, to rub myself against every hard ridge of his body, makes me whimper.

He finally steps away, putting some distance between us. "When I was coming of age, I almost did terrible, despicable things. And the only way I could find I could control myself was via more unconventional means." My eyes drifted down to the restraints. "I apologize for how they force you to the ground, but I typically come in here when I can't control my wolf. You don't shift. You have the same cycles and impulses that I do. But as long as you are in here, you can't do anything you'll regret. I don't know what it's really called. Maybe there is some official name."

He runs a hand through his hair as if suddenly anxious. "But I didn't have a pack by the time it hit me when I turned sixteen. The several days leading up to the full moon I'd have the desire to fuck and hunt like nothing else. So I —" he eyes the chain around me, "—found ways to control myself. It lasted until I was twenty-five and then the intensity lessened. You're twenty-four? Usually Weres mate before they're twenty-five, and if you haven't, the urge will only become more insistent. The craze helps Weres find and fuck someone. You were right to keep your distance, Red. If you fuck someone in this state, you are in danger of mating with them."

"What does that even mean?"

"You are bound to them. They become your pack, and if separate for too long a time, you die."

I shake my head. "I had sex with Hunter. His rejection broke my heart. I guess at times I felt like I'd die, but I don't think I'll actually die without him."

He shrugs. "I don't know all of how it works. I left my pack too young. But I do know it's something like that. It's incredible we've escaped mating thus far, but I can't risk it on a full moon." His gaze rises to the skylight. "The wolf moon, no less."

Brexley turns away. "I'm afraid it's partly my fault. I should have seen it sooner, but I believed you about your parents, and thought you'd been so pent up that it explained your sexual appetites. I'm the fool here, not you. And my presence, I think it may make it worse because part of you knows what I am. The same as you."

"No," I say quietly and without conviction.

"You never met your father," he says, pointedly.

"No," I scream it this time.

"It's going to be okay. We'll both feel more in control in six or so hours."

Six hours?

"I have finals," I whimper. How the fuck can I take them if I'm strung out and chained up in here? "Brexley, I need to come. If I don't I–" I literally feel like I'm going to die. "Please fuck me," I beg.

I'm so hot, so anxious, so turned on I can't stand it. It's so bad I don't care that he can see me reach down and play with myself. It's not enough, not even close to enough.

"I can't, Red," he says, his brows drawing together as he breathes more heavily. "Think of it as an extension of my duties. I'm here to protect your body. Even if I'm protecting you from yourself."

He can't leave me here, not like this.

"But I know what it feels like." His eyes sweep down to where I'm relentlessly rubbing my clit. "And, I think I have a solution."

I need him. Is this the feeling he was talking about? Like

I might die if I can't touch him. "Yes, anything, please Brexley," I beg.

He stands then circles me, stalking like he's about to make the killing move.

"You need to take the edge off, little Red. And I think I found a way for you to do it." My eyes follow his gesture to what's laid out on a small table. He drags it over so it's in my reach.

I groan in both disappointment and anticipation. A mini orgasm shudders through me, as I've yet to stop touching myself.

"How do you happen to have women's sex toys on hand?" I ask, trying to distract myself from the hot prickles sweeping along my skin.

Picking one up, he says, "It's amazing what one can get delivered in this city. And at any hour no less."

He bought delivery sex toys for me?

Am I angry? Insulted? Turned on? Touched by the consideration?

Horny. I'm fucking horny.

"It's not enough," I say in a low tone.

I mean it in more ways than one. The orgasm did next to nothing to give me any relief or satisfaction.

"I think you can make do," he says before he starts for the door.

Anxiety grips me and I rush to say, "You do it. You don't have to fuck me, but what if you helped me?"

Brexley pauses. His tongue pokes the inside of his cheek as he considers my proposal. I have a thousand uses for that tongue right now, but I keep quiet, not wanting to ruin my chances.

At last, he says, "Fine, but we do it my way. If you step out of line, I'm stopping it right away and you're on your own." He moves to the table and picks up a sizable sex toy.

"Aren't you going to unchain me?" I ask.

"Not a fucking chance," he shoots over his shoulder. Then he rounds behind me. I start to turn but he barks an order. "Get on your hands and knees."

I do as he says and almost sob in relief when I feel the fat tip of the toy run up and down my lower lips.

I half growl, half groan as my hips try to buck back onto it. "Don't tease me, I can't take it."

He chuckles darkly, right before he pushes it in me. It's not as satisfying as his cock, but I let out a long moan as I'm filled. Instantly, I'm slamming myself back on it. In moments I'm coming again, but it still isn't enough. Why isn't it enough?

Because it's not Brexley.

"I need you," I whine.

He pulls the toy out and I half scream half whimper.

"We do it my way," he stresses.

"If you don't stick that thing back in me, I'm going to fucking kill you."

My threat turns into a high-pitched yelp of surprise as he gives me what I want.

"I'm trying to keep this professional," he says through his teeth.

"You're offering to get me off with sex toys and you're worried about being professional?" I ask, losing myself to the fullness and rhythm he's set.

Turning slightly, I find Brexley has his cock out and in hand. As he fucks me with the toy, he jerks himself off hard and furious.

My hips stall as a strange, choking sound escapes me. I'm coming. My body wraps and squeezes around the toy.

"Let me suck you off, Brexley. You need it too."

"We can't," he says, his voice tight. "No touching, that's the rule." A look of wild desperation is on his face. Like it pains him to hold back. Good, I want him in pain.

My hips go nuts as I sob my way through another orgasm. This time it cracks through the surface of my need, but just barely. I need so much more.

He slows the pace. "No," I beg. "Don't slow down. For fuck's sake, I'm going to come again. Please let me come again." I practically sob the request.

Suddenly he leaves the toy in me to return to the table. His hard cock juts out from his body. I lunge at him as he passes by. He steps out of reach, his eyes glowing. "Bad girl."

Grabbing something else off the table, he gives me a wide berth as he returns to the toy he left in me.

"Don't you mean bad bitch?" I taunt.

With a click, a vibrator comes alive against my clit. Oh sweet fae lords and all that is holy, I am completely overwhelmed. Brexley manages to attend to my clit with the vibrator while pumping the other toy in and out of me.

He pistons the toy and turns up the vibration setting until I'm trapped in one long, endless orgasm. Tears run down my face as I lose all sense of time. I ride a rollercoaster of sensation that may kill me. After what feels like years, my body collapses. My legs are covered in my own wetness, my entire body trembling, and I'm as thirsty as if Hansel has sucked me dry with his devious power.

Brexley moans behind me. I turn to see him laving a tongue against his desire covered hand.

"Fucking hell," he mutters.

I see he's gotten some satisfaction too, and his dick softens before my eyes.

"How do you feel?" he asks gruffly.

"Exhausted, spent, and ... "

He raises an eyebrow. "And?"

I fucking hate to say it. "Still horny."

Brexley shakes his head and sighs. "Guess we'll need to rehydrate. And start again."

CHAPTER 31
THE FINAL COUNTDOWN

RED

Three gallons of water and countless orgasms later, we are both dripping in sweat. I'm on my back, wrists and ankles tied down because I got too "overzealous."

So, I tried to jump him a couple times. So what? Tying me up is a disproportionate response. A super hot, if not disproportionate response.

"How long have we been in here?" I ask, my voice little more than a bag of gravel.

With a quick glance at his watch, Brexley says, still panting, "Three and a half hours. How are you feeling now?"

"Like. . . like I can think again." It's true. A clarity has returned to me that I haven't felt in days. Since before I met Brexley.

He nods. "Good, let's get you some sleep. After all, you have finals in six hours."

Turns out we don't have to go far to get to his apartment. He opens the door and I find myself back in his living room. When I saw the closed door initially, I would have guessed it was a closet, not a soundproofed room of chains. My life has gotten so weird.

Passing by my rabbits, I see they are set up in a pen with a litter box, food, water, and treats. Am I in some kind of alternate universe?

Brexley leads me to his master bath. He points out the clean towels and extra clothes.

"I'll be downstairs if you need me," he says, heading toward the door.

"Don't you need to clean up too?" I ask, sounding too earnest.

"There's another bathroom downstairs."

Panic rises in me at the thought of him going. I feel strange, anxious, and uncomfortable now that logic has returned to me. The things we did. . .

"Will you sleep in the bed with me?"

He pauses at the door, giving me a long, hard look. I can't tell what he's thinking, but regret and shame swirl in me. I don't want to be left alone right now.

"Get some rest, Red. I'll wake you up in plenty of time." The bedroom door shuts with a click, leaving me to my own thoughts.

SOMEONE GENTLY SHAKES my shoulder and I open my eyes to a massive coffee cup from the Book and Bean. Brexley stands next to the bed with a mocha and a ham and cheese croissant. "Don't worry, it's decaf so you don't tweak out. But it's time to get up. Your test is in an hour."

I fell asleep fast and hard and I feel like I got a full night's rest. My body is sore but satisfied.

Dressed in a tight black t-shirt and jeans, Brexley looks delectable. But his expression is closed off.

This is familiar. You are used to this. To being brushed off after the fact, so focus on you, that's all you can do.

A strange calm comes over me as I revert to doing what I've always done. Throw myself into the parts I can control. I eat quickly, then borrow some more of Brexley's clothes. My hair is only a third dried from last night, so I plait it into a braid.

I find my phone on the bedside charger. Thirty missed calls, mainly from Goldie and Cinder. When I open up my text messages, I see they've been freaking out at the news my apartment building burned down since early this morning. But I didn't have any missed messages on my home screen because Brexley must have gotten my phone open and responded to both of them.

He identified himself in the messages, and that yes it was true my place burned down, he took me to his place, and that I was safe and resting. He assured them I would call them as soon as I was able.

My heart squeezes tightly in my chest. Not only did Brexley take care of my rabbits, but he also made sure my friends weren't freaking out. I call Goldie and find Cinder is already with her, so I only have to explain things once.

I give them a brief rundown of escaping the burning building. I don't tell them about the fire mage, or that I'm half werewolf, or how Brexley 'took care' of me last night. After agreeing to a girls night with drinks later this week, I hang up. None of us can afford to talk longer, we all have finals today.

As soon as I set foot downstairs, Brexley says something about having some work to do and calls his car service again. Tom, the kid from the night before, shows up to escort me to campus.

Before I get in the car, Brexley takes me by the shoulders. His touch no longer sets me off like before, but it does cause a warm coil in my tummy.

"Remember, you got this. You just need to relax and get out of your own way." For a moment, I think he'll kiss me, but he doesn't. "After your exam, Tom will bring you back here until your shift. You'll be safe, I promise."

Then he takes off, leaving me no chance to respond. Not that I know what I'd say. Thanks for drugging me, chaining me up then giving me a hundred or so orgasms before giving me a cup of decaf in your bed?

The next few hours go surprisingly fast. I breeze through my first final, sociology with Goldie. But before I head off to my next final, she hugs me so tight and promises she and Cinder are here for me in whatever way I need.

Normally I'm a bundle of nerves, walking into Dr. Langley's lecture hall. So eager to do well, while feeling like I've already failed. But as I take my usual seat, I can't deny that I feel different.

The last several days have changed me, and I'm having an out of body experience. It's as if I'm walking on air. Nothing is real, especially not the worries that weighed me down before. It doesn't make a lick of sense, but Brexley helped set me free.

Right now, I suddenly don't care so much about my performance. Dr. Langley passes out the test, giving me a nod. She's waiting to see how I do, knowing what's on the line. I realize the scary dragon doesn't scare me anymore. Maybe repeating her class wouldn't be the worst thing in the world.

Guess I should have switched to decaf a long time ago.

Yeah, that's why I feel like this, my inner voice mocks.

After I turn in my test, a heaviness returns with my every step as I exit the lecture hall.

I'm not the same girl. Hell, I'm not even *what* I thought. I haven't fully accepted the fact that I'm part werewolf, but I won't deny it either. The context somehow makes me feel less crazy. I'm not too much. It's part of my nature.

But does Gigi know? Surely my mom did. Has everyone been lying to me my whole life?

Before the myriad of questions bring me crashing down to earth, I put all of them in a little box and put them on a shelf in my mind. I'll deal with them later.

Outside, I find Tom outside by his parked car, waiting for me.

"How'd you do?" he asks, opening the door for me.

"My best," I say, feeling a weight lift off my shoulders.

Even though my heart and conscience are in tatters, for the first time in as long as I can remember, I truly feel things are going to be okay.

CHAPTER 32

DANCING IN THE DARK

BREXLEY

I thought we could be done. That I could chalk it all up to the moon craze. Now that I'd satisfied her itch, she'd lose her hold over me. But as I enter the Poison Apple, I'm struck by the sight of Red.

I followed her at a distance to make sure she got to her finals all right. Then I tipped Tom extra to pack some heat and have me on speed dial, while I got some distance. Once Tom informed me she was safely back in my apartment, I knew she was secure. Later, he drove her the short distance to work without incident. I trusted Rap as much as I trusted my own security measures.

I needed to find Grandma, but damned if Theodore Dunkin wasn't as paranoid and efficient as I was at hiding someone. All my attempts to unearth either of them came to zilch.

Red drops off the carefully concocted drinks to a group on the lounge couches, allowing me the perfect view of her confident stride. Whether she knows it or not, she owns this place.

It pained me to be away from Red for so long. It developed slowly through the day, but a pressure built around my chest with each hour, threatening to cave it in. Now that I'm in the same room as her again, it's like I can breathe.

Cinder must have dressed her, because she's wearing a strappy black bodysuit and knee-high boots over fishnet stockings. Her hair is pulled up in a more sophisticated updo than what I've seen, and her lips are blood red. She looks like a dominatrix. There is an ease about her that wasn't there before. I hope it means her test went well. I don't see how it couldn't. She proved to herself she knew the material.

When she turns and sees me, the ease I noted in her flees. She stiffens and turns cold.

I don't blame her. She wanted me to stay with her, reassure her with emotional intimacy. And damned if it didn't kill me to walk away. But I couldn't be sure it wouldn't cause us to mate. I'd been so careful not to touch her while wringing her out of all her built up animal needs. I wanted nothing more than to curl her into my body and hold her afterward, but I walked away.

I can't walk away now, though.

Before Red can return to the bar, I intercept her at the edge of the dance floor. I back her up into the mass of writhing people. She turns away from me, and I step up until I'm right behind her.

"Your boyfriend is back," I say into Red's ear.

She stiffens, her eyes scanning the room until they land on Hunter. He doesn't push his way over. The stupid sonofabitch wouldn't debase himself. He's been playing pseudo security guard the last couple hours, staying out of sight, but always nearby. I'm not sure if he's waiting for me to slip up, or if he wants Red alone. Either way, I don't intend to give him the chance.

"He's not my boyfriend," she says, her voice tight.

Anger snakes through me, despite myself. "Right, because you weren't good enough for him."

"I—" she seems at a loss.

"What? It's okay for you to say it, but not for me to say it? Maybe that's because you know he's wrong. Hearing that bullshit mirrored back makes it clear what a douche nozzle the boy is."

"Don't call him that," she says, but it lacks the usual vehemence when she's defending her precious Hunter.

My hand wraps around her waist, and I pull her close.

"What are you doing? Don't touch me." Panic flares in her voice, but she doesn't push me away.

"Maybe I'm helping you?" I direct her hips in a slow sway to match mine. "After all, it's safe now."

That's a lie. Nothing about this is safe. She is dangerous to everything I've wanted. Still, I don't let go of her.

"Everyone can see us," she protests.

"Good, because I'm your boyfriend, right? We need to sell this if we don't want people questioning your past and finding out more than you want them to."

"You're an asshole."

I squeeze her hips harder, and a gasp slips out of her. I worked her so good last, I'm surprised she can stand.

"Yes, I am, and it's important that prude sonofabitch knows what he's missing."

Red may think this is some pissing match between me and the goodie two shoes, but it's more than that. He needs to see all he had, all the sexuality and power that swirls around her. How he didn't appreciate what he could have had. I've seen all of her power and sexuality and I'm still in awe.

Red needs to know the truth. She can't see it, but I've got a full view now. "He wanted you then, he wants you now. But on his terms. Hunter thinks you aren't powerful enough for him, but he's wrong. You are far more powerful than he can imagine. Seeing you like this, confident, in your element, he's drawn to you. And that scares him. It should."

Even from here, I see Hunter's eyes darken with lust, anger, and jealousy.

Perfect.

That's when I dip my lips to the slope between her neck and shoulder. Unable to help myself, I nuzzle the soft skin there. My tongue darts out and I taste her. A low hum escapes me. "You are far sweeter than any of those little cakes your Gigi could make."

"You're being ridiculous," she says, though it's breathy. She doesn't even realize she's adopted my favorite adage.

"Now I know you are this sweet everywhere." I muse, before latching my mouth to that spot again, swirling my tongue against her warm, soft skin. I lift my gaze to meet Hunter's in an open challenge. His jaw clenches.

"And to think that prude boy has no idea what heaven lies at your lower lips, has no idea what you sound like as you scream for more. What a fool." My hand slides down her side, curving to slide down her backside. The bulge of her phone, tucked in her back pocket, keeps me from squeezing the perfect globe of flesh. I want to take a bite out of it right here.

Electricity zips off her skin and races through me. Again, that deep part inside me opens up and beckons her flesh as if it were the home I never had.

"Stop," she says, but it's so faint, even she doesn't seem to believe she said it.

The energy continues to come alive and wrap around us. This crazy little redhead is unlike anyone I've ever met, and the things she makes me feel. . . There is still something between us, something unsatisfied. I don't want to fuck her or get her off. I want to make love to her slowly, thoroughly, and look deep into her eyes and feel like I'm not alone.

My teeth grate across her skin, and I'm possessed by the intense need to mark her. "I don't know if I can stop," I confess before dropping another light kiss to her neck.

Hunter turns on his heels and walks out.

Good boy. Leave rather than make a scene, you fucking idiot.

But Red is worth making a scene over.

"I hate you," she whispers.

"No, you don't."

"I hate me too, for giving into your sickness."

I grab her arms and whip her around. "Don't you feel better? I can even touch you right now and you don't dissolve into a puddle of need. Because of me, you can focus on your surroundings, and you can focus on your ridiculous little life."

She pulls out of my grip. "My life isn't ridiculous." Her eyes meet mine and I don't try to hide the fire blazing in them. I let her see all my need, my desire. She may be sated, but nothing will ever get the taste of her out of my mouth now. Even though we avoided mating, I'm well and truly fucked.

"I. . . I," she falters, as if pulled into the gravity of me. "I need to take out the trash." She stalks past me.

I grab her arm, stopping her. She is so wound up, she doesn't notice my other hand slipping the phone out of her back pocket. I lean over and whisper in her ear. "Admit it Red, you're still as hungry for me as I am for you, heat or not."

The fuck am I doing admitting this? Still, I can't stop myself. I need to hear her say it.

She rips her arm out of my grasp again. "I need some fresh air. The presumption in here is suffocating." Then she throws over her shoulder before she stalks off, "Don't follow me."

I have no intention of abiding, but my phone rings.

Faefucks.

Weaving through the crowd, I find Rap's office empty. I shut the door and lock it.

"What?" I growl.

Jameson's voice grates in my ear. "You have the audacity to ask me what I'm doing calling you? Why are you fucking around, Brexley? Kill the old bat, clear the debt."

"Listen, you want me to do the job, I will do the job. You know why I'm so good at hunting people? Because I have patience. But every time you call, it thins, old man. So stop fucking calling and let me do my job." I end the call without waiting for a response.

Fuck that old man.

Even though I *have* lost focus, and I sure as hell have been fucking around.

Still, the other sources I've been using to shake down where Grandma is has led to absolutely zilch. So if I can't go to her, I need to make her come to me. Holding Red's phone in my hand from where I took it off her person just now, I send a message to her Gigi.

Let's see if the old lady can stay underground now.

We need to finish this once and for all.

266

CHAPTER 33
TRAPPED BY TRASH

RED

The trash bag is only half full, but I needed an excuse to get away. I prop the door to the back alleyway open so it doesn't lock behind me and toss the bag in the dumpster.

But I'm not ready to go back. I didn't wear a coat, but I welcome the biting cold air. My blood runs hot with arousal.

No, anger. I'm angry.

The fucking audacity of Brexley. The way he turned so cold on me then heats up to use me in his pissing match with Hunter again. I have to push away the powerful preen I felt at having Brexley practically rubbing me in Hunter's face. Showcasing me like some precious gem that sparkles under the club lights.

I hate to admit it, but it felt so fucking good. Hunter's jealousy was undeniable. I chased after him for so long, and to have him see how special I am, satisfied a deep part of me I didn't know existed. Dark desire shone from Hunter's eyes, and he seemed angered by it. For once I didn't try to pull back or shy away. I didn't make myself less to accommodate him.

Or I did, but Brexley wouldn't let me. He coaxed my hips and body into swaying, into falling into a rhythm of confidence and sexuality.

Fuck, it was amazing.

As much as teasing Hunter felt amazing, all I wanted was to pull Brexley into the back of the bar and lock him in Rap's office. I'd sit on the desk and make him kneel before me, lift my skirt and lick me until I came.

He would if I asked.

But this has got to stop. Our toxic cycle of seduction, sex, anger, and cold distance. I'm better than this, and I intend to start acting like it.

The door slams shut behind me, making my bones rattle from the nearby impact.

"Well, hello Red, out here all alone?" A familiar female voice taunts.

My insides freeze as pure fear takes over. I force myself to turn around.

From the shadows of the alley, two pale forms emerge. Hansel and Gretel. Their faces twisted into hateful, evil smiles.

CHAPTER 34
THE TORTURE TWINS

RED

S uddenly I'm back in the halls of FFA, alone, unprotected, starkly aware of all the pain I'm about to endure.

Gretel is like a deranged hyena and she enjoys causing pain when her brother fully lets her off her leash. But he's the one to look out for. Hansel is far more deadly than Gretel. He's calculated and controlled enough to draw out the pain. Or worse yet, he continues to give you hope that he will give you some kind of release, but he never does. It's an effective way to break someone.

And I've been broken more times than I can count.

"Where is your wolf now?" Hansel asks with a grin that makes my stomach churn.

Don't panic, don't panic, I tell myself, but my hands are ice cold and sweaty. My heart jackrabbits and my brain fuzzes, trying to fight the inevitable.

"He'll be out in a minute," I lie.

Gretel tsks. "What a lying little wolf fucker you are."

"Yes," Hansel says, observing his cuticles as they both saunter toward me, boxing me in. "How did you end up with such a rare specimen? I think we'll draw him out later and force him to shift, just so we can make a pelt out of him."

"I want to have fun," Gretel hisses at him.

"I'm sorry, my beloved sister, you're correct. I digress." Hansel turns to me. "Now give us what we want or there will be pain."

There's always pain, even if I give them what they want. Still, I can't help myself. "What do you want?"

"Don't play coy with us, your grandma's newest recipe. We want it. We've already enjoyed a hostile takeover of one of her farms in Costa Rica, so we have all her ingredients at our disposal. Now, we need the recipe for her new product. A baseline for our designs if you will."

Before I can answer, Gretel shoots a hand forward, magic sparking off her eyes.

A sharp pain spikes through my stomach, sending me to my knees. I clutch at my torso, trying to find a way to ease the torment. The worst part is I know Gretel has only begun "playing."

"Are you fucking kidding me?" I manage to speak through clenched teeth. "I knew you were sadistic assholes, but I didn't know you were stupid."

Gretel's face further contorts in fury. It's like there's a knife twisting in my gut. I gasp, doubling over. Unbearable hunger hits me full force. I'm so hungry, I'm tempted to rip open a nearby trash bag and shove its contents into my mouth. Gretel has pushed me to that before, driven me to eat trash, simply for her amusement.

But I fight the impulse. I refuse to give her the satisfaction, though my guts feel like they're caving in.

Hansel picks at his cuticles. "Don't play coy with us, Red. We know you have it."

I fight the pain, and my words come out choppy. "I have nothing to do with my Gigi's business. I never have. Why the fuck would I know what she is working on?"

"Stop playing dumb," Hansel snaps. "It's clear you are as much of a human lover as that old bitch. We know she gave you the recipe. The secret one she's about to roll out that will change the world as we know it." He sounds like he's quoting something.

"We had her email hacked. She sent a package with the recipe to you before she vanished. Now tell us where it is." His eyes flash as his palm stretches out, sparking.

Then a horrible twin force snakes around the stomach pain. It's as if someone is sucking all the moisture from my body. My throat and tongue turn dry as sandpaper. I'm literally dying from thirst. Despite the immeasurable pain, I begin to laugh.

"Why bother hiring all the low-budget kidnappers?" I croak.

"Aside from the fact we are trying to keep a low profile?" Hansel replies.

Insanely enough, I know he's serious. Though their disturbance at the Poison Apple the other night made the human news, it likely hasn't touched the mage cities. And the Ogre had been chalked up to a random incident, a fae gone mad who attacked a college campus. Who would possibly believe a fae and a couple of mages were working together? And I'm sure they covered their tracks with the mercenary mages too.

"We are very busy running our new business," he explains in a patronizing tone. "If one wants to be success-ful, one must learn to delegate."

"And if you didn't have your rotten little guard dog, you would be easily plucked," Gretel adds.

I hate that she's right. Per fucking usual, Red is a powerless pawn.

I'm sick to death of it.

"Oh yeah, the business you murdered your own family for. Tell me, did the Gingerbread Witch see it coming?"

"Grand Ginger's passing was tragic, but she did have a tendency to stick her head where it didn't belong." Hansel shoots Gretel a glance which she returns with a terrifying grin.

"Yeah, the pressure was too much, and she had a tendency to lose her head."

I know I shouldn't egg them on, but I'm so faefucking angry to be back in this position, it overrides my common sense.

"You think your tiny little Gingerbread company is going to make you into something important? My grandma's business makes yours look like a joke, like an EZ bake oven—tiny, fake, and running off cheap light bulbs."

Hunger and thirst strike me like whips. A scream tears its way out of me as I fall to my knees, my forehead hitting the pavement. As soon as the pressure eases, I press my hands against the cold asphalt until I can look up at them.

"You can do your worst; I still won't know whatever recipe it is you are after. I know nothing about her business."

Hansel scowls. "It's the recipe for pure power. It's going to change everything if she distributes it the way she does Magic Morsels. How can she not share that with you? Her precious granddaughter."

"Because I want nothing to do with power or magic,

and especially anyone like you two. I don't know a damn thing."

"Then we resort to holding you hostage until the old bag gives it to us," Gretel says a little too gleefully.

"I don't know, Gretel," Hansel says coolly. "I daresay she may still be holding out on us. Let's make sure." His open hand closes into a fist and I scream.

I'm not sure if it's possible for a person to concave into themselves, but I'm certain in moments I'll be nothing but dust. My vision goes black, and I silently beg to pass out.

The snarl of a pissed off animal barely registers in my ears. Then, like a light switch turning back on, the pain is gone. I gasp and fall on the ground, my cheek scraping against the dirty asphalt.

"What the fuck is he doing, Hansel?" Gretel hisses.

"I. . .I don't know, Gretel."

For the first time, I hear uncertainty in Hansel's voice. I force my eyes to open. They are so dry at this point they feel gritty and everything is blurry. A muscular form stands between me and them. A black shirt falls to the ground next to me.

"Which one of you fuckers wants to die first?" Brexley growls.

"Hansel," Gretel hisses in panic again. "I can't use my power."

"I know, Gretel, but keep trying."

"Oh, do you both suddenly have a case of impotence? Oh dear." Brexley taunts. "Why don't you let me put you out of your misery?" Then I hear the crackling of bones and a savage roar. He takes a couple steps toward them.

Both the mages pull out weapons. Gretel's is a chain with two blades at either end, while Hansel's is a longsword.

My eyes flutter shut and I groan even as I hear yelling and fighting. There is the blunt contact of flesh meeting flesh, the whipping of weapons through the air. I can't move. I can't speak.

Then I hear the retreat of designer heeled-boots clacking away.

Brexley shouldn't have chased them off, but I can't tell him. I can't tell him they would have fixed me only to break me again. But now, I'm so dehydrated and malnourished, I might not make it. And I can't even laugh at the irony of wanting to call my tormentors back.

CHAPTER 35
DAME KIKI ELEGANZA

RED

I'm not sure how long has passed before I'm scooped up into warm, strong arms. The strong, masculine scent of Brexley mingles with the coppery sting of blood. I vaguely register the slickness of liquid on the chest my head is pressed against.

Flesh against flesh, electric sparks still snake through me. But it's dampened by my current state.

"Fuck, Red," he growls. "Don't you fucking pass out."

"Or what?" I say back in a thready voice. Fae lords, it hurts to speak, to breathe.

"Or I'll eat Bangs and Bombs for dinner." His voice is far too soft to back the threat.

"No, you won't," I croak.

"You better stay awake to make sure I don't. I bet they'd be delicious served with carrots."

"You love them, despite your best efforts. They got to you."

"Yes, they did," he says in a contemplative voice that seems far away.

When did we get in a car? I fall in and out of consciousness, but Brexley never lets me go. And even in my wretched state, I find a way to revel in his touch. The feeling of being held makes me want to cry. There were so many nights at the Academy I longed for Hunter to just hold me. But he was always off in training or studying, working to be the top of his class. He sometimes managed to keep the twisted twins away with threats, but he did his best to put distance between us.

I should tell Brexley he could take some tips from Hunter on that point. Since he's so dead set on being alone. He's doing a terrible job keeping away from me.

If I had any moisture left in me, a tear would fall from my eyes.

How stupid is life? That I would be killed over a damn recipe I know nothing about.

I DON'T REMEMBER FALLING asleep, but when I wake I'm surprised how good I feel.

"There she is," an unfamiliar voice says. It's a deep pitch, but there is an elegance to the person's speech.

I find myself on Brexley's couch, a heavy blanket wrapped around me. Instead of the binding bustier, I'm wearing loose clothing. The strong scent of an expensive perfume I can't name washes over me. A woman removes her rather large hand, with elaborate acrylic nails, from my stomach. She steps back, and I get a better look at her.

The Black woman has a massive mane of hair, outrageous, blue sparkly eyeshadow, and the longest fake lashes

I've ever seen. To match the drama of her hair and makeup, the woman flaunts a sequin dress and platform heels that must put her at seven feet. A lime green boa is wrapped around her arms. She clip-clops back to stand next to Brexley, towering next to him. I can't help but notice her thick, carved calf muscles flexing and lifting in those heels.

She, whoever she is, appears to be a drag queen.

"Hi," I say, feeling confused and out of sorts. "Who are you?"

The woman smacks Brexley on the chest. "Aren't you going to introduce me?"

Brexley stands next to her with a bandage wrapped around his bicep. He opens his mouth, but she cuts him off. "Right, I guess I'm used to an emcee giving me all my cues. I am Dame Kiki Eleganza!" she says, extending her arms with a flourish. I can't help but smile at her zeal and drama. She was clearly made for a stage.

"She's a Level Four healing mage," Brexley says gruffly. "I called her when I realized how bad off you were."

Dark circles drag under the wolf shifter's eyes, and it looks as though he's been tugging his hair every which way. He wiped blood off his bare torso but missed a few spots.

Pushing myself up into a sitting position, my hands drift to my stomach.

"What did you do to them?" I ask Brexley. I vaguely recall Hansel and Gretel screaming about their magic not working.

"A werewolf trait is the ability to temporarily nullify or cancel out magic within a certain radius. Mages hate it," he says with a smile that is closer to baring his teeth.

"Whoa," I breathe.

"The twins didn't seem to care for it and resorted to hand-to-hand combat with me. While they are well trained, it did not go well for them." Delight and violence sparkles in his eye as he twists the ring around his forefinger. He delighted in kicking their asses. I would have certainly enjoyed the show, if I'd been able.

"How do you feel, honey?" Dame Kiki asks, putting the attention back on me.

I don't feel moments from death anymore. "I feel like I could down a pitcher of water and a couple bacon cheeseburgers," I admit. "But I'm okay."

Tears sting the backs of my eyes with a sudden ferocity.

Kiki's drawn eyebrows scrunch in sympathy as she sits at my feet on the couch. "Oh honey, you've been through a lot, haven't you? This isn't the first time this has happened," she finishes softly.

I look up at her in surprise.

She gives me a small smile. "I'm also an empath. I can feel the age of emotional wounds as well as physical ones. I'm just glad the Big Bad Wolf here was smart enough to give the best of the best a call." Kiki shoots a steely glance at Brexley who rubs the back of his neck, clearly uncomfortable.

"How do you know each other?" I ask.

"Oh, well . . . " Kiki pauses, casting Brexley a look as if asking permission. He nods, and she goes on. "A while back, my family tried to, let's just say, erase me from the family tree."

"They wanted to kill you?"

"You can't choose the family you are born into, a pity for all parties involved. So I hired the big bad over here to watch over me and handle my *problems*. And if I do say so myself, the big sexy lug is worth every penny. Even if at heart he is a crotchety old man with more emotional issues than Hamlet and Liza Minelli. Not to mention, when I knew him, he wasn't even house trained yet."

"Kiki," Brexley warns.

Dame Kiki shoots me a saucy wink. I can't help but laugh.

Brexley shifts even more uncomfortably, watching me with a frown.

Tears spill from my eyes though I feel numb inside. I must be doing better, normally I don't have the capacity for tears after Hansel is done with me. I don't even care who changed me into Brexley's shirt and boxers. Being able to lay out on the couch in comfort and safety gives my emotions space I desperately need.

Dame Kiki suddenly straightens before looking back and forth between us. "Oh, I see." A smile twitches at the corner of her mouth.

Before I can ask what she sees, she jumps up. "Well, I must be going. I have to grace the stage of the Pumpkin Coach Club with all my fabulosity in forty minutes and as lovely as y'all are, I can't deprive the masses of the Fairy Godmother."

"Fairy Godmother?"

"Oh yes, dear, it's the nickname everyone has given me. Something about how people's dreams come true when I'm around. But honestly, I'm just not afraid to give people a good kick in the rump when they need it. That's all most people usually need." She shoots an indiscernible look at Brexley. He frowns.

"Listen," she crosses over to poke Brexley in the chest. "You give that little girl over there whatever she wants. Whether it be a truckload of cheeseburgers or a whole chocolate cake. I helped her, but the soul and body need the immediate hit of sugar and antioxidants to recover and soothe from a thing like that."

Brexley nods and pulls out a thick wad of bills from his back pocket.

"Don't even think about it, wolf boy," she warns, while waving a long nail in his face.

"Please let me pay you, Kiki," Brexley nearly grits his teeth. I get the impression this is not the first time they've had this fight.

"Absolutely not, sugar buns."

"Kiki, I'm serious, you know how I feel about—"

"Yes, yes," she waves her boa in his face impatiently. "You can't abide favors or ties. I get it." She grabs the wad of money and tucks it in her bosom.

Then Dame Kiki swoops back over to land a big kiss on my forehead. "Don't worry, honey. You'll be alright," she whispers.

"Thank you," I say in a scratchy voice. Part of me doesn't want her to go, but I lean back, exhausted.

"The best thank you is to just be fabulous," she casts over her shoulder while walking away as if she were on a runway. The door slams behind her.

CHAPTER 36

THE PACK OF THE PAST

BREXLEY

I hand Red a large bottle with a plastic straw filled with cold water. Then I sit on the coffee table so my knees almost touch the couch.

"I'm so sorry, I'm sorry I wasn't there." I plead for her forgiveness, knowing I can't give it to myself.

"I sent you away," she says before sipping some water. I allow a beat of silence while she takes a sip of water before asking what I need to know.

"How many times?" My voice is low, dangerous. But not to her.

Red looks up, not understanding at first. But I give her a hard look.

"Oh," she breathes before playing with the straw so she doesn't have to look at me. "There really is no counting, to be honest. After something like that happens so many times, it's better not to count."

I grip my kneecaps to keep from running out and hunting those bastards down. "I'll kill them."

Red doesn't protest. I don't think she hates the idea.

"I thought Fairy Fine Arts was an institution meant to teach magic users how to be helpful and useful to society, not sadistic tormentors."

"It is."

"Oh really? What in the fuck use is someone whose magic is thirst and hunger?" My words are harsh, but my tone isn't. I don't want to risk Red thinking I'm upset with her.

"There are lots of good applications. Hansel could use his powers to rehabilitate alcoholics by slating their thirst. Gretel could use her powers over hunger to help people lose weight to improve their health. She could help people who are on the brink of starvation or help those in chemo or hospice regain their appetite to give them strength."

She looks away. "But as soon as the professors weren't looking, they went as far in the other direction as they could."

"And you were their favorite target."

She rears back as if shocked I figured it out. I didn't need what Kiki said to qualify the guess. The compulsive manner in which Red licks her lips, especially when nervous, explained so much.

Red doesn't realize how resilient, how powerful she is, wolf's blood or not. But the moment those two re-entered her world, just like when Hunter showed up, her power drained away. With Hunter, she gives it away; with the twins, they take it from her.

Part of me whispers that I would do anything to help her stay in her power.

"Yeah, I was their favorite punching bag." She gives me a humorless smile, still unable to maintain eye contact. As if she can't let me see all the pain behind her morning mist eyes.

"Hansel would enjoy dehydrating me for the duration of a class. The thirst would be almost unbearable. The way it would grip me, it would be difficult to focus. So not only did I not have any magic, but I couldn't even pass a history course."

Suddenly her extreme desire to pass her class came into perspective. The tireless hours she put in were also an attempt to break with the past. She never got a fighting chance to succeed. I knew the feeling.

"I was at that school for three years before I was kicked out for not showing any magical aptitude and flunking all my classes. In truth, they should have kicked me out before the first year was over. But they kept me in deference to Gigi." Her hands tighten on the bottle. "And I should have left long before then. But I didn't have the backbone. I still held out hope that my magic would show up. That I would finally be good enough for Hunter. Usually, magic ability appears in childhood, but it has been known on rare occasions to manifest as late as nineteen."

She pauses to sip some more water. "Staying at FFA almost killed me. The first party I attended, Hansel made me so thirsty that I couldn't stop chugging whatever was in front of me. I ended up in the hospital with alcohol poisoning." She sighs and hangs her head. "My Gigi was nice about it, but I could see she was disappointed. Then for three months, Gretel wove her magic around me, until I never felt hungry. Slowly but surely, food became repellent until I was skin and bones at the end of my sophomore year."

Unable to internalize these horror stories anymore, I

shoot to my feet. "Why the fuck didn't you tell someone what they were doing?"

A dry laugh escapes her. "Oh I did, but I learned very quickly that it only made things worse for me."

I pace back and forth, running my hands through my hair.

"It seems stupid in hindsight, okay? But some part of me still so badly wanted to belong. I wanted to make Gigi proud. I wanted Hunter to really fall in love with me. I wanted too much." She settles deeper into the couch cushions and closes her eyes.

"I . . . " I swallow over the lump in my throat. Something rising from my depths that I haven't experienced in over a decade. "I get it. You know it's a shitty situation, but you've made your home in that shit place. Even if you leave it, part of you will always want to belong to it."

"Your pack," she breathes, as if worried she'll spook me. And she's right. I'm not sure how the words are coming out of me right now.

"I was only nine when I was excised from my pack."

Her face contorts as if it pains her. "Why? Why would they do that to you?"

I scrub a hand along my face, and then go to sit in a chair next to the couch. Red turns, curling her knees up, still sipping on the water. The gallon jug is half emptied.

"I was out chopping and gathering wood for my mother when I saw her. A woman came through the woods like fire on snow. Her hair was red, like yours," I say with a half-smile.

Maybe that's why I find Red so irresistible. I have a thing for fiery haired women. The woman's eyes were a brilliant aquamarine, and at first, I thought I'd stumbled on a mermaid out of water.

"She was a witc—a mage," I instantly correct myself.

Her magic had a pungent smell, like rubbing alcohol and dead flowers, but she was so nice it didn't matter so much, because I was instantly addicted to talking to her.

"When I asked her why she was out in the Alaskan wilderness, she said she was looking for someone she lost. While she helped me carry the wood back to my pack, she asked about my studies. We homeschool in the pack, and I was very much into. . . " I pause, feeling stupid before I even said it. "Classic literature. It was part of our English studies, but for a wolf like me, it wasn't considered an alpha quality. Even my mother would take my books away and shove me outside to go hunting. Then this woman pulled a book out from her coat and gave it to me right there. She said it was one of her favorites." I swallow over the lump in my throat.

"She wanted me to lead her back to my pack. I warned her they didn't like outsiders, but she was certain they would help her find who she was missing. I left her at the center of our settlement to unload the wood at the back of our cabin. Then I heard the screaming and roars. I ran back to find the alpha towering over the woman, about to deliver a killing blow." I still remember the defiance in those aqua eyes as she waited for the death strike. "Before I knew it, I jumped in the way and took the alpha's hit."

My fingers drift up to the raised scars, the constant reminder of how I betrayed my own for a woman. "He pulled back just enough to not kill me. Even bleeding and unable to see out of one eye, I got back up and told the alpha he couldn't kill the woman. Already angry, he became incensed, screaming that I chose a human over my own kind. Then the book she gave me fell out of my coat. I said she was kind, but that only made things worse. He ripped the hardcover volume in two pieces. It took years for me to find that book again and finally read it. The alpha proclaimed I'd committed the ultimate betrayal and I clearly didn't respect the pack or how things are done. Then he ordered me out of the way so he could kill the woman."

"No one stopped him?"

I remember the other Weres gathered around us, observing the scene. None of them stood up for the woman or for me.

"My own mother watched this all happen and did nothing." The pain of that hurts more than I can admit.

"What about your father?" Red asks.

A twisted little half smile plays at the corner of my lips. "The alpha was also my father."

A small gasp of horror escapes her.

"I lunged at him, ready to fight for her life still. I was too young, too weak, and he took me out in no time. When he was done, he left me bruised and bleeding on the frosted pine needles. I could do nothing as I watched him stalk over to the woman and strike her down in one blow." Bile rose in my throat. I still remember the last look she gave me. A mix of gratitude and apology, that tore at me to this day. "It was the last thing I saw before I passed out from the pain and blood loss. When I woke, I'd been thrown over the edge of the border of the pack's territory. They even left a dead rabb—" I stop myself to eye the two rabbits cuddled under the coffee table. "a dead animal for me to eat, in a mock attempt to provide for me. It was a death sentence, and they knew it."

"How did you survive then?" Red asks, licking her lips before drinking greedily from the bottle.

"I could hunt and fend for myself in the absence of a pack connection, but I was wasting away. I traveled South, closer to the towns of man. Finally, I crossed paths with another hunter, a werewolf. But he had no pack. I was near death, and he took me in. Showed me how to survive, like he had."

"Sounds like a better dad than your real one," Red mutters.

"No," I snap. "To survive as a lone wolf, one must avoid all connections. He wasn't my family or even my friend, he simply taught me how to survive."

"Sounds like something someone would do from the kindness of their heart, otherwise why do it?"

We were coming far too close to the reason I was here, but now that I'd opened the floodgates I couldn't stop. "It was an exchange. My survival in exchange for a favor he would call in one day. It has hung over my head for years, my last tie, and as soon as it's resolved, I can go back to being truly free."

"Freedom without friends or family," she says in a low voice. "Doesn't sound like a great time."

I sweep a hand to the apartment. "I do okay on my own."

A frown tugs at her lips as if she is lost deep in thought. Finally, she asks. "Is it dumb to still want to be part of that world? To belong to where you came from?"

"Yes."

Her head snaps up.

"Dumb, meaning it's illogical. Those situations were hostile and had either of us stayed, we probably would have died. But the bond of a pack, the need to belong, it's a biological imperative. Instinctually, we want to belong, we want others to agree with us, to like what we like, because that means we are working as a unit and will likely survive. And in my case, it literally meant death without it. But what I've learned is sometimes the harder path, the lonelier path, gets us where we need to be."

"Is that why you took the security for Dame Kiki? Because her situation was like yours."

I hadn't analyzed why I'd accepted that job. Lord knew I went to her and paid for healing magic many times since then, which was invaluable. But in the beginning, yes, it was likely that. "When Kiki is out of drag, he goes by Robert. His family rejected him for his lifestyle choices and when I met him, he was on the verge of becoming what he is today. Then, he'd been a sad faced young man who had this other side that would flare out like the rays of a sun. Some part of me couldn't stand to see that extinguished. I knew once Robert got on his feet, he'd be able to stomp any threat back down on his own. Robert, Kiki, just needed a chance."

"What happened with the family?"

"I intercepted some hired guns. The family wanted to take care of their *problem* quietly so as not to bring shame to their family name and reputation. After the third attempt, I paid them a visit and convinced them it was better to leave Robert, Kiki, be. If they didn't, I would pay a second house call. They were not keen on that." I knew my smile was vicious, but I relished their fear. I struggle to abide magic beings, but the bigoted ones absolutely disgust me.

"And does the past, the original place we come from, do we ever stop mourning it?"

My tongue pushes against the inside of my cheek as I consider that. "No. Or at least, I haven't gotten there yet."

She nods.

A tiny nudge at my ankle draws my attention. It's Bangs. Bombs is still loafed in a lazy pose. The cinnamon girl stands up before setting her front feet down to nudge my ankle again.

"She wants you to pet her," Red explains.

The rabbit springs onto my lap before I can respond. I'm so surprised, my claws emerge by instinct on the chair arms. Mindfully, I retract them as the bunny twitches her nose in my face.

I run a thumb along her face and she instantly calms, settling in my lap.

Fucking ridiculous.

"What was the book?"

"What?" I ask, entranced by the soft nose pushing up into my hand.

"The book the woman gave you, what was it?"

I don't answer.

"Brexley?"

"Pride and Prejudice."

She chokes on her water, violently coughing.

I level a glare at her and continue to pet the rabbit.

"You got a problem, Red?" I dare her to say, realizing how utterly ridiculous I look on every count now.

"No, no, not at all. Wait, did you read it?"

"Yes, I did," I say, shooting her an imperious look while still petting the rabbit in my lap. "It's one of my favorites. You got a problem with that?"

Her expression turns serious as a heart attack. "I would never book-shame someone."

She's saved by the bell, literally, the doorbell. I ordered a fleet of bacon cheeseburgers from an app, the moment Kiki commanded it. Red devours two burgers and an order of large fries before she even starts to slow down.

Halfway through her third burger, Red pauses to say, "I'm glad you learned to survive on your own, but I'm sad you have to. Making a new family at the Poison Apple, it's helped. It's healed wounds in me. At first, I told myself I wanted nothing to do with my old life, but it only became true when I made a new one, with friends who care about me."

I don't respond, and it's not long before Red passes out on the couch. At some point, Bombs wondered where his wifebun went and joined her. I doze off, petting the two rabbits nestled in my lap.

For a moment, I entertain Red's idea–the idea of belonging, companionship. But the pain of losing all that is too sharp. The pain is literally etched in my face. I can't forget, and therefore I'll never risk it.

I promised I would kill Grandma so I could get back to my reclusive life.

But as I watch Red lightly snore, and the two rabbits cuddle in my lap, I realize I can't do it. Hurting Red would be like gnawing off my own arm. Despite my best efforts to keep her at bay, I care too much about her.

If that makes me a dead wolf, then so be it.

CHAPTER 37

MATED AND SATED

RED

I wake up before Brexley, who is still asleep in the chair next to the couch. My rabbit babies have returned to their pen where they are snuggled up next to their litter box. Feeling out of sorts, I take to the stairs and head to the master bath for a shower.

Unlike my dinky bathroom, I have no problem washing the soap out of my hair here. The powerful shower head helps me emerge clean and refreshed. And I don't hate that the scent of Brexley's soap clings to my skin.

There is a knock at the bedroom door as I rifle through a drawer of clothes, trying to find a pair of pants I can roll down at the waist to wear. I have some money put aside for emergencies, and I know my friends are happy to lend me clothes as well. But I really need to go shopping soon.

"Come in," I say, and Brexley enters.

"You feeling okay?" he asks, even as his eyes rake over me. My hair is wet, and I've got one of his big fluffy white towels wrapped around my body.

"Yes, much better, thank you."

There is something soft around our interaction now. Usually there are barbs and spikes, but the edges between us are all smoothed over. I'm not sure if it's because I'm out of heat, the full moon has passed, or because we laid all of our most private pain out in the open.

"Do you," he stops to clear his throat, "need anything?"

"No," I say. We stand there for a moment longer.

"Okay then," he says, as the awkwardness intensifies. He turns to go, but then abruptly changes course and crosses until he stops in front of me.

His brows draw in a scowl as he rakes a hand through his hair. "Fuck, Red. Why do you have to be so—"

"So . . . what?" I prompt.

He doesn't say anything. Instead, he grasps my chin with one hand. Then he slides his lips along mine. The kiss is tender and deep, and it triggers all of my feelings at once. Unlike the violent frenzies we've given into before, there is no urgency, only deep, passionate feeling. My hands grip the knot holding up my towel.

When Brexley pulls back, I'm breathless. "I'm so what?"

Pressure builds in my chest. I'm hoping for something, so badly. But I'm not even sure what it is I'm hoping for. I only know we are on the cliff's edge of that hope coming true.

Suddenly it's as if I can see to the depths of his soul. I see every emotion in him and he lets me in.

I reach up to gently touch the scars that run down his face. He doesn't stop me or pull away. Tracing the flesh, I feel like the most important person in the world for getting to touch him like this. I'm touching his vulnerability, his pain, his past. He pushes it so far away yet keeps it so close.

Like me. The bubble of feeling in my chest threatens to burst.

Don't cry, you big ninny. You'll scare him off.

He says in a low voice. "You're so under my skin. I thought I could get you out, but I can't. When I leave you, it's painful. It's too painful." His eyes search mine, and I realize he's trying to tell me something.

"It hurts me too," I confess. I felt it. When he leaves, a pressure builds around my chest the longer he is gone. Then at the Poison Apple last night, I could suddenly breathe. I didn't know what gave me relief until I looked up and saw him standing there.

"Maybe, maybe we accidentally–"

"Mated," I finish for him.

His throat bobs up and down as he swallows. I've never seen him so vulnerable. "I tried to stop it."

"I think you were too late," I say quietly.

"I think so too," he agrees, then tunnels his fingers through my hair. He doesn't kiss me again, and I realize he's waiting. He's waiting for me to say something more, do something more.

And then I realize, I can't scare him off. He's seen me completely unhinged–possessed by lust, wild, and even violent at times. All the parts of myself I've been ashamed of for so long. But he never balked. Brexley only ever wants more of me and made it safe for me to allow my true nature.

No one else would understand, how could they? Hunter always wanted me to shove those parts of myself away. For him, I desperately worked to cram those parts of me inside, but it was like trying to punch oversized pillows in a tiny handbag. And the anxiety I felt at not being the "right way," left me a neurotic mess.

Something thickens in my throat. Brexley may say

harsh things, but his actions have spoken every word I ever longed to hear from Hunter.

I never really knew Hunter. He always kept himself at a distance, and no amount of pushing got me any closer. He was an idea I wove myself.

But Brexley is real. He did his best to push me away too. He's lashed out and caused me pain, and made me face painful truths. But where his words were sharp as knives at times, his actions were so much louder. Getting me my favorite table, being kind to my friends, helping me study, and fae lords, even the way he treats rabbits.

A werewolf taking care of my little house rabbits? It's ridiculous! Ridiculously adorable. Every time Bangs and Bombs run up to Brexley looking for attention and he reaches down and ruffles their ears, my ovaries are in danger of exploding like pop rocks.

As fucked up as it is, he also didn't need to help me with my near insatiable itch last night. But he stayed and pleasured me, gave me relief, repeatedly until I was satisfied. And then he made sure I got to my finals in as good of shape as possible. Because it matters to me.

The Big Bad Wolf cares for me.

So I drop the towel, leaving myself bared, not looking away from his eyes. I'm too scared to release the words lodged in my throat. It's too soon. It's been mere days, but my feelings are almost too big for my body. But I'm beginning to realize that's part of my wolf nature. If only I could shift into some animal and run off that energy the way Brexley does. But I suppose Brexley gives me other means of working off that excess.

So instead of saying the words, I take his hand and rest it on my bare chest, right over my heart. It pounds at the contact. If I can't bring myself to say the words, maybe he can decipher the message my heart is beating into his palm.

Brexley's pupils dilate even as his irises flash a white blue. "Why Red, what a big heart you have."

"All the better to love you with." The words slip out before I can think.

Holy fae lords, did I really just say that out loud? A shock of cold slams into my body as I realize how vulnerable I made myself, yet again. I seem to be unable to help myself when it comes to falling in love. No matter how scared I am, I can't help but love, hard, hopeless, and with abandon.

I'm not sure if I love or hate this about myself.

Brexley's fingers tighten in my hair, pulling me closer to him. Heat cuts through the cold fear gripping my body.

Searching my eyes in earnest, it's as if he is trying to find the lie. In his gaze, I see a scared little boy, one who is dying to love and be loved. He's been starving, and he's learned to live with the hunger like I have. But maybe we don't need to be skin and bones. Together we can be more.

"I think," he clears his throat a couple of times, "I think I love you, too." The words are gruff, and unsure. His hand presses harder against my chest. I'm not sure if it's to steady himself or press the meaning directly into my chest.

The bridge of my nose prickles intensely, the need to cry gripping me. And then just as fast, it disappears. I'm all over the place.

The tips of my fingers skim along his chest, and I run them up to cup his face. Then I rise on my tiptoes and slant my mouth over his.

Our moans entangle with each other as we succumb like never before.

He gently draws me in to press my naked body against him. His tongue pushes into my mouth, both filling me and making me feel empty between my legs. I can't help but notice how well we fit each other, as if made for one another. Warmth and love flows from my head to my toes like heated honey.

This time, this isn't a fight where one or both of us lashes out or tries to gain dominance. This is about acceptance of the scariest fucking thing ever. And we are holding onto each other for dear life as if we're afraid one of us is going to fall too hard and splinter into a million pieces.

He kisses me deeply, adamantly. I return it with everything I have in me, plastering myself against him. At the back of my mind I plead, *please don't destroy me. Please don't let me destroy myself on you.*

But it's too late to avoid that. This wolf has the power to decimate me, and he knows it.

Hunter is a bare speck of dust compared to the whole planet-sized presence of Brexley. The Were crushes me to him so tightly, I can barely breathe.

"Red, I need you." The way the words are ground out through his teeth, I can tell he wanted to use the 'L' word again. But it was scary enough the first time. He's letting me know I could destroy him too.

I kiss him fiercely, digging my nails into his shoulders, showing him I'm not going anywhere.

He picks me up, my legs naturally winding around his waist. My center slides against the thin material of his pants and the ridged bulge underneath. I bite his lip as heat shoots from my sex straight to my head, leaving me fevered.

Brexley walks us over to the bed. Laying me down, he makes quick work of his pants. Standing before me, naked, his erection proudly jutting from his unreal body, I still can't find my breath.

What if? What if I got to have this for real, for always? Isn't that what we're doing here?

Brexley traces the tip of his finger along my tattoo, tracing the lines and the wolf face.

Even though we confessed our feelings, fear grips me tight like a vindictive anaconda.

Brexley drops between my legs, giving me no time to prepare. He easily slips a finger inside me, and sucks on my clit sending white hot sparks blazing through me. I clutch at the sheets, my hips rolling as he eats me like a starving wolf. My desire jettisons up so fast, I'm dizzy from the speed.

In no time, I'm breaking on his tongue and fingers, my pleasure flooding Brexley. All too soon that pleasure grates as his speed doubles and he gives me more than I can take.

"Brex," I gasp and plead, yanking at his hair to get him to stop. I madly twist, trying to break free, but he uses his forearm to push down my lower belly and trap me.

It's too much, it's just too much.

He lifts his head, eyes glinting with power. "You can take it, pet." Grinning like the devil, his tongue dips into my navel, toying with the ring there.

I don't believe him, out of my mind to get away from the unique torture. He presses even harder on my lower stomach, pistoning his digits into me. I curve forward in a half-sit-up as my experience of the friction turns on a dime.

I gasp like a fish out of water when Brexley goes back to torturing my clit. He growls into it, sending sharp vibrations into my most sensitive parts. The second orgasm hits hard like an earthquake, leaving no part of me untouched. Tears leak out of my eyes. The pleasure is so intense I'm not sure if I want it to end or never stop as I ride it out.

Fuck, I love him. I love him so hard, my body threatens to fall apart.

When he finally releases me, I flop back on the bed, boneless and wrecked.

I continue to twitch with aftershocks, as Brexley kneels between my legs. Towering over me, he licks my desire from his covered fingers.

A shudder rips its way through me at the erotic image. Werewolf or sex god? Wait, why am I or-ing? He is definitely both.

"So sweet, little Red, I could eat you all up." He growls.

I don't have the voice to tell him that's exactly what he just did. Instead, I reach out to him. He's too far away, and the space makes me vulnerable. As soon as he covers me, I push his shoulder. Understanding my cue, he rolls until I'm on top. I'm half surprised I can sit up even as my thighs shake around him.

Touching the bandage around his arm, I silently ask about it. He unwinds it to show me his skin is healed now. I drop a kiss on the spot. He looks at me in amazement, his mouth parting. That's right, Big Bad, we can be rough *and* sweet.

Then I push back on my knees and envelop his hard cock in my hot mouth. I lick and suckle the velvety soft mushroom tip until Brexley's head falls back.

"Fuck, Red," he rasps, like he's praying. "I've been dreaming of fucking these perfect lips. Fae lords, it's even better than I imagined. I can't decide if I want to shoot it down your throat, on those perfect decorated tits, or inside your heavenly cunt.

I can't help my lips from curving around him.

He props up on his arms, to get a better view of me and I give him a show. I take him all the way to the back of my throat and moan. My hips grind on one of his hard, muscular thighs. I trace every vein and ridge with my tongue and lips, licking up the shaft like it's a dripping ice cream cone. The taste of his skin mixed with the tang of his precum makes me moan. Brexley hisses through his teeth, eyes glowing brightly.

"I'm going to fuck you so hard my pet, you won't be able to walk for a week."

My center throbs in anticipation. Oh fae lords, I want that so bad. I double my efforts sucking him hard and fast, while my own fingers sneak down to rub at my aching clit.

Brexley pushes me away and grips the base of his cock, eyes shut tight. "Fuck, fuck, fuck, no," he chants. "Not yet."

I lick my lips like a cat who ate the canary. I luxuriate in getting to run my hands along his hard muscles, to kiss and lick along the deep impressions along his hips and abdomen. Then unable to help myself, I bite into his hip, not holding back.

Mine.

He jerks hard and grabs my hair, yanking me away.

"I was helping," I say with a cheeky smile.

Brexley frowns at me, but I can tell he's not really angry.

"Come here." He picks me up as if I weigh nothing, and angles me over his cock. I slide down, letting him fill me nearly past my limits until I'm seated at the hilt.

Oh. Oh fae lords. It's so good, so satisfying, I could die. I mindlessly rock forward on him, needing more. I need all of him. All the time.

More than my body, something at the center of my very being feels sated and complete with him. Nothing has ever felt so right.

Our groans of pleasure surround us as heat and friction spark every feeling in me. Brexley lets me set the pace, but his eyes burn into me. As if they are silently swearing that if I ever try to run away, he'll hunt me down. His gaze is so possessive, it wraps around me, branding me and making me his. I try to return it with the same sentiment as best I can.

Perspiration coats our skin as I rock on him faster, grinding my clit on his pelvic bone. Reaching up, he pinches my nipple piercings, sending shoots of pleasure to my center.

Brexley stills my hips, forcing me to look at him. "You have to know I would never hurt you, right?"

"I know," I say, running my thumb along his cheek. I lean over and kiss him, rocking again.

It's so much more than release with him. It always has been. Brexley truly sees and accepts all of me, even the wild parts. And I do the same for him. The comfort it gives me is profound.

Brexley grabs my hips, his pelvis slamming up into me. The weightlessness of him holding me up combined with the barrage of power has me flying. My love for him powers my imminent orgasm with rocket fuel, and it's about to blast me directly to space. My inner muscles clench over and over, trying to keep him in my body, until they've worked into a frenzy, fluttering on the edge I'm scared to go over.

Oh fae lords, I'm going to come. My moans and gasps grow louder. I fear he's going to split me in two, but suddenly I welcome the prospect of him breaking me in this way.

"That's it, pet," he urges.

"Fuck Brex, I'm so close." I hold onto his shoulders for dear life as he pounds into me. My body fractures and my heart goes with it. A pain and pleasure so addictive, I never want it to stop.

"Look at me," he commands hoarsely, slowing as I rock jerkily on top of him. I do what he asks, working to keep my eyes open as my sighs and screams carry through the bone shattering release.

Then he comes with a loud groan, eyes fighting to stay open and on me. Heat floods my center, causing another shudder to rock me.

Brexley's right there with me, forcing me to surrender everything along with him. And I gladly do so.

"Fuck, you're gorgeous," he breathes, running a thumb along my lower lip.

To him, I'm not a freak, I'm not a broken, talentless nobody, living in the shadow of someone else. To Brexley, I'm everything and it causes a sob to catch in my chest.

I collapse on him where he envelopes me in strong arms. I've died and gone to heaven.

We stay that way for a while, with his softening cock inside me as he strokes my hair. Prickling starts at the backs of my eyes. I've felt alone for so long, deep at my core. I've kept even my friends at a distance, but Brexley takes all of me and the gift is beyond anything else.

"I love you," I murmur into his pecs.

"I love you." His words are muffled in my hair.

Considering all we've done, I can't help but laugh at our sudden shyness.

I don't have another final until tomorrow, and I'm prepared enough for that. So we spend the rest of the morning making love and taking time just to touch each other. Brexley only disappears to receive the massive food orders we send out for. Between my being on the brink of starvation and him being a hungry wolf, we plow through a scary amount of Chinese food.

At last, when afternoon comes, Brexley suggests we shower. I insist I need to check on the rabbits and then I'll join him. So I throw on one of his t-shirts and pad downstairs. After refreshing the rabbits's water and petting their heads, I catch sight of my cell phone on the counter. I grab and see there is a missed voicemail from Rap.

Maybe she needs to change the schedule for the night shift. That's usually why she calls.

I hit play and listen.

"Red, it's me. I don't know how to tell you this. But I did some digging on your boyfriend, and I thought you'd want to know. He goes by another name." her voice is hesitant as it is clipped and determined. "The Big Bad Wolf. He's a notorious assassin, Red. He's killed a lot of mages, even his share of humans and fae."

I reach down to pet Bangs soft ear. This is nothing I don't know. I don't think too hard on why it doesn't freak me out.

Rap goes on. "And Red, he's here on a mission. He's been tasked to kill your grandma."

My fingers pause on Bangs as I take that in.

"I can't betray my confidant, but I need you to trust me. Come to the Poison Apple right away, we'll work this out. I'll get the ward redone to keep him out. We'll keep you safe, I promise."

The message ends. I straighten and hold out my phone, staring at it.

It's silly. Totally wrong.

Why does my body feel so cold?

Have you heard from Gigi?

Do you know where she could be?

302

Is it normal for her to go this long without contacting you?

So many little nudges to tell him about her. I found Brexley in Gigi's bathroom, no one else around. Hunter didn't know who he was. Numbly, I walk upstairs.

This can't be right, but something in my gut tells me it is.

Brexley looks up, startled when I open the shower door. Then his face morphs into a seductive grin. "You going to get out of those clothes and join me or what?"

"You came here to kill Gigi?"

The expression on his face tells me everything in less than a second.

My world was on fire and turning to floating ash. Shame clogs my throat.

"Red, I—"

I don't let him finish, my brain races a mile a minute. "What was I then? Just some fuck toy to amuse you until you could find the most powerful mage and take her out?"

"Red, no, it's not like that. Or, it was in the beginning. But we're mated now. I could never--"

"Are you working for Hansel and Gretel?" I demand.

His face darkens and I know he isn't, but it changes so little, too little.

"Red, it's true, I needed you to get close to your grandma, but then you were attacked and the twins got in the way. It changed things. It changed me."

"Stop." I hold up a hand. "How do I know everything out of your mouth isn't a lie now? You tricked me, you used me, you want to kill my only family. I'm half surprised you didn't kill Bangs and Bombs, or were you saving that for last? The final bullet to riddle me with?"

Having said my peace, I retreat to the bedroom. I shuck on a pair of pants before rushing downstairs. The rabbits are already in a pet carrier. Some part of my brain knew what was going to happen.

"Red, listen to me," he says, following me down the stairs, still naked and wet.

"No, I can't. I won't. Stay the fuck away from me." I slip on my shoes.

A hand grabs my arm and he spins me around. Brexley's mouth crashes over mine. The heat and desire pulses there like a live entity. But it doesn't erase the ugly truth. I wrench myself free then slap him across the face. My palm stings from the contact, and his head remains poised to the side, a red mark across his cheek.

Before, our violence had been about being uninhibited, a game that led to sex. But this time, the act leaves me cold and stiff.

"If you come near me again, you'll wish you'd died when your pack banished you." I packed as much punch as I could in those words. The slight flutter of his eyelids let me know I hit my mark.

"Leave me and my family the fuck alone." Then I pick up the rabbits and leave. It's time to rely on the only people I can trust.

CHAPTER 38
CRYING OVER C**OO**KIES

RED

I call the girls to meet me at Poison Apple. The bar is the only safe place for me and the buns right now. When I get there, of course Rap is working in her office. She tells me the ward has been reset and to go lie down because I look like shit. She'll be out in a bit and we'll talk about a plan.

I set up Bangs and Bombs in a storeroom and head out front.

Making myself a double mocha from the espresso machine, I prepare myself to lay it all out there with Goldie and Cinder. It's time I told them everything. Brexley did nothing to deserve my trust while they have gone above and beyond.

I refuse to be like him. I'm not going to keep my walls up to make sure I stay alone and miserable.

Though it's hours until we even need to start prepping for our shift, first Goldie then Cinder come in and grab their own caffeine of choice, then join me on the lounge couches under the lighted tree.

"Bad day?" Cinder asks stiffly.

"The worst," I nod with a sniffle. "And no one can fix it. No one, except my best friends who deserve to know everything."

Goldie and Cinder exchange a look before crossing over to crowd in on the couch with me. Our legs intertwined, I tell them everything. About where I come from, who my grandma is, and about my time at FFA. About how I met Brexley and how I was terrified of letting my new life fall to pieces.

I bite back tears while the girls listen patiently. Then I share how Brexley figured out I was a hybrid when even I didn't know. I gloss over the chaining me up in a private room and making me orgasm within an inch of my life.

When I'm done catching them up, I say, "I'm sorry I didn't tell you all of this sooner. It's not that I didn't trust you, it was more I loved living this new life, as the new me. And if I let all this old bullshit in, it would destroy what I've become. And I really like who I am around you guys. I don't want to be the heir to Grandma's House, a magic dud, a powerless desperate hybrid. I just want to be Red. I want to get tattoos with you guys on weekends and do face masks while we watch shitty reality shows."

Brushing angrily at a tear that escapes my eye, I'm not even brave enough to look at them. Instead, I stare into my chocolate-stained mug.

A long pause ensues.

"Well," Goldie starts. "That is all . . . a lot. That's a fuck ton to absorb. And honestly—"

My body tightens. Here it comes. I brace myself against the anger and accusations.

"—I don't know how you've been dealing with this all on your own, you poor thing."

I let out a little breath, but Goldie was always the quickest to forgive. I chance a look at Cinder who has a completely unreadable expression.

"Now that you've told us everything," Cinder starts, "it makes perfect sense why you would keep all this to yourself."

"So, you don't hate me?" I say a little too hopefully.

Cinder rolls her eyes. "I could never hate you. The truth is, I've had some experience with mages and their bullshit. As much fun as watching those reality shows is, I know there is almost zero reality about them. And leaving everything you knew to start over must have been terrifying."

I shrug one shoulder. "Sort of, but it also felt so right. Moving and starting over gave me a sense of freedom I never had from under my grandma's shadow."

"Hey," Goldie says, nudging my shoulder with hers. "Fuck that. You've got your own power. You kick ass here every single night, you are a great friend, and the fact you can learn to trust us after all that is the true power. And so help me, if I see that dog again, I will set his tail on fire and shank him." She grinds her teeth. Brexley really pulled the wool over her eyes, and she won't take it lying down. I almost feel bad for him.

"Speaking of reinventing yourself," Cinder adds, "Have they posted grades for your finance exam?"

My heart leaps up to my throat. I'd forgotten all about it. "Yeah," I croak.

"Hey Red," Rap calls from the hallway leading to her office. She emerges a second later with a box. "Another package from your grandma came in."

My heart jumps even higher. I half expect Gigi to trail in behind Rap, but it's just my hope creating delusions.

I recognize the format of the box. So do Goldie and Cinder. Goldie shoots up like a rocket. "I got it. I'll take care of these," she says with a cheeky grin at Rap.

Rap raises a skeptical eyebrow. "If you keep getting those sent here, you are going to have to share with me one of these days," she warns before leaving us.

As soon as Rap leaves, Goldie turns and holds up the box. "Cookies!"

On my feet, I ask, "Is there a note? Maybe this is what everyone is looking for."

She rips it off and hands it to me. I'm desperate for any clue it can provide. And while it contains Gigi's usual message, there is an added line I don't understand. Then I take the box and rip it open. It's just a pile of delicious cookies. I grab a platter and empty the cookies onto it, checking the box for clues. Goldie pushes the cookies around to see if anything is among them.

"Nothing," she reports.

My shoulders slump as I drop back into my seat and set the box aside. I didn't find anything either.

"At least we still have cookies," Cinder gives me a weak smile.

Investigating one of the round, crumbly sweets, Goldie says, "How did I not see that these cookies are from the same baking genius who makes Magic Morsels?" Then she pushes them back into the original box.

"Because Magic Morsels taste like trash compared to the homemade cookies from the big G, herself," Cinder points out.

Goldie sits down next to us on the couch. "Does your grandma use magic to make these cookies?"

I shake my head, showing them the tag. "Nope, just love and lard."

Cinder leans over Goldie and takes the tag from me and reads the extra line. "And a little something extra."

"That's different, usually it's always love and lard," Goldie says.

Something extra. I have no idea what that means. It doesn't tip me off on where Gigi is, or what this is all about. But I can't wait to march up to Theodore Dunkin and cram this note down his gullet until he tells me where my Gigi is.

The *special package*. Suddenly it clicks in my head. The email my Gigi's assistant received. The twins intercepted it and thought it was her latest recipe, not the monthly stipend of homemade cookies. The recipe—love and lard. I'd delight in telling them what absolute idiots they are, but I'd prefer to never run into them for the rest of my life.

They are losing their minds over a run of the mill, monthly gift of cookies I get from my grandma. What a couple of absolute delusional cretins.

"Go on," Cinder nudges me.

I put down the note and pull up the University website on my phone. My finger hovers over the button. I don't want to see the grade. I don't want to risk feeling powerless and worthless. I've been jerked around too much the last week.

As if sensing my apprehension, Cinder says, "If you fail, you'll just try again. That is a strength most people need desperately, but won't give themselves."

I nod and swallow past the lump in my throat.

Goldie holds up three cookies like they are playing cards. "And no matter what, you'll have some chocolate chunk for celebration or solace."

Cinder and I take our respective cookies and I know

they are right. Everything will be okay, and I can't help but think of what Brexley said. They are my pack.

Pushing Brexley out of my mind, I hit the button.

"Oh," I say, registering the number on the screen.

"Oh, good? Or, oh, bad?" Goldie sounds like she might expire any second from the suspense.

Unable to speak, I hand the phone to Cinder.

"Ninety-two percent," she reads.

"I passed the class," I whisper.

There is a hush before the explosion of excitement. We are all on our feet and both girls hug me fiercely from either side.

"Fuck that other school. You are a total genius! They just didn't appreciate it," Goldie yells.

More quietly, Cinder says, "Well done."

Then we step back to cheers in the center with the cookies from my grandma. We each bite into the perfect blend of chocolate and sugary dough.

"Oh my fae lords, these are the best ones yet," Goldie moans. "How do they taste so fresh?"

I can't help but agree with her. I'm unsure if it's finally confiding in my friends, my passing grade, or the cookies, but I feel better than I ever have in my life. My body lightens and I feel like all the potential inside me has been unlocked and I might fly off the ground.

Cinder has chocolate smeared on her lips.

We laugh as I try to wipe it away. In no time, we devour the cookies.

"You sure your grandma doesn't put magic in these?" Goldie asks, her pupils dilating. "I feel supernaturally good."

I wave a hand. "She knows I hate that stuff and

wouldn't do that." Though I have to agree with Goldie, these are uncommonly good.

"Goldie," Cinder gasps.

"What?"

I turn to look at Goldie and gasp. "Uh, what the fuck?"

Goldie frowns. "What the fuck, what? Oh my fae, Cinder, you are glowing."

"I'm glowing? *You're* glowing," Cinder points.

A hot pink cloud of energy surrounds Goldie, while a dark purple one surrounds Cinder.

"I thought you said there was no magic in here?" Goldie said, then her eyes widen at me.

I look down to find a red and white energy misting from my skin. "Your eyes are going wolfy," Cinder points out.

A few moments later, the energy fades away. None of us move.

The building shakes with a boom. The tree limbs sway over us as the bottles on the display shiver so hard some of them slip and fall to the ground with a crashing shatter. A gust of cold wind sweeps through the bar, like someone has ripped a blanket away from over the building.

"What was that?" Cinder asks.

I'm not sure if she's talking about the colorful energies or the boom, but I don't have time to answer.

"It's time for the bullshit to end, and for you to give us what we want," Gretel announces, flanking Hansel on their way in.

CHAPTER 39
EATING THE SPECIAL COOKIES

RED

A girl from FFA I vaguely remember follows Hansel and Gretel in. The Indian girl is barely five feet tall and petite with bronze skin. She wears dark green leathers like Hansel and Gretel. She's the one who broke the wards. She wields kinetic energy like a cannonball, and that's why they can all waltz right in here. The boom was the ward breaking.

Panic crawls up my throat. The twins nearly killed me last time, and they would do the same to Cinder and Goldie, to put pressure on me, or just for fun.

"You guys need to run," I mutter to Cinder and Goldie without taking my eyes off Hansel and Gretel. "Go out the back."

"We aren't leaving you with these psychopaths," Goldie says.

"Not a chance," Cinder adds as they square up next to me.

Dumb, stupid, wonderful friends.

"We hear you received a package?" Hansel says, examining his cuticles but there is a new intensity around him. Losing to Brexley has put him on edge. "We'll take it now."

The cookies. The cookies that made us glow, they were different somehow. It's the package my grandma sent. They weren't normal.

"I ate the package," I say, leaving Goldie and Cinder out of this. "They are all gone, and the recipe was merely a love note from my Gigi." I extend my hands out. "There is nothing for you here."

The twins exchange a glance. "Oh dear." Hansel says as casually as if we are discussing dinner plans. "Then it looks like we will just have to cut you open and fish out what we need." His dark eyes glitter maliciously.

"Oh dear, no more wolfy to save you," Gretel says with a nasty grin.

A spike goes through my heart. Even though I tell myself I hate Brexley, he is the only one with the power to make me feel safe right now.

"I wouldn't be so sure about that," a male voice says from behind me.

Brexley saunters in from the rear entrance. He stops next to me. I'm a jumble of fear and feeling, but my heart soars to have Brexley near me again. I hate how right it feels to be with him, knowing what I know.

"We still need to talk," he insists to me in a low voice. Then he claps his hands and rubs them together. "Now, who wants to get their magic neutered?" he asks with dark promise.

Brexley lifts off his feet, until he is dangling in the air. He struggles, but continues to remain suspended. I reach for his hand, trying to tug him down to no avail. Panic grips my throat as I throw my entire body weight into it, and he doesn't budge.

That's when Hunter enters from behind Hansel and Gretel, hand outstretched in Brexley's direction.

Disbelief hits me like a high-speed train for the second time today. "Hunter, what the actual fuck?"

CHAPTER 40
HUNTER & THE WOLF

BREXLEY

"They hired me to keep the wolf away from them," Hunter says, still keeping me dangling in the air. Little prick. The second he lets me go, I'm going to tear a new hole for him to breathe out of.

The twins are back to grinning evilly. I intend to teach them a lesson as well. Nullify their powers and beat the unholy faefucks out of them. The stench in here is near unbearable.

"Hunter, what the hell are you doing?" Red demands.

"I'm protecting our way of life, Red."

"What the hell do you mean, *our* way of life? I don't understand."

His face contorts with barely repressed rage. "Your grandma is more interested in helping humans than her own kind."

I knew the boy didn't like me, but I didn't quite pick up on the fact he's bigoted against humans and fae.

"This recipe she wants to unleash into the world, it will unlock powers for humans, but what about me, I mean us?"

He stepped right into that one. Hunter's nasty side can't be contained anymore.

"So this is about you needing more power? Like them?" she gestures to Hansel and Gretel.

"For you, too," he urges. "Red, you have mage blood coursing through you, just like me. But we are imperfect, unexpressed. My father fired me from security because I'm a Level Two on the cusp of Level Three. He said I'm destined to spend my days working on a construction site, moving metal bars for minimum wage." Anger twists his face. Sweat droplets pop out on his forehead. He's having to work to keep a hold on me.

Red gasps. "Hunter, you are so much more than that. You are better than what he thinks."

It pains me to see her try and comfort him. Her caring side won't let him go on some level. Either he's too embedded in her past, or she is really that good of a person. Either way, it rankles me. Hunter doesn't deserve her consideration. He doesn't deserve to lick the mud off her boots.

Neither do you, a nasty voice inside me whispers.

At the far side of the bar, there's movement and a flash of banana yellow. Rap slowly creeps her way toward the twins. She may not have magic, but she wouldn't approach unless she intended to inflict some damage. Retraining my gaze on Hunter, the twins and the tiny energy mage, I make sure not to draw attention to the sneaking bar owner.

Hunter is still going on. "Oh, I will be. After Hansel and Gretel tweak the magic of your grandma's recipe, I'll be a Level Five. You could be too. It's the recipe for power."

I finally interrupt. "You really think the wonder twins

318

here are going to share power with you? They murdered their own grandma for leverage. They are going to toss you as soon as they get what they want. Like the garbage they know you are."

Hunter's face turns purple, and my body drops a few inches. A Level Two mage can't hold me forever. He's weakening the longer he holds me up. I'm counting the seconds.

Hansel takes over. "Well Red, looks like it's time you give us what we want."

"Or you become as hungry as we are," Gretel promises.

"How do you like this?" Rap says, popping up from behind them, and smashing a skillet to the back of Hansel's head.

The room explodes in activity.

Cinder and Goldie rush forward and attack the tiny energy mage, while Red goes straight for Gretel, kicking her in the stomach before she can do anything.

Hansel stumbles forward and Rap smacks him again with a resounding *Thwang*. The mage goes down like a ton of bricks.

Hunter loses his hold on me.

Red screams as Gretel unleashes her power.

I hit the ground running, tearing straight for the group of mages. The second I get in range I can nullify their magic and it will be quick work with them.

A loud groan precedes a nearby bar table dismantling. The metal bar rips right off the bottom of it. The steel bar flies across the room and slams into me. Red screams, and my vision goes black.

My body is numb at first, then pain begins to blossom from my torso. Blood fills my mouth with a cooper tang. Disoriented, I blink hard to get my eyes to open. It takes a minute to realize I'm pinned against the wall. The metal sticking out from my stomach is buried into the wall behind me. I swallow hard as I note my blood circling the bar. My feet are still on the ground, but I have to work to keep from sagging and causing myself more damage.

Hansel staggers to his feet, his hand stretched out as he unleashes it on Rap who is now grasping at her own throat.

The energy mage sends Cinder and Goldie back with a blow, and they crash into the ground.

Red's eyes meet mine through the chaos. My advanced healing is good, but it's not this good. Blood dribbles out of my mouth as I try to convey with my eyes all my regret and the love I hold for her.

I'm sorry, little Red.

"Looks like the Hunter did kill the Big Bad Wolf," Hunter gasps from where he clutches onto the bar counter-top. He's used too much of his power and it's drained him.

Red's face twists in anguish and tears drip down her cheeks. Then her eyes flash white, but this time it doesn't ebb. They grow brighter and brighter until she is nearly blinding. A scream rips its way out of her.

Her honey cinnamon scent intensifies far beyond its usual potency. It oddly helps me breathe a little easier.

Energy explodes from her, forming a massive white wolf's head. The magic avatar is a vicious visage that hovers over the room like a ghost, filling it with a terrifying power. A howl sweeps through the bar and everyone stumbles, staring up at Red's projection.

Red also looks up at it, but her eyes are unseeing. As I struggle to hold onto consciousness, I find myself both fearful and in awe of her.

The wolf face howls and surges up, then dives back down. It opens its massive jaws as it descends on Gretel. The spirit snaps its jaws, closing down around her body.

Gretel twists and contorts. It releases her and she drops to the ground, unmoving.

The scent of spoiled milk disappears.

"Gretel," Hansel cries out in anger. He trains his hand on Red, who has yet to move. Before he can unleash his magic, the wolf spirit whooshes over him, closing its massive jaws around Hansel. He screams and like his sister, he struggles against the avatar, falling to his knees. The layer of spoiled meat evaporates until there isn't even a whiff of it left, and I can breathe a little better.

Werewolves can nullify a mage's magic, but Red is devouring it. Gretel's magic is gone.

The avatar makes quick work of the energy mage who is left passed out on the ground. Then the wolf turns its attention to Hunter.

Hunter attempts to stumble away, headed toward the door, his face stricken with terror. The wolf dive bombs him, and Hunter hits the ground. The remnants of diesel lingering in the air fade away.

The wolf spirit withdraws back into Red. She blinks rapidly as if coming back into her body.

If it weren't for the crackling pop rock sensations in my lungs, I would smile. She's a Level Five mage. One of a handful in the world.

Red is suddenly at my side.

"Don't you leave me," Red says, holding my face. "If you do, I'll let Bangs and Bombs piddle all over your apartment."

"They love me too much to do that," I say before dissolving into a coughing fit. A weight presses on my chest until it's as heavy as an elephant. I fight to breathe against the pressure.

Red reaches into my pocket, pulling out my phone.

Frantic, she takes my hand and presses my finger on the screen to unlock it. She thinks she can save me. She always was ridiculous. Ridiculously kind, ridiculously smart, ridiculously beautiful.

"Red," I say, but end up coughing more.

"Shut up, Brexley. I'm trying to save your life," she says, still focused on my phone.

A chill spreads through my veins. I want her to touch me again. I'm so cold.

"I have to tell you something," I rasp.

"You can tell me later," she says, tears falling faster down her face.

"Red," I say, putting as much power as I can into it. Consciousness is a losing battle, and I don't have much time here.

Her head snaps up. I finally have her attention, so I attempt to smile, though I can feel blood coating my teeth.

"My, what big powers you have."

Then I succumb to the bliss of darkness.

CHAPTER 41

A FABULOUS WAKEUP CALL

BREXLEY

"Bibbidy bobbidy bup, wake up little pup."

I wave off Kiki's voice which is right in my ear. "Five more minutes."

Then I feel the pressure of someone's body on mine. "Oh, thank the fae lords," I hear Red say.

That gets me up. I blink hard until my eyes fully open. My arms automatically fold around Red's body and I hold her to me.

"Is this heaven?" I ask. I'm laid out on the couch in my apartment. My shirt is gone, but there are remnants of blood on my torso.

Dame Kiki responds. "The both of us are angels, so I can see why you would think that."

She is dressed in a hot pink glitter bomb of a dress with matching makeup. She wears a platinum blonde wig and smiles at me kindly.

"I called Kiki and Tom and both came at once," Red explains.

"I'm grateful." She waves me off with her boa while dabbing at a tear with her other hand. I'd have to thank Tom later. "I'll find a way to repay you," I tell Kiki.

She purses her lips and pops an eyebrow. "This time I'll take my repayment in friendship, if you don't mind."

It means I'd be in debt to her, tied to her always. But not in a bad way, a manner that goes both ways in reciprocity without keeping score. I nod, my throat suddenly too tight to speak.

Her glitter lined eyes widen a little as she breaks into a massive smile. Then she covers up her reaction. "Good boy."

I can't help the chuckle that escapes me.

"Well, I'll let you two recover, but as soon as you can I expect you to come visit me at the Pumpkin Coach Club."

Red gets up and goes to give Kiki a hug. "You can count on it." She walks Kiki to the door and lets her out before returning to sit at my hip.

"How are you feeling?" Red asks, anxiously searching my face.

"Hungry," I say, letting my hot gaze travel down her body. She's wearing my clothes and is a rumpled mess with circles under her eyes. I could eat her right up, anyway, anywhere.

She gives me a light smack on the chest.

Admittedly, I could use another long nap and there is a soreness in my torso. My fingers trail to my stomach where I find flushed, freshly knitted skin where there was once a hole.

"Where is Hunter?" I growl. I have some mages to take apart.

"He's been taken into custody along with Hansel, Gretel, and Nala, the energy mage."

"I'm going to fucking kill them," I promise.

Red looks down at her hands in her lap. "I don't think that will be necessary. After devouring their magic, they're in agony. They keep describing it as a fate worse than death, like being stripped of their senses."

"That's my girl," I say with no small amount of pride.

"Rap, Goldie, and Cinder are still with the authorities so I could take care of you." Then I sense a hesitancy come over her.

"Do I smell bad to you now?" Red asks, lines drawn between her brows.

"Yes." I confirm and her face falls. "You are even more fucking intoxicating. Better than a donut shop that's been dipped in caramel and cinnamon." It's true. She already was a delectable little morsel.

A grin breaks across her face. I reach out and pull her to me so I can press my lips to hers. I can't help but sigh against her mouth, feeling like I'm home.

There's a knock at the door.

I pull back enough to say in a low voice, "I believe that's for you."

I don't need my sense of smell to know who's already at the door.

Red frowns before going and opening the door. "Gigi! Wait, who the hell are you? Get that knife away from my grandma!"

Something clatters to the ground.

I have to work to hoist myself up. I limp my way toward the door, still feeling like my stomach is on fire.

Gripping the kitchen island, I see Jameson fill the doorway. His wide, muscled frame and deep scowl might as well be a dark cloud, threatening to snuff out the little old lady currently in his crosshairs. His salt and pepper hair is as rumpled as the

325

plaid shirt and jeans he wears. As if he'd spent the last forty-eight hours traveling straight from Washington state to Boston. I'd no doubt that's exactly what the old bastard had done. He got impatient and thought I couldn't finish the job.

All the better for what was coming next. Which is exactly why I gave him my address when I realized he was on his way.

Red hugs her grandma protectively. The infamous matriarch from Grandma's House meets my gaze. There is resignation in her eyes, as if she always knew this day would come but hoped it would be later.

That's right old biddy, the jig is up.

"Your timing is impeccable, old man, though I expected you later. Won't you both come in? I think you all have a lot of family matters to discuss."

Red's head bobs back and forth, not understanding. But she will soon.

"Red, this is the man who tasked me to kill your grandma, Jameson Sturgeon. Jameson, before you kill Eloise Rogers, I thought you would first like to meet your daughter."

"What are you talking about?" Red breathes.

Jameson has a face like a slapped ass, and I can't say I don't enjoy it.

"It's okay, Scarlett," Gigi reassures her, leading her inside.

Scarlett. Scarlett Rogers, nicknamed Red. No wonder I couldn't get the proper background on her. I didn't have the right damn name. I run a hand down my face. It's amazing how a detail like that can make it almost impossible to dig up what I need.

Something nudges my heel. Bombs is asking for attention. I reach down and pick up the gray fluff ball. He immediately starts licking my bare chest. "Missed you too, little thumper," I murmur before I head back to the couch with him.

Soon enough I'm reseated on the couch. Eloise assumes a chair across from me. Red and Jameson remain standing at opposite ends of the living room, both wearing identical stormy expressions. Red grips the back of a chair, as if it's the only thing holding her up.

Red's grandma wears a loose pant set in cream along with a sizable pearl necklace and matching earrings. Eloise Rogers's lips have thinned and wrinkled with age, but she has the same pale eyes as her granddaughter. This close I can also see a similar sprinkling of freckles mixed with age spots. Her short hair is perfectly styled, and the color is somewhere between platinum and white. The lady is elegant in every way. But she has gotten her hands dirty and it's time for her to wash them clean.

"I'm glad your security found you and passed along my message," I say to Eloise, scratching Bombs's ears where he sits in my lap. The cinnamon rabbit, Bangs has also joined us, pushing her head under my hand for attention too. Bombs begins to lick her face.

A wolf petting rabbits. Still ridiculous.

I can't help the smile tipping up the corner of my mouth.

"Where have you been?" Red asks her grandma. Betrayal shines from her eyes. "I thought something terrible happened to you."

The old woman shifts uncomfortably. "Mexico. Theo sent me."

From some digging, I knew she was talking about

Hunter's father. Theodore Dunkin, head of grandma's security.

"I've been working on something big, very important, and frankly dangerous."

Her gaze sweeps between us. "But I suppose you know all that now." She folds her hands in her lap and continues on. "Someone hacked our servers, and we knew the threat to my project was imminent. Ted insisted I was also in danger, took my phone, and ordered me to Mexico and said not to tell anyone. He was the only one who knew."

Theo has a shit son, but the guy knows how to secure an asset.

"I never imagined they would come after you, Scarlett," Eloise said in earnest, her eyes pleading with her grand-daughter. "Had I known, I would have been here. But you must know I did all of this for you. I saw how torn up you were over not being able to access your magic."

"You knew it was her werewolf side dampening her powers, didn't you?" I ask.

Eloise nods. "I figured it out eventually."

"Why didn't you tell me?" Red asks, her voice thick. "Why didn't you tell me I'm half werewolf?"

Eloise Rogers heaves a heavy sigh. "I didn't want you to die the way your mother did."

"She died in a car accident," Red says, but her voice wavers. She already knows it's a lie.

Jameson stalks forward a couple steps, intense concentration. "Tell us everything. You owe us that."

Eloise blinks back a sudden glittering in her eyes. "What would you like to know?"

CHAPTER 42
FAMILY REUNION

RED

"Why didn't Samantha tell me?" Jameson demands. "Why didn't she tell me I had a daughter?"

Emotion clogs my throat. I see the resemblance, but I still can't believe I'm in the same room as my father.

"Samantha, Sam, that's who you named your tavern after," Brexley comments from the couch.

Jameson doesn't answer, but his eyes soften. He named a tavern after my mother? Instantly, I want to see it.

Gigi settles back into the chair carefully, as if her bones are so fragile she's in danger of breaking. Her fingers clutch the arm, bracing herself. "It started when Samantha wanted to take a trip to Alaska. She always had a great interest in animals and wanted to see the grizzly bears in their habitat. There was a boat tour and she . . . "

"She fell overboard," Jameson finishes for her.

My grandma nods and waves her hand. "The tour guide

was an idiot and hit a patch of rocks, and the boat went down. Everyone was recovered except for my Samantha."

Jameson turns his attention to me. "I found her on the shore, half frozen and near death. I'd been out in my wolf form but changed, picked her up, and took her back to my pack. They agreed to help her, so we nursed her back to health. She was touch and go for the first several days, but I couldn't leave her side. Especially because many of the others didn't care for her. Not only was she an outsider, but she reeked of magic."

"That didn't bother you?" I ask.

Unnamed emotion fills Jameson's eyes, making them glitter with moisture. Maybe it's remorse, or nostalgia, or possibly love? "No, it didn't. Several years prior there had been a forest fire. To save some of our pups, I dove into the fire, but came out with a burned snout." He taps his nose. "After that, I couldn't smell a thing." His voice turns husky with the same emotion welling in his eyes. "My Samantha. When her eyes opened, the entire room lit up. She was sweet and kind, and she saw the good in everyone and everything."

A hard lump forms in my chest as he describes my mother. It's how I remember her, but I sometimes wondered if it wasn't just the fantasy of a child.

His eyes close as if he's searching the past. "She saw the good in me. We fell in love in a matter of days, no, hours." Then he walks over to the window and runs a hand over the window frame as if needing to find something to ground himself. "But the pack said she had to get gone as soon as she was well. But after two weeks together, I knew Samantha and I had done the impossible. We had mated. Something fae can't do with those outside their race."

Is that why I didn't mate with Hunter or anyone else when I was in what Brexley called the moon craze?

He continues on. "I went to the alpha and explained. She had to stay, I needed her."

"And they were okay with that?" I ask.

A humorless laugh escapes him, as he looks out the window. "He was livid, angry, and confused. The alpha threatened to kill her, but pack law forbids anyone from killing another's mate. Not to mention, they owed me a debt for saving the pups from the fire. There was nothing they could do. So she stayed. And despite the rumblings from some of the other pack members, I can easily say it was the best time of my life. We were happy in my little cabin. We took long walks in the mountains, went fishing. I cooked for her while she read books by the fireplace. She found every corner of my soul and cast her light on it. And I felt as if heaven had bestowed an angel upon me. It was pure bliss." The wood window frame creaks under his crushing grip. "And then she left."

Jameson whirls around and stalks toward Gigi who continues to sit, placid, in the chair. "I went after her. It took months of hunting, but then I found her, with you. I ended up on your doorstep, but you turned me away."

As if he can't bear to look at my Gigi any longer, he turns to me to explain. "The old witch, she tells me I can never go near her daughter ever again. When I refuse to leave, she offers me money. As if I could be bought. When I refuse again, she says that her daughter had to choose between me and her family, and she chose family. It was then I knew you were the one who kept her from seeing me."

Gigi's eyes close as if bracing against a phantom pain. Part of me wants to go to her, to comfort her. But I'm frozen to the spot. If I move, I might explode, unable to hold the torrent of information overwhelming me.

Jameson lets out a humorless laugh. "Your security detail was plenty thorough. No matter how many times I tried to break my way through, you wouldn't let me even see her. Not once." His voice grew hoarse with rage and grief. "Finally, I had to return to my pack. After being away for months, I barely made it back before dying. I needed my pack's connection to survive, especially after being rejected by my mate. I thought my heart couldn't break anymore, but I was wrong. When I returned, the alpha cast me out. He said I had betrayed our pack by leaving. That I made my choice when I chose a witch over my own pack."

Jameson scrubs a hand through thick dark hair, generously peppered with gray. "I thought I could have both my pack and my mate. I ended up alone. Banished from my pack, I began to waste away. Do you know what it's like for a wolf to go rogue? It feels like your soul has been ripped from your body, and all that is left is to lay down and die. But I have one thing to thank your grandmother for. My hatred for her stewed in my depths, keeping the embers of my will to live stoked enough to go on. She turned the woman I loved against me, and when I heard Samantha died, my hatred grew. With each passing year, I learned to live as a lone wolf, but my heart darkened with contempt for the woman smiling from every aisle of the market. I festered in my never-ending grief as I saw her face plastered across billboards."

Jameson's expression cools as his back straightens. "So, I called in my one favor. I'd held onto it for years, waiting until it was the right time. The pup I saved grew up to be one of the most effective assassins. It was the perfect opportunity, as if made by fate for me. So I sent the Big Bad Wolf to kill Grandma."

I swallow hard. This is too much to take in. At some point, I lowered myself into a chair. My legs can't hold up the weight of all this. Brexley is still petting my fur babies but watching me closely. His presence is reassuring and grounding, even as I reel into outer space like a spinning top.

"Gigi?" My voice is hoarse. This is only one piece of the story. And the other woman in the room likely has some of the missing pieces. Can I handle it? I have to. I have to know everything, even if it destroys me.

Gigi shuts her eyes, as if in pain. When they open again, an apology is deeply etched in her pale blue irises. I know whatever I'm about to hear, I won't like it.

"When Samantha returned home from Alaska after the accident," she starts slowly, "she told me all about you. About mating with a werewolf."

"And you couldn't stand it, could you?" Jameson yells. I flinch. He sees and regret crosses his face.

Gigi doesn't rise to the bait, instead her tone remains even. "She also told me she was pregnant. And that she had to leave to protect you for your own good."

All the color drains from Jameson's face. I watch him carefully. The shock for both of us rocks the earth beneath our feet. Again, I'm grateful I already decided to sit down.

My grandma turns to meet Jameson's gaze. "She loved you more than anything. And before she could tell you, your alpha cornered her. He scented that she was with child and was enraged. He called the baby an abomination and Samantha's presence a curse. But he said he still respected you, which is why he'd give her a choice. If she left, he wouldn't exile you."

"No," Jameson growls. "He wouldn't."

"Samantha seemed quite knowledgeable about what would happen to you if you were cast out. Heartbreak and certain death, is what she said."

"She would have told me," Jameson protests, despite the evidence of my presence.

"If she told you, you would have fought your alpha and likely died. If she stayed, you both would have been cast out and she would have had to watch you die as your baby grew inside her. My sweet Samantha, she couldn't bear the thought of you wasting away, knowing it was her fault."

Gigi reaches up to fiddle with her pearls. "Then you showed up," a small smirk pulled at her lips. "You were a determined bastard, I'll give you that. I even vouched for you. I told Samantha we could find a way to keep you alive. She wouldn't hear of it. A wolf without his pack will die. That is what we knew with certainty. So, I sent you away again and again. I too watched the fatigue and distance from your pack wear on you. You seemed to fade away before my very eyes. Though I wanted my daughter to speak to you, I knew she was right. If you knew she was pregnant, you'd never leave. If you stayed, she would have to watch you die. But then you finally left."

"That's ridiculous," Jameson snarls. "If they had exiled me with Samantha, we would have been fine. Samantha and the baby would be my new pack."

Grandma shakes her head slowly. "She didn't know that. Not until years later."

I realize I'm clutching my chest. My heart shatters into pieces. For my mother who desperately tried to save the love of her life. For my grandmother who tried to protect her child, and for Jameson who was left alone and confused. So much love and so much pain existing in one story.

Gigi pushes her way out of the chair and walks to stand by Jameson. He's a full foot and a half taller than her. Next to him, Gigi is a tiny, fragile bird. My breath catches in my throat as I fear he will claw her face right off. She reaches out and touches his arm. "She never stopped loving you. Not for one single moment. But it wasn't until years later that she found the solution. It had been so simple, but so little is documented about Weres . . . but she discovered that with a new family you could form a pack. She told me she couldn't keep your child from you any longer, and that she was going to get you back. Samantha was going to fight the alpha for you if need be. I tried to get her to take some of my people with her, but she was adamant she wouldn't be able to get near the pack if she didn't go alone."

He straightens in alarm. "I had already left. They wouldn't know where I'd gone."

"She went and never came back." Tears freely flow down Grandma's face now. "I knew when I didn't hear back after a week, she was gone. And it was just me and you, darling." She turns to me, and I realize I'm holding my arms tightly, tears streaming down my face too.

I have to push my words out through the lump in my throat. "You told me it was a car crash."

"It was meant to keep you from following her footsteps. To keep you from following her to Alaska in search of your father. I was terrified. So, I tied up the loose ends and told you that she died in a car accident and your father was a human who left before you were born."

I hate her lies, but I understand her logic. Would I have left home to find my father? After feeling like such an outcast in my own world, I likely would have tried to seek out my biological father.

"I hated you too," Gigi says, turning back to Jameson. "I wondered if maybe it wasn't you who killed her. One way or another you took her from me, but I had Red to think about. And I couldn't live in hatred if I wanted to raise this sweet little girl. I had to turn to love. And when the bitterness threatens to blacken my soul, I throw myself into work. And somehow, I drove my granddaughter away too."

"Oh Gigi, no," I say, running to her and throwing my arms around her. I fight the soft sobs to say. "It's not you. It's never been you. There were so many other things. The academy, Hunter, and I was so ashamed of not having magic. I was sure you were too."

Since meeting Brexley, I've come to realize that her shadow wasn't too big. I simply made myself small. But having the permission to be myself fills me, makes me bigger than I could have imagined. I knew striking out on my own path could help me find my way, but part of me knows I'm strong enough to be myself anywhere now. Even if that is in the background of Gigi's awesome empire. As long as I love me, all of me, no matter how emotional, or needy, or neurotic, I can be larger than life.

Gigi pulls back so she can run her soft, crepe paper thin hands over my face, smoothing my hair back. "Oh darling, I never cared about that. You have always been perfect to me. I knew I didn't make an easy life for us, with so much attention and fame. But my work has never been about money or acclaim. It has always been about holding onto the thing that kept me alive after Samantha passed. But by choosing work, I turned away from what mattered most. You've always been here, and I should have held on tighter to you." Her delicate arms wrap around me to prove her point.

"Sam could still be alive," Jameson muses, hope sparking in his eye.

"If she was, she would have come home to us," my grandma grips my shoulders.

"She's right," I say. "My mother . . . she didn't make it. The alpha killed her."

Jameson raises an eyebrow. "How would you know that?"

It all makes sense now. When did Brexley put it together?

"Because Brexley was exiled, like you."

"Yeah, so? What does this have to do with him?" Jameson shoots a skeptical glance at the werewolf covered in rabbits.

I step out of Gigi's arms. "You never asked him? Asked him why he was cut off and kicked out?"

Jameson shakes his head. "Lone wolves don't ask questions. It was one of the first things I taught the kid. Asking questions is a gateway to connections. You can't survive as a lone wolf with any kind of connection."

I want to tell him he sounds like an insensitive bastard, but I push down the feeling. He did what he had to do. But my dislike of his callousness, and my instant need to be loved by him are jerking me all over the place. "Brexley was nine when a woman showed up to his pack. She had hair like mine." How could I have not seen it before? But I knew so little, it was impossible to put it together until now. "He didn't know why she was there, but he knew the alpha was about to attack her. Brexley was just a kid and he knew it was wrong to attack an unarmed woman. He jumped in the middle and tried to save her. The alpha beat him to a pulp, slashed his face and killed my mother anyway. Then Brexley was cast out for disobedience. His own mother didn't even try to fight for him."

Jameson sits down this time, as if numb. Gigi braces herself against the chair she was in. It's one thing to guess for years, it's another to know for certain.

Jameson studies Brexley a moment before his dark eyes widen. He tugs on his beard, and I wonder if that's what he does when he's nervous. I know absolutely nothing about my father and I instantly crave to know everything. Where does he live, what does he do, what's his favorite food?

"You're Rafael's son. I remember you," Jameson says, "You were so tiny when I left."

"The runt of the pack. For what it's worth, I don't remember you either, old man." Brexley confirms, seeming to be more at peace with all the revelations. But I guess he's had the most time of any of us to process.

The room falls silent as we all share a grief so profound, so entwined. So much confusion and pain clogged the past and now that it's clear, the anguish pours through like a rushing river.

"How did you figure it out?" I ask Brexley. He's the one who brought us all here.

"In pieces," he confesses. "I have some contacts who were trying to help me find out more about your grandma so I could track her down. Little bits here and there, but when I discovered you were half wolf, so much more made sense. Even if I didn't want it to."

Jameson stands again, his face a blank mask as he turns his attention to me. "I would have done anything for your mother. I would have . . . I would do anything for my daughter." His voice cracks as he addresses me. "Maybe that's the real reason I've stayed alive all these years. I knew my pack was out there." Despite his words, he looks unsure, as if preparing for me to reject him.

"I would like us to be a pack. All of us," I say, gesturing to my grandma. I can't very well have my father trying to kill my grandmother. Her eyes are shiny with tears still, but there is a softness in her face, as if she is experiencing some kind of relief.

"I'd like that too," he says.

Then I fly at him, throwing my arms around him in a big hug. Large arms close around me, and I feel wetness atop my head.

I have no idea what the future holds, but I know I won't have to go it alone.

I catch Brexley's smug smile from where he still sits on the couch. He is pleased with himself. Normally, I'd try to bring him down a notch or two, but right now, I owe him everything. And I don't mind that.

CHAPTER 43
MY, WHAT BIG LOVE YOU HAVE

RED

The door no sooner closes behind Jameson and Gigi, when Brexley turns and says, "I understand if you hate me, but I wasn't lying when I said I love you. I was willing to die to protect you from Hansel, Gretel, and that dickweed, Hunter. Or anyone else who even looks in your direction wrong. Admittedly, it didn't start out like that, but I can't help but love you."

I don't answer right away, and his face contorts in pain. "Please, Red, say something."

Closing the distance between us, I run my hands up his chest. "My, what a big apology you have."

A wolfish grin curves his mouth before he pulls me to him in a kiss that makes my toes tingle.

"What were you talking to Jameson about?" I ask, having watched an array of emotions cross Brexley's face when they adjourned in a corner.

"I asked him about the mechanics of mating."

"A bit late in life to ask about the birds and the bees

isn't it?" Okay, that might have been too much of a touchy subject.

Brexley gives me a dirty look but doesn't seem truly offended.

My fingers slide up and down the back of his neck. "What did he say?" I ask, truly wanting to know.

"He said I was correct that Weres joining under a full moon will most certainly do the trick. Most in the pack mate as young as sixteen, and the need to mate does get worse the longer you wait."

"But we didn't . . . "

"When Weres meet they can mate at any time. And you heard him, it's practically unheard of to mate with someone outside of that. Him mating with your mother was against all odds."

That was the reason I didn't mate with Hunter or anyone else during my periods of heat. Thank the fae lords for that.

Brexley continues, "He said when it happens there is this sense of coming home. And if I'm being honest, little Red, I think I felt that the first time I met you. Somewhere between caging you against that window and fighting off that ice mage."

"You mean when you were balls deep?" I chirp.

He growls. "I'm trying to be romantic, but yes, I also felt it when I was balls deep in that sweet little pussy." His head dips so his lips can latch onto my neck. Goosebumps rise along my neck and arms as he applies just the right amount of suction to get my engine going.

"Am I doomed to repeat this cycle of heat every month still?" I ask, trying to fight closing my eyes and giving into him. I still have more questions.

He pulls back and shakes his head. "The only one who will be heating you up from here on out is me."

I suppress my smile, not willing to reward his pun.

"But no, it's done its job, hitching you to me." He cups my face and gives me a positively devilish grin. "You poor little dear."

I surge up on my toes and kiss him to soften him for my next question. "So if I ever try to leave you, I'll die?"

Brexley's expression turns somber. "I would die without you." A flicker of fear shows in his eyes. It's the thing he's been running away from his whole life, and now he's fallen into the most vulnerable position with me. I don't take it lightly.

"What are the limits of that? If I try to leave the state to visit my grandma on a plane, I'll drop dead after so much distance from you?"

Some of his anxiety eases. "No, but it will be painful to be separated, at least for a little while. After a time, we can separate for longer periods of time and longer distances."

I did recall my father – how weird is that to say – left his pack for a while to seek out my mother.

"But what does that mean?"

"It means," he picks me up so fast I squeal. "You must be in my bed every night. It means, if you feel like taking a trip, I will likely tag along. But if you recall, I have my own life. I won't impose."

"You plan to stay an assassin," I say, not sure how I feel about that.

Brexley ascends the stairs. "Baby, you knew I was bad."

My fingers curl around his shoulders.

"But maybe I opt for more security jobs than wetwork. If I need to stay close to you, tied to geography, I don't want to scorch the ground I walk on anyway."

Brexley deposits me on the bed before covering me with his body. He nuzzles my neck.

"Aren't you still healing?" I ask, my breath quickening as his fingers make their way down my body.

He only responds with a hum, as he tugs my pants over my rear.

"My, what a big sexual appetite you have."

He tugs at the hair at the base of my skull, forcing my back to arch some. Looking into my eyes, his irises glow. "All the better to eat you with, my dear."

Then he snakes down my body and shows me exactly how bottomless his hunger is for me.

EPILOGUE

BREXLEY

"It's a Hobbit hole."

"It is not a Hobbit hole," I argue.

Granted my west coast cabin has an overabundance of wood beams and possesses a lot of stonework to create a rustic, cozy feel. But the doors aren't round, which any bookworm would know is a defining feature of any hobbit hole. Also, I'd rather eat my own tongue than admit I designed my favorite home from Tolkien's framework.

Red juts out her chin. "It is, and as long as we are here, we need to make sure we have second breakfast every single day."

"And it should be accompanied by champagne and orange juice," Goldie chimes in, returning from the room she set her bags in.

After the spring semester concluded, Red insisted she get to see my primary home in Washington State. It's also only an hour drive to Jameson's tavern, so she can visit the bar named after her mother and spend more time with her father. Our relationship is still gruff, but I feel we finally allowed the natural progression that we halted all those years ago. It's like having a father for the first time, since my own was such a massive alphahole. I have no desire to ever see him again.

The physical distance between Red and her father hasn't been as much of a confining or painful factor, and I wonder if that has either to do with the fact that he has been on his own for so long, or perhaps because she is only half werewolf. Either way, I haven't been willing to risk the extra space, but Red doesn't seem to mind. We've happily cohabitated in my condo. We even use Tom to get around. He's a good kid and enjoys having us as regulars. And especially loves when Red's hot friends come along for the ride.

This home is the heart of me, and while we are finding a place to live closer to Boston University so Red can finish her degree, I refuse to give this place up.

Well, that's not entirely true. My heart belongs to the girl rifling through my things. Red is in the sitting room, going through my near bursting bookshelf by the stone fireplace.

"Brunch, we're describing brunch, right?" Cinder asks, having emerged from her room as well.

I scrub a hand over my face.

Gigi – who insists I call her that – claps her hands together. "Perfect, I'll make scones."

Cinder and Goldie look at each other like they've hit the jackpot, and I can't deny that my mouth is already watering at the prospect of eating her food.

"Any news on that miracle cookie you created?" I ask Gigi, referring to the very recipe that unleashed Red's magic potential. Red refused to return to FFA to train, but promised never to use her magic again. A lot of mages let out a collective sigh of relief when they discovered all she desires is to work in finance.

Gigi's mouth quirks to the side. "The FDA rejected it. They said the product is too volatile."

I knew better than to agree, but unlocking powers in humans could result in a sharp tumble into chaos.

"The FDA is nothing but a bunch of Nazis," Gigi mutters while opening a window. The fresh spring breeze sweeps in through the room. I appreciate it, since her magic scent still slightly nauseates me.

Gigi is a woman possessed when presented with a problem or challenge. She swears she will concoct a recipe that will help my senses because she can't abide the idea that she smells bad.

"Any new developments on what powers you've manifested?" I ask Goldie and Cinder.

If you told me six months ago my pack consisted of three girls, an old woman, and Jameson, I would have died laughing. But the truth is, I feel at home being near them as well. I am invested in their happiness, and they are invested in mine.

Both girls frown. "Nope," Goldie says popping her 'p.'

"But we'll likely find out," Cinder says, her violet eyes flashing with intrigue. There is a lot under the surface of her quiet demeanor, and I still haven't quite figured it out.

Both Goldie and Cinder occasionally glow or say they feel strange, but nothing concretely magical has manifested . . . yet. They are considering attending FFA in the fall, to help them with whatever powers Gigi unlocked in them.

I told them I don't recommend it.

"Aha!" Red cries out in triumph, holding a massive leather-bound volume. "You love the Hobbit. Look at this special edition. There are two more like it down here."

I cross the room and pluck the book from her grasp before setting it back on the shelf. Then I throw her over my shoulder. She lets out a surprised yip as I give her behind a sound slap. Bombs and Bangs have snuggled down in their makeshift pen in the corner, having been fed a metric ton of treats for enduring the plane ride so well.

Rabbits riding in a private jet, ridiculous.

"What do you say Gigi, want to get a piercing or tattoo with us when we go to Portland?" Goldie says. They've been working on her for a while.

Cinder grins. "I know the guy who runs the parlor."

"Yes," Gigi taps her lower lip thoughtfully, her pearl bracelet falling down her wrist. "I can't decide between a cookie with a bite out of it, or maybe Scarlett and Samantha's names?"

Cinder's grin turns positively feral. "We can get my guy to make a design that incorporates all three."

Gigi's eyes light up.

"Are we going to take a walk down by the ocean or what?" I prompt, still not having let Red down. She is currently poking my butt, hoping to annoy me. Little minx.

The women immediately get in line, grabbing their jackets, ready to enjoy the staggering views my remote abode offers. Before I turn, my eyes catch on the copy of *Pride and Prejudice*.

Red must have snuck it here in her suitcase. She knows I like to keep it close by. My heart squeezes.

Red gave it to me at Christmas. She got it from Gigi's house, and it had belonged to her mother. So while I lost my copy to the alphahole that is my father, I got the piece of her back. It mattered more than ever. I tried to tell Red it's not because I'm a sap, it's because I've got wolf level loyalty. The truth may lie somewhere between.

I'd spent a fair amount of time regretting ever helping the woman who got me banished from my family. But now, I see how the pack I have now is a million times better. I send up a quick thank you to wherever Samantha is and duck out the—albeit, *slightly* circular–doorway with Red still over my shoulder. The ring digging in my pocket will be sealed with the promise of her happily ever after–finance degree, rabbits, friends, family and all.

Want to read about the lost girls night at the Pumpkin Coach Club with Dame Kiki?

Head to www.hollyroberds.com and check out the bonuses to read!

LOVE THIS BOOK?

Enjoy more by this author
Vivien woke up with no memories and a terrible thirst for blood.

The Grim Reaper must destroy all blood suckers.

The reaper dogs just want to get pets and loves in between fetching the souls for the Afterlife.

Read this COMPLETE trilogy and you'll laugh, you'll cry, you'll absolutely die.

LOVE THIS BOOK?

Vegas Immortals: Death & the Last Vampire

*Available on Audio and Kindle Unlimited

WANT A FREE BOOK?

Join Holly's Newsletter Holly's Hot Spot at www. hollyroberds.com and get the Five Orders Prequel Novella, The Knight Watcher, for FREE!

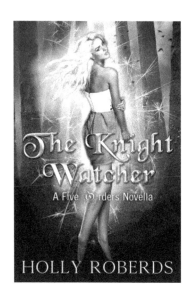

Plus you'll get exclusive sneak peaks, giveaways, fun lil' nuggets, and notifications when new books come out. Woot!

ACKNOWLEDGMENTS

There are SO many people to thank, and first off I have thank my mom, dad, brother, and the rest of my family for not reading my books. Way to not make this weird. *two thumbs up*

BIG thank you to *Calliope's Children*, my monthly plotting group. To Kim K., Kim M., Brooke, and Venessa, y'all have assisted in me getting so characters killed and laid. Thanks for plotting my books, k thanx bye!

To my online sprinting group - Ellie Pond, Amanda Berry, Elena Lawson, Danielle Romero, Sara Massery, Ivy Nelson, Selena Blake, and Kathy Obuszewski. You are one of the few BEST things to come out of Covid!

Thank you to my beta reader Sarah Urquhart! You are the best emotional support Canadian I could ever asked for. And I absolutely how you turn into a feral wolverine when I ever suggest pulling back on the spice.

Thank you to my editor Theresa Paolo. You hone in exactly to the spots where the book feels wrong in my gut. You helped make this book go from good to Amazing!

Thank you, thank you to my proofing team. I am so damn sick of the typos that sneak by and you are a bunch of damn proofing NINJAS!

To my special reader fangroup, *Holly's Hellions* - you fill my cup, feed my creativity, and make me laugh. I definitely write these books for you. Let's always Read Books and Raise Hell!

Thank you to l'husbun, love of my life. You are a constant support, beacon of love, and I am giddy whenever you prompt me to explain to the normies about what I do!

A Letter from the Author

Dear Reader,

Thank you for reading!

I got super jealous of all the Fairy Tale retellings I was seeing and just had to join in the fun! I swore to myself it would be a one-off standalone.

...you can see how well the went.

Loved this book? Consider leaving a review as it helps other readers discover my books.

And never let it be said I don't listen to my readers. You want Goldie, Cinder, or Rap's story? Let me know! And I'm likely to oblige. PBS was right about the dangers of peer pressure.

Want to make sure you never miss a release or any bonus content I have coming down the pipeline?

Make sure to join Holly's Hotspot, my newsletter, and I'll send you a FREE ebook right away!

You can also find me on my website www.hollyroberd s.com and I hang out on social media.

Instagram: http://instagram.com/authorhollyroberds

Facebook: www.facebook.com/hollyroberdsauthorpage/

And closest to my black heart is my reader fan group, Holly's Hellions. Become a Hellion. Raise Hell. www.facebook.com/groups/hollyshellions/

Cheers!

Holly Roberds

About the Author

Holly started out writing Buffy the Vampire Slayer and Terminator romantic fanfiction before spinning off into her own fantastic worlds with bitey MCs and heart wrenching climaxes as well as other errr climaxes...

Holly is a Colorado girl to her core but is only outdoorsy in that she likes drinking on patios in Denver.

She lives with her ever-supportive husband and surly house rabbits who supervise this writer, to make sure she doesn't spend all of her time watching Buffy reruns.

For more sample chapters, news, and more, visit www.
hollyroberds.com